THE WHITE PIPES

NANCY KRESS

W9-CKC-051

B®

BERKLEY BOOKS, NEW YORK

This Berkley book contains the complete
text of the original hardcover edition.

THE WHITE PIPES

A Berkley Book / published by arrangement with
Bluejay Books Inc.

PRINTING HISTORY
Bluejay Books edition / January 1985
Berkley edition / August 1986

ISBN: 0-425-09107-4

A BERKLEY BOOK ® TM 757,375
Berkley Books are published by The Berkley Publishing Group,
200 Madison Avenue, New York, NY 10016.
The name "BERKLEY" and the stylized "B" with design are
trademarks belonging to Berkley Publishing Corporation.

PRAISE FOR NANCY KRESS

THE WHITE PIPES

"Unrelenting ... it rings true thanks to Kress' skillful creation of characters and setting ... an apt scene for violent confrontations between rivals for the spoils of sorcery and love."

—*Locus*

"Nancy Kress is fast developing into a major talent!"

—*Romantic Times*

THE GOLDEN GROVE

"Sensitive, highly original fantasy."

—*Xignals*

"Explosive ... Kress infuses fantasy with the force of raw passion."

—*Locus*

"Obviously a talented new writer!"

—*Publishers Weekly*

"Gracefully written . . . convincingly evoked and sustained."

—*New York Daily News*

"A fine tapestry of a tale!"

—*Fantasy Review*

"Strange and compelling ... keeps one reading."

—*Isaac Asimov's Science Fiction Magazine*

THE PRINCE OF MORNING BELLS

"A fine yarn and a grand entertainment!"

—*Twilight Zone*

"Witty, endlessly diverting and beautifully written ... a classic medieval fantasy world."

—*Heavy Metal*

For my sister Kate,
who listened to me bitch

1

THE SERVANTS HAD PUT JORRY AND ME IN AN ANTE-chamber, a small stone room hung with a gaudy arras, until dinner should be over in the Great Hall. As I waited I inspected the arras, there being nothing else to inspect. Indifferent weaving, gorgeous imported fabric, crude design. The figure of a warrior—I thought it a warrior, but he had been decapitated and what I took for a helmet might have been a cooking cauldron—was as primitive as the drawings Jorry used to make with pointed sticks in beach sand. Primitive and rich. The arras might have stood for all of Veliano.

"Are you nervous, Mother?"

"No. Yes. Don't talk to me, Jorry, I have already drunk the First Flask."

I heard him move behind me, and then his small hand slipped into mine. It stayed only a moment; he was too perceptive and obedient a child to risk breaking even my First Flask trance. Even the pressure of his warm fingers was a distraction, but one I was glad for.

The noise beyond the arras rose, a burst of shouted laughter followed by bawling snatch of song. Not too drunk, I pleaded silently to No One—please, not too drunk. My illusions, such as they are, are delicate ones, far from the drinking bouts and bearbaiting and acrobats that I guessed to be the usual entertainment in a mountain kingdom as remote as Veliano. If the local nobility were drunk, they might not appreciate my city tricks. Too drunk, and they might not even *see* my city tricks. It has happened before.

The arras lifted and a servant entered, a sullen half-grown lad who had recently taken a blow along the side of the head. His cheek and left eye were blue and purple. "They be removing the sweet now, Harper Fia. You said to tell you."

I am not a harper, but I let it pass. This mumbling boy would not know what I am if I told him. He hung at the arras, scowling, obviously hoping for some small coin in return for his information. I had none I wanted to spare. I lifted my chin and stared pointedly at the border of the arras, garish with the four-leaved gillyflowers of the Four Gods Protector. After a moment the boy cursed and went away.

But my trance, always fragile, had broken. I would have to start again.

Sighing, I pulled the First Flask from one of the secure, hidden pockets sewn inside my tunic. All my flasks were light, small, and of cheap metal, even during those rare times in the Silver Cities when I might have afforded better. Tin does not attract thieves. I raised the First Flask to my lips, but then broke my own ban on speech before a performance and knelt down next to my son to bring my face level with his own. Smooth brown hair fell over his forehead into his eyes; I smoothed it back with my palm.

"Jorry, hear me. You know to stay here until the performance is done and I come for you. You can watch from behind the arras, but not come into the Hall."

"Yes, yes." He frowned, impatient at hearing instructions he had listened to so often before, at so many other halls. But few as rich as this, or as remote. And summer would not last forever.

"Jorry, would you like us to stay here, in Veliano?"

I had his attention now. "You mean, stay for always?"

"For at least the winter. If this king likes my stories, I could ask for a place in the Household. They do not have a master of revels here."

They had probably not even heard of a master of revels here. I would be asking for what did not yet exist. But that

2

might make it all the easier. Not to have the scheming jealousy of an established master who knows his tales have all been heard, who fears the stories of a rival who is also a woman . . .

Jorry nodded vigorously. "I want to stay! Did you see the big fires in the kitchen and smell the meat roasting?"

Was it really that he was born to be so skinny, or hadn't he had enough to eat? In a panic, I ran my hands over the bones in his arms. But, of course, my panic was silly; Jorry and I might be badly dressed and we might have spent our share of nights on the cold floors of tavern kitchens, but we have never actually starved.

My Storygiving, indifferent as it is, had always kept us fed. Still, seeing the light in Jorry's dark eyes I felt a pang that my ability and training were not enough to have earned for him more of the world's riches or a more settled home. The ponies on which we had ridden to Veliano with a trading caravan had shanks as spindly as Jorry's own.

Perhaps it was not too late. Here, in this miniature kingdom with its newfound wealth from gemstones and its provincial eyeing of the luxuries of the Silver Cities, in this just-completed palace so determined to look rich that the inept arras were all woven with gold threads, where there was no master of revels to judge the quality of my performance . . .

But first that performance would need to please the provincial king.

Quickly I drank the First Flask, stared at the arras until I felt the light trance film my mind, and then drew from my tunic the Second Flask and drank it.

The effect was immediate. The helmet/cooking pot on the arras wavered, swirled, steadied. A rush of sound, a single elusive note almost but not quite music, beat around my ears and then died. Warmth flooded my body, and I broke into a light sweat, which evaporated into cool air. Then the first wave was past, and I saw what was actually in front of me, heard and felt what actually existed in the antechamber. But it was a subtly heightened actuality. Colors were a little brighter, shapes a little vaguer, sound more melodious but slightly muffled, like the singing of cyrets in a distant room. I closed my eyes and felt the drug take me. More time passed, but I could not have said how much.

The arras rustled again. Another servant, not the sullen lad but a richly dressed woman, motioned me into the Great Hall. With a last glance to be sure Jorry was safe, I went.

Not only the meal but the very tables had been cleared from the Great Hall. Lords and ladies of the court sat on pillowed benches under yet more huge, garish wall hangings. Veliano's blue and red gems flashed everywhere: on rings, set into wine goblets, from headdresses and candelabra, without restraint or suspicion of restraint. The trader who taught them to weave stones into arras, as the women do far to the east of here, could become a national hero.

I approached the central bench and bowed low before Rofdal, King of Veliano. A huge fleshy man in his middle years, he wore no crown and dressed no more richly than the rest of his court, but it was not possible to mistake him. This was the king. Peasants' awe, servants' behavior, street ballads in the town, and innkeepers' gossip—everything I had observed since entering the pass to Veliano five days ago—said that Rofdal was a lord whose whims and rights were one. Beside him sat his queen, but I saw nothing of her save that she was young and far gone in pregnancy. Nerves and drugs made a blur of all but King Rofdal, on whose pleasure could depend a change of fortune for Jorry and me.

"So you come from the Silver Cities, Harper," he said, pleasantly enough. I listened carefully to his voice; my ear is good. The voice was deep and rich with that slight note of petulance that comes to men whose will is never successfully opposed and who would be outraged if it were.

"Yes, I come from the Silver Cities, Your Grace. From Frost. But I am not a harper, Your Grace," I said respectfully, "but rather a Storygiver, which is quite a different thing, and one I most devoutly hope will please you."

"Whatever you are, begin," Rofdal said, drank off his goblet, and gazed around his court from eyes that seemed too small for the broad fleshy expanse of his face.

I bowed again. "I need a table, Your Grace. One as long as my outstretched arms."

One was brought. Meanwhile, the servants gawked and stared, although as yet I had done nothing worth looking at. A few ladies tittered. Rofdal lounged, not too bored.

"*Now* begin, Storygiver Fia. If you are finally ready."

"Yes, Your Grace. I am, Your Grace."

I spread my arms over the table in a great curve, palms down, fingertips just brushing the lacquered surface, and closed my eyes. The usual stab of panic—what if, this time, *nothing occurs*? But I pushed the panic back, concentrated, and in a moment I felt the familiar tingle in my fingers and then up my inner arms.

A gasp from someone in the audience, a rising murmur, a breath indrawn in sudden fright.

I opened my eyes. On the tabletop, between my outstretched fingers, the pink mist was forming. It swirled, throwing off tiny sparkles of light, then began to coalesce into more solid masses. Two of them this time. I looked down on the two masses from above, which foreshortened them, but even so I guessed, with a gust of disappointment, that they would form into the Crone and the Lad, one of the oldest and easiest tales. They did.

"Aaahhh!"

"Look at that!"

"What can it *be*!"

I could not look up to see it, but the amazement and excitement in the Great Hall were palpable. People crowded closer to the table in astonishment; people backed away from the table in fear. The noise rose to a deafening pitch. And all this for the tired old story of the Crone and the Lad, which in the north would have raised only yawns! I had been right to join the trading caravan for the arduous mountain trip to Veliano, where the commonplace art of Storygiving was a miraculous novelty. Veliano, untried by Storygivers, and unsophisticated, and rich enough not to notice her own gleanings nor to exact for them any price . . .

The Crone and the Lad took definite shape; she dressed in

shapeless black and with warts on her nose, he tall and straight and young; both seeming to the minds of the audience—and to mine—to be as solid as the table beneath them. I concentrated harder, the peculiar concentration of the Storygiver, in which one tries to *not* think, to make one's mind empty and glowing, so that the story may be given. Given from where? From the drugs, from the arts of the mind, from the very air. Not even the Storygiver can always be sure how the story will proceed, although nine givings out of ten it will be merely one of the familiar pantomimes with nothing added.

My audience had quieted. I risked a brief glance away from the table; Rofdal watched intently as any child—more intently than my Jorry, who had seen his mother perform this trick all his life. It amused me to see the king's powerful, imperious face with his eyes wide and his mouth open. One side tooth was blackened.

On the table the Crone had just given the Lad a magic apple, and the Lad stood examining it. He held it toward the edge of the table, as if to offer it to the audience, and you could have heard a puppy whimper, so intent were the watchers. I smiled to myself. Although at first I had been disappointed that the story to emerge had been only the Crone and the Lad, now I decided that it had been a happy giving. The plot was so simple that even an audience unused to Storygiving could understand it. Moreover, it contained as villain an old woman, always a safe target for calumny. A story with a king's son or a queen as villain might have been riskier; I did not know the politics of this court, nor what intrigues might be unknowingly mirrored.

The tale between my palms was nearly done when something new began to happen.

A third mist formed near my left hand, swirled, coalesced. I stared in surprise; there was no third character in the story of the Crone and the Lad. The audience, not knowing this, watched expectantly.

All at once a tingling itched my palms. I could feel my face flush, as with heat or great effort, although I felt no strain. The third mist took shape: King Rofdal, miniature and complete, dressed as he was as he sat the bench before me. The figure strode to the center of the table. Immediately the Lad drew a sword—a sword he did not in my story even possess—and turned on the king. And chaos erupted in the Hall.

Men shouted, a bench crashed to the floor, men-at-arms sprang forward. Rough hands seized me from behind, and suddenly I felt the point of a dagger pressed against my throat. When I struggled I was dragged backward, my palms left the table, and the figures still between them rose into the air and, whirling wildly, began to once again come apart into pink mist. The Crone's face became a rotating blur, the Lad's legs dissolved into mist, Rofdal thinned as grotesquely as if he had been exploded from within; at the sight of their king's face expanding and thinning in queasy swirls over their heads, ladies began to scream.

Someone wrenched my arms behind me and pinned them. The point of the dagger bit into my throat. I tried to scream and could not.

Suddenly a solid mass catapulted at my captor, striking him on one of the arms that held me. Jorry, hurling himself in one long run from the antechamber, shrieking like a gale.

"Let my mother go! Let my mother go!"

The soldier kicked him. Jorry's solid little body hit the floor, and at that moment my terror vanished and I began to kick and writhe and scream, working one hand free and trying to gouge his eyes, to knee his groin, anything to tear loose and run to where Jorry lay still on the stone floor. Had I been armed, I would have killed; had I been truly a magician, I would have sent the man into agony.

I was neither, and the rough arms pinned me until a voice roared across the din and dwarfed it all.

"Restore order!" Rofdal bellowed.

And order was restored. As neatly as that. Screams and shouts ceased, and the arms that held me trembled and relaxed slightly—just enough that I kicked my way free and ran to Jorry.

He was already staggering to his knees, crying. His sobs

were the only sound in the room. I gathered him to me, and he clung to my neck like the child he was and not the warrior he had tried to be for my sake. The man-at-arms' boot had caught him on the thigh, and I could see that he had no broken bones, only a nasty bruise. He buried his face in my shoulder, and I crouched on the floor and held him, glaring at the company in the Hall, trembling with anger and sickeningly aware of how powerless we were, my son and I, in this remote Hall where Storygiving could cause such superstitious fear.

But Rofdal was not afraid. He towered above us, his fleshy face shrewd but not accusing, as if what I had done—whatever it was—was beneath his accusation, worthy only of his curiosity. That was the first time I sensed how actually powerful this lord was, that he felt no need to fear what terrified his subjects.

"Why did you make that illusion of me?"

I took heart that he called it an illusion and not a mockery, and so gave him the truth. "I did not make it, Your Grace. It made itself."

He did not answer. I could not tell what he thought. I should have said something else, should have said the figure came somehow from the minds of the audience, intruding on my mind as it gave the story, flowing from my fingers but not my will. Some such lie might have shifted the blame from me—but would he have understood it? I did not understand it myself. Storygiving did not work thus. My control over my own illusions had always been imperfect, but not inventive—Never. Never inventive.

"I meant no offense, Your Grace," I said and heard my voice totter from fury to fear. My arms tightened around Jorry. What would he do to Jorry, what would he do to me?

A lord standing at the king's elbow said softly, "Landril . . ."

Rofdal's gaze raked my face and then those of all his court. His expression blackened as if their silence—and mine—offended him, as if because he looked questioningly, someone must give answer. The name Landril hung in the air. The moment turned long, and then dangerous.

Suddenly, before I could stop him, Jorry had pushed

himself from my arms. He scrambled to his feet before King Rofdal and glared upward.

"Don't hurt my mother!"

The high young voice rang, the small face glared defiance. I grabbed wildly for Jorry but some instinct, some instantaneous shrewdness about the hidden facets of the moment, made me stop my grab for my son. Instead I clutched my hands together; nothing else could have stayed them.

Rofdal put his huge hand under Jorry's chin and raised it. I crouched on the floor, looking straight up at the king's face, seeing it from a vantage shared by no one else in the room. Its expression was complex: wistfulness laid over something I could not guess, frustrated anger, displeasure that boded ill for someone, although the instinctual clarity was still with me and I sensed that it was not for Jorry or me.

"A brave lad," he said. "A strong and brave young warrior." He raised his eyes and this time there was no complexity in his look nor its object: it was pure warning and directed toward his pregnant wife.

"The Storygiver is a guest," Rofdal said. "She is to be treated with courtesy. I see no offense in what she has done, nor—" and his voice took on the warning that had been in his look at the queen "—any resemblance to ought save myself, and that harmless enough. Tomorrow night she may perform again, and I will judge this entertainment without all this caterwauling."

A last contemptuous glance around and he strode from the Hall, and on either side of his path men and women sank to their knees like so many flowers mown by a scythe.

I staggered to my feet, clutching Jorry's arm. A servant hastened forward with a goblet of wine. I gulped it, even though I knew I should not. The last of the Storygiving drug, unexpended when the tale had been cut short, still flowed in my veins, and the drug went ill with wine. I drank anyway and then gave a few sips to Jorry. He looked puzzled, knowing ordinarily I did not drink when I performed. But this was not ordinarily; my son was there under my hand, solid and damp and smelling like a small boy, and at the thought that he might not have been had Rofdal's whim been different, I began to tremble. Storygiving had never before led to this. Storygiving was an ill-rewarded but not a dangerous occupation; never before had I taken my child into danger. I would take him out of it instantly; we would walk from the Hall, mount our ponies, and ride from Veliano.

But we could not leave Veliano. The king had commanded I appear before him again, to give another story. Another story, and the Four Gods I did not believe in alone knew what would coalesce this time.

I looked up. And staring at me from across the Hall was a tall man dressed in rich black: the man whom I had once robbed and fled from, the man for whose sake I had avoided giving stories in the courts and mansions of the Silver Cities and given them instead at country villages and remote halls and poorly paying street fairs—*here*, at the butt end of the world, where he could not possibly be.

I turned Jorry's face toward me, as if to hide it—a stupid, because revealing, mistake. But it did not matter. When again I looked up, Brant of Erdulin was gone. I motioned to the serving woman who had brought me the wine.

"We must rest. Take us to some quiet room, away from all noise." She bowed and led the way, and I followed as casually as I could, Jorry's hand clutched in mine.

The room to which she brought us was not part of the servants' quarters, as I had expected, but of the public rooms of the palace. Obviously Rofdal's use of the word "guest" had confused the woman; itinerant harpers would not ordinarily be brought to such an antechamber. It was small, furnished with a pillowed wooden chest, a lacquered table inlaid with Veliano gems, and the ubiquitous tapestries. Most important, it had one window. I dismissed the woman and pulled Jorry toward the casement.

"Mother? What are you doing? We can't go down there!"

We could not. I had not noted closely enough the terrain around the new palace. It had been built beside Veliano's old citadel, now the Priests' Hall, and between the two the ground fell away into ornamental dells and gardens. Below this window the construction was evidently not finished; leaning far out from the casement, the fresh summer twilight cooling my cheeks, I saw sloping ground covered with rubble and loose rocks. An athletic or strong woman might have leaped down safely and then caught Jorry, but I was small and not athletic. There would have to be a rope, of knotted cloth if nothing else. Before I could search the chamber to find something to make it of, the door opened and closed and Brant stood in the room, his back to the door, mine to the wall.

He had not changed. The boy I had known ten years ago at Mother Arcoa's had become a man, but I recognized still the first thing I had ever noticed of him: the incongruity of mouth and eyes. It may be that the incongruities of men define them more than their harmonies. Brant's mouth still set in the line of his youth: straight, cruel, unwavering. His eyes still shadowed, in their blue depths, a barely glimpsed and unspoken pain. The eyes watched Jorry. Only once did he glance at me, stunned. Then his gaze moved back to Jorry, and when he spoke it was not to me but to my son.

"How old are you, boy?"

But I had prepared for this possibility, prepared for it for years. "Eight," Jorry said. His voice carried some fright of this powerful and richly dressed man who stared at him so intently, but it carried no uncertainty about the question. He believed he was eight, because I had taught him so.

Only I knew he was nine.

Brant went on staring at Jorry. Jorry was small, like me, and he looked like me: straight brown hair, brown eyes.

"Not mine," Brant said, and under his hard voice I heard the splinter of old pain, and I braced myself.

"No," I said, and kept my voice steady as I lied.

"How did you come here, Fia?"

"With a trade caravan. Five days ago."

"Why?"

"To give stories."

"No," he said, and moved swiftly toward me across the full length of the room. I had forgotten that: how swiftly Brant moved. I drew Jorry behind me, although I knew Brant, no matter what he might now feel, would not strike either of us. He had always been too subtle for violence against the unarmed.

"No," he said. "You didn't come here to give stories. Here is too remote for a wandering Storygiver to just happen upon, unless the Storygiver is either seeking something or seeking to avoid something. Which, Fia?"

I stared dumbly, not wanting to tell more than I must. He was both wrong and not wrong. What I had sought to avoid in coming to a place as remote as Veliano was Brant himself, but not because I had ever thought to see him again. Avoidance, flight—they were how I existed, begun that winter day ten years ago at Mother Arcoa's but now the nature of my existence. I have existed as a free woman by being mostly in motion, unpinned, unknown to the rich and powerful except as a Storygiver who appears for a night or a season to give tales and is gone from their halls before she is known. But I was not unknown to Brant. In his rich clothes—Brant, whom I had never known but in threadbare wool like my own!—he towered over Jorry and me, and from him I caught the scents of horses and rich wine. The last light from the window glittered on his dagger and on the clasp on his shoulder, a clasp set with Veliano stones red as blood; and under the clasp the muscles of his body shifted in a hard mass.

I had known that body.

He said softly, "Seeking to avoid something, of course. Who are you fleeing this time, Fia? Whom have you stolen from now?"

"That was long ago, Brant. And you stole as much from me as I from you."

"Did I? What?"

"Trust," I said, to say something, to at least try to attack.

He laughed, a sharp laugh that startled me. I have a good ear; this man was dangerous. The restless hardness of the boy, that had given me so much unease at our lessons and so much pleasure in his bed, had been tempered into something more subtle, less malleable. As I have become more temperate—and it is Jorry who has made me so, not the mere presence of years—so Brant seemed to have become harder, with a tightly leashed hardness that made me afraid.

"I'd have thought," he said, "that it was you who stole trust from *me*, along with the gold you perhaps have forgotten. It was you who disappeared, Fia, the day after I told you my name. Or perhaps you have forgotten that as well."

"Not for a moment, Brant," I said and looked straight at him. Something flashed between our eyes, some many-layered look of rage and pain and the memory of desire, and I knew that I had been right to be afraid. Even as a youth, Brant did not forgive. And now he was a youth no longer.

"Fia," he said, in a soft voice that chilled the flesh on my neck, "I will ask you once again. Is this child mine?"

Jorry looked from Brant to me, his small face furrowed. "No," I said.

For a long moment Brant's gaze held mine. Then from his tunic he pulled a flask and drank it off.

I could only watch, helpless. Brant closed his eyes, stood immobile a long minute, spread his hands over the lacquered and gaudy table.

The pink mist formed, swirled, coalesced. I knew, appalled, what he must be going to do, but I did not know how well he could do it. How long after my flight from Mother Arcoa's had Brant remained there, mastering the arts of soul and mind that I had only begun to learn?

I wanted to run to the door; Brant stood between me and it. Jorry watched the table, his lips parted in childish curiosity, his hand warm in mine.

From the mist between Brant's palms came two figures: he and I ten years ago, youth and maid. The tiny Fia wore the ill-fitting tunic of an apprentice bound to the seedy Storygiving House of Mother Arcoa; the boy Brant wore his own nondescript homespun in which he had one day appeared at the door, demanding instruction but giving no references, the gold to pay clutched in his hand. Both figures looked solid and so real that I gasped. Only accomplished Storygivers could will which figures would form from their minds or create them so solidly, but it was not that which caused my stifled

cry. There had been a rumor, at Mother Arcoa's, of masters
who could do more than pull and direct stories from their own
mind. Once, the pupils whispered to each other in the
darkness of their beds or in the rustling intimacy of the forest
at night, once Storygivers could pull stories from the minds of
their audience . . .

I had not believed it. I did not believe it now. The tiny Fia
and Brant on the table embraced, lay down, began to caress.
She removed his tunic, kissed his chest. He ran his hands over
the curve of her thigh, tenderly cupped the swell of her new,
barely budded breasts.

A slow heat flicked through me.

The tiny figures coupled. I could not look away. It was
unbearable, obscene, to watch this reenactment of remembered caresses—how well remembered!—across the table
from Brant with Jorry beside me. I felt Brant's eyes on me and
knew that if I looked up I would see again that haunting
incongruity: cruelty in the mouth, pain in the eyes. I did not
look up; I could not.

The boy was speaking to the girl, talking excitedly, his
hands on her shoulders. The pantomime on the table of course
gave no words, but I knew what he said. I have never
forgotten it, not for a moment, any of it. He pleaded, she
shook her head dumbly. This went on for a great while; it
seemed to go on forever. Beside me, I felt Jorry grow restless.
The figure of Brant fell asleep, exhausted, on the table. The
figure of Fia took, from within a carved altar with a secret
drawer, gold, more gold than she had ever before seen in her
miserable and orphaned life, and left him there, asleep. Her
figure disappeared.

The boy awoke. He looked for her, searched for her. He
was desolate and then possessed. He tore his hair, he ordered
out armed men, he gave out gold, a hundred times more gold
that she had stolen, searching for her. At one point, he held
his dagger against his own body and then cast it away in tears.

Tears pushed against my eyes. I had not known.

Suddenly the figure of Fia appeared again. She carried
Brant's shoe, a ridiculous and youthful piece of folly, the most

pathetic thing I have ever done. Behind the stupid shoe was clearly visible the curve of her pregnant belly. She pressed the shoe to her cheek, and she cried.

The man Brant clapped his hands violently. All of it, the whole dumb show, disappeared.

I stood as stone. What Brant had done was not possible. He had willed the rest of the story from my mind, had robbed me of it as easily as I had once robbed him. He knew, now, that Jorry was his. I looked at his face, and I knew that not until this moment, that never before in a life spent creating the cool lies that are stories, had I so clearly seen the searing heat of the unshielded truth.

"Why?" Brant said and his voice was like a blade.

"You told me your name," I said. "Brant of Erdulin—the family of a lord! You were a fool, but I was not. You said you wanted to take me back with you, back to your lands—" curse him, how had this happened, when I had spent ten years never venturing near Erdulin "—and . . . and marry me. Marriage! Already I was carrying the baby, Brant, and *I* saw how it would be even if you did not, you who were only playing at poverty at Mother Arcoa's for the adventure of running away to the Silver Cities. You could not see how it would be—but I could. Not a boy and girl playing at love, but an heir of the nobility who wanted to marry a street foundling with a bastard talent for Storygiving, who was already claiming to be with his child. Would your father have permitted it? Would I have sat at your table, nursed your son? Or would the baby have been sent to a wet nurse, held in reserve until your other sons were born, a bastard of the blood, and I sent to the kitchen until you had wed elsewhere and I no longer crept to your bed at night, hoping for a glimpse of my sleeping child in the guarded corridors along the way?"

Jorry whimpered. He did not understand all I said, but he had never before heard me speak in such passionate fear. I put my arm around his shoulders and pulled him to me. Brant watched silently, his eyes cold.

"You believed—or pretended to believe—that the difference

in our ranks made no difference, and that a mere boy could choose how his life would be ordered. I knew different, Brant. I was a street child, remember. I had always known different. And sons are the properties of their fathers and their fathers' families. Your delusions would have lost my baby for me."

"So rather than risk that my delusions—or my fickleness— would have lost him to you, you removed all risk and lost him to me. And yourself as well."

"Yes," I said, and knew I had not told the whole story. But how to recall the follies of youth, the touchy pride, the terrifying willingness to throw one's whole life after one careless action, and count the throwing some sort of virtue? Barely can I remember the hungry impulses of youth; I cannot explain them.

Jorry shifted against my side, raised his small face to mine. I felt his fear. "Is that . . . is that man my father?"

"No," Brant said with such swift hardness that Jorry recoiled. "I am not your father. I was not permitted to be."

As steadily as I could, I said, "We'll leave now, Brant. This hour."

"You will not leave at all."

I stared at him and then launched myself away from Jorry and toward his eyes. I am no fighter, no athlete. But a blind panic had seized me. I had heard in his words immovabilities I could not guess at, and I stuck all my fingers out to gouge his eyes in the way I have seen market fighters do, because it was the first thing that occurred to me. He would not let us leave, he would keep us, he would keep Jorry, and everything in me screamed No!

Brant caught my wrists and pinned me without trouble. I kicked and writhed, screaming stupidly, "Run, Jorry! Run away! Run!"

Jorry stood rooted. Brant clamped a hand across my mouth and, when that did not muffle me enough, across my throat. His voice in my ear was rough and low.

"Fia. Hear me. I will not hurt you, nor the boy either. Hear me!" And then, "Hear me before I break your neck."

It was because I heard in his voice that he would not do it—

could not do it—that I stopped struggling. Perversely, I sensed reassurance only in his lying.

Brant kept his arm across my neck, but loosened its press as soon as I stopped struggling. He held me from behind, and I could not see him. Without sight, and in my fear for Jorry and myself, awareness of him heightened in all the rest of my senses: his smell of horses and wine, the press of his hard body against my back and buttocks, his voice, rough and quick, less than a hand's span from my ear.

"You have seen my Storygiving. Didn't you wonder, you fool, that the court thought your performance so miraculous? My abilities, Mother Arcoa's, the mind arts, Storygiving itself—none of it is known in Veliano, and neither am I, for reasons that have nothing to do with *you*."

"I will say nothing," I said, inanely enough. The grip across my throat tightened momentarily, then loosened, as if a spasm of emotion shook Brant and he struggled for control.

"You are a thief, and a liar, and very possibly a whore," he said. "I do not take the word of thieves, liars, or whores."

For a moment I could neither see nor breathe. I had told myself, through how many nights of years, that this is what Brant would, must, think of me now. But to hear it, and in that hard and relentless voice, was another thing. Some stupid youthful hope I had not even known I still harbored, stood pierced to the heart and dying in anguish, and I shuddered along the length of my body.

"Let my mother go!" Jorry cried, but he did not launch himself at Brant. He stood trembling and afraid, and I saw that my child remembered the feel of the man-at-arms's kick upon his thigh and stood now in his own anguish of loyalty, cowardice, and fear.

At Jorry's voice, Brant did let me go. He stood looking bleakly at the boy, and I don't know what he would have said to him had not the door abruptly opened.

A manservant entered, bearing a tray of smoking food. The servant could see Jorry's face, my face, and Brant's back. He stopped in confusion and stared. Probably he had expected to find only the Storygiver and her child, resting. Certainly he had not expected to see Jorry's face wrinkled in fear, mine twisted with rage and tears, a lord's back stiff as a sword.

Brant's gaze rested on Jorry. For a moment I thought I saw on this older face all the desolation that had flickered beneath his eyes at fifteen, now come scorchingly to the surface. Then the expression vanished, and an overdressed lord used to command turned toward the servant.

"Coryn, leave that food and send a page to his Grace. Tell him I have examined the Storygiver and am convinced she meant nothing by the armed figure that appeared in her illusion, and that she is ignorant of how it was misinterpreted. Say I await his Grace's pleasure to relay all she has told me of this strange art."

The servant's surprise relaxed; he had had my agitation satisfactorily explained. Lord Brant had been questioning the Storygiver about her politics; Lord Brant had possibly not been gentle.

"Yes, my lord," the man said. "Immediately, my lord. And, if it please your lordship, your lady wife awaits you in her chambers."

Your lady wife.

Brant nodded and preceded the servant from the room. He did not look back.

Jorry made a small noise. Old as he was, I picked him up and sat upon the wooden chest with him on my lap. Before me the jewels set into the legs of the table flamed red; the long summer sun was finally setting. In the north, I thought irrelevantly, in the north of the Silver Cities it would already have set and the crowded streets would be full of lighthearted idlers looking for entertainment. Jugglers, Storygivers, the play, harpers, magicians. In the Silver Cities.

In my arms Jorry quieted. Soon, then, would come his questions, and I would need to have something to give him in answer.

But I had so few answers myself. How long would Brant hold us here, and what steps might he take to convince himself that my knowledge of his Storygiving would not threaten him?

My knowledge. I had no knowledge. I did not know how Brant had done what he had done in this room, pulling the story of Jorry's parentage from my mind to his fingertips, nor how he had done what he must have done in the Great Hall, intruding the figure of Rofdal into my story. Nor why. I did not know the range of his arts, nor their purpose in this remote mountain kingdom, nor the reason for his secrecy. Erdulin lay north of the Silver Cities, in lands placid and fertile and dreaming under soft sun. It lay a long distance from Veliano. What could be the nature of Brant's position here?

Your lady wife.

I held Jorry tight and rocked him in the gathering twilight, and ached inside with confusion and fear.

"I'm hungry," Jorry said.

"Then you shall eat," I said, trying for lightness. My voice broke on the last word.

Jorry looked at me with troubled eyes. "Mother—is that big man my father?"

I stood him on the floor, off my lap, and spoke as solemnly and with as much force as I could. "Yes, Jorry, he is. But he doesn't want to be, and so you must never tell that to anyone. Do you understand me? You must never, never, never say that he said so, or that you saw him give a story, or that he and I had a quarrel. This is very important, Jorry, the most important thing I ever told you in your whole life. Never say anything to anyone about Lord Brant. And if you do—" I steeled myself, knowing this was necessary for his safety, yet still hating it— "if you do, I will sell your pony, Slipper, and you will never see him again."

He turned red and then white, as if I had struck him. I saw from his eyes that first he did not believe me, and then he did and thought I was hateful. I made myself hold firm, spurred on by the remembrance of the line of Brant's mouth.

"Do you promise, Jorry?"

"Yes!"

"Then hold to your promise."

I cut him some meat pie, cheese, bread. In a moment he was

chewing hungrily. I could eat nothing; even wine would have choked me.

Your lady wife.

A thief, a liar, possibly a whore.

His hunger slaked, Jorry looked at me with troubled eyes. "If that lord is my . . . father, then do I belong to him? I heard you say sons belong to their fathers."

"You belong to me, Jorry. To *me*."

"Because he doesn't want to be my father?"

"No. Not because of that. Because you are mine."

"I will not tell anyone what he said."

"I know. I have your promise, remember?" I said.

"I remember. I don't want that lord, either. Kalafa is not so mean."

Kalafa—the caravan trader, whom I had been bedding. It took a moment to remember that, or him. He would not come to seek me. He would assume I had found more interesting bedding elsewhere, and he would do the same, shrugging lightly.

The chamber darkened. Outside the window the first stars appeared, and I saw that although this far south their night would be brief, it would be brilliant. The summer stars shone as sharp and clear as Veliano gems, with nothing of softness about them: the hard unsentimental stars of mountain heights.

2

IN THE MORNING, I FOUND MYSELF CALMER.

The idea that Jorry and I should instantly flee the palace, which had kept me awake much of the night, looked foolish now. What would be gained? The trading caravan with which we had ridden to Veliano would not leave for five more days, when its profitable exchange of goods from the north for stones from Veliano's mountains would be finished. It was true that Kalafa and I had found each other amiable, in an unruffling sort of way, but not so amiable that he would even consider leaving before he had made his profit, or if King Rofdal wished otherwise. And the king wished me to give a story tonight. That, too, was a powerful reason to stay where I was. I had seen men like Rofdal before—men used to being obeyed so completely and so instantly that it gave them a childlike reasonableness, a willingness to play fair, until they were crossed. Then all that obedience served to convince them that nonobedience was monstrous, unnatural, to be raged against—as Jorry did when I, whom he expected to devote myself to him, crossed his will. Rofdal was a king and thus an extreme, but I did not think there was much difference, except of degree, with most men.

With Brant?

No. At least, not as a boy—as a boy, thwarted will did not drive him. I did not think it drove him now. But what did I know of what drove Brant now?

His presence provided the only reason not to stay my five

days in the palace. His presence, which hurt—I would admit as much to myself—and his meddling in the story I had given. Why had Brant brought into it the figure of the king, why had he made the Lad draw steel on Rofdal, and why had both those occurrences thrown the court into such havoc? Landril—the courtier at the king's elbow had used that name. Who was Landril?

Everywhere, at every hall and palace and tavern and market tent, there is scheming for position and power, even if it be only position as first of the kitchen maids or power to choose the dinner wine. For the most part I disregarded the whole sorry game, since game it did indeed appear to me, as hazardous and pointless as the game boys play of baiting a boar large enough to castrate them should they miscalculate. Jorry and I stayed beyond range of boar and boys alike. A Storygiver is too small, too much a harmless and foolish diversion, here one month and gone the next, to count in anyone's games.

Until last night. Still, I could discover the political situation easily enough. That required only questions.

Jorry stirred on his pallet next to mine. We had not been allowed to remain in the small rich room of last evening, but had been given this empty storeroom off the kitchen, with pallets on the floor. I had not minded—the room was clean and the pallets thick and sweet-smelling—until I noticed the window of the room was barred. I was going nowhere, at least until morning. Rofdal's order—or Brant's?

Brant had no reason to wish us here. If he had ever wanted to take Jorry, his son, from me, he did not want to now. Never venturing farther north than Frost, the southernmost of the Silver Cities, the pathetic trick of falsifying Jorry's age—none of it was necessary any longer. Brant had looked at Jorry as at a mongrel whelped from a straying bitch.

A night, ten years ago in an attic room at Mother Arcoa's, it had rained—I remembered vividly the rain, how it had blown in the open window, bringing the scent of the sea, how I had marveled in my dazed wonder that it did not cool our skins but seemed as hot as my own young blood, and we had said . . .

I swung off the pallet and toward the door. Dwelling in the past was like the stories I made between my spread hands: useful only when simplified for idlers and children. Swift stories, not tangled ones, caused the crowd to throw its coins. At the door someone had left water for washing and our bundles of possessions brought from the antechamber of the Great Hall, and I told myself that both were worth more, this morning, than all I could remember of a time ground out of existence.

"Sleep," Jorry murmured.

"No, you must wash. Come, Jorry, it's morning."

"Sleep."

I made him rise and wash. He grumbled, lagging sullenly, so unlike himself that my heart felt sore. I would need to find the right time—this was obviously not it—to talk more with him of what had happened last night. I would need to try to imagine what Brant's words had sounded like not to me, but to Jorry.

Another tangled story.

The door to our small room had not been bolted. I was just in the act of opening it to go search for something to eat, when Jorry screamed.

He stood at the tiny window, pointing. I rushed to him. Beyond the bars, a story below us, was a rough courtyard formed by this unfinished wing of the new palace and the gray rock bulk of Veliano's old fortified citadel, now the Priests' Hall. In the courtyard stood a gibbet and from it, upside down, hung the bodies of a man and a woman. They had been flayed. Blood had blackened and dried on their skinless bodies, all but the faces, which had not been touched. The wind blew them a little and the face of the woman, lighter, bumped against the man's in an obscene parody of a kiss.

"They are dead, Jorry," I said as steadily as I could. "They are dead now. They don't feel any pain." I knelt and put my arms around him. His first fright had passed; he stared at the bodies with horrified, fascinated eyes, his right hand clutching the cloth at my shoulder.

"Who killed them, Mother?"

"I don't know."

"What did they do wrong?"

"I don't know."

He considered, and his voice shook a little. "They must have been very bad to be hurt so much."

The innocence of protected children, to believe that only wrongdoing earns pain. My fault—but should I have taught him otherwise? I know how easily, once a child knows the severance of crime from suffering, he may decide that to avoid the latter he must turn to the former. I had wanted Jorry to be neither victim nor persecutor. I wanted him to live as I did, mostly unnoticed, between the cracks of the world's walls. It is safest there.

I said, "I don't know if they were bad, Jorry. I don't know what they did."

"Find out. I want to know." And then, "I don't like this place."

"Come away. Don't look. We need to go find breakfast."

The wrong words—he looked queasy. I felt queasy myself. That horrible windblown brushing of flayed faces—

Unbidden, the memory came again of Brant and me in the tiny upstairs room, wrapped close on a pallet meant for one.

Flaying was a punishment of centuries ago, of wilder and more barbarous times. To see it here, now, was more than shocking—it seemed unnatural, as if time had slipped its leashes.

Jorry gripped my hand as we left the storeroom.

It was better in the kitchen. The court had not yet been served breakfast and so the kitchen was a pandemonium of rushing servants, boiling pots, spitting grease, fragrant smells of baking. The rattled cook glanced at Jorry and me and apparently decided we ranked somewhere above the kitchen maids and below the pages. We were directed to a smoky corner with a small table and food brought us there. It was good food, hot and plentiful. Rofdal, or his steward, was not mean with his servants. I was not surprised: rulers can only keep absolute power over their nobles if they are popular with their servants. Servants and peasants make armies.

After breakfast I begged water from the cook and mixed it with a few pinches of the powders I always carried on my person. I filled the First and Second Flasks. As I corked the Second, I wondered what story would emerge from my mind tonight—and whether Brant would leave it alone. After last night, he must realize that tampering with my story put me—and Jorry—in danger.

Or was that what he had wanted?

For a second I stood still, unseeing, in the noisy kitchen. But—no. If he had still wanted Jorry, he would just have taken him. He was a noble and I an itinerant Storygiver; sons, even illegitimate ones, are the property of those fathers who chose to claim them. As for the possibility of vengeance, I pushed it away. I did not know what Brant had become from the wild boy he had been, but in my experience men did not devote much vengeance to old loves. To old debts of money or old slights of rank—yes. But not to old loves. My fleeing Brant, whatever pain it had cost him as a boy, was not a humiliation of rank. It could even be argued that I had flattered it. I had been afraid of his height.

But all this reasoning—it was foolish. I did not believe Brant would hurt Jorry and me purely because I did not believe Brant would hurt Jorry and me. The mind had its own perceptions.

"I want to see my pony," Jorry said, and my heart smote me. Was he thinking of my threat of last night?

"Then we shall go see your pony," I said.

A young girl sat plucking chickens against a wall on the sunny side of the stable-yard. For a while I watched her surreptitiously. She was not very deft at her task, setting a plucked fowl onto her tray with several pinfeathers still intact, once missing her bucket of entrails entirely with a tossed gob of internal chicken. As she worked she hummed wordlessly, but not badly, the same four or five notes again and again. From her actions and face I thought that she might be a little simple. But a simple informant is sometimes best; no one would think it odd that I spoke to her, nor think that anything significant could have been said. So while Jorry curried and exercised his swaybacked pony, Slipper, I pulled feathers from chickens and learned about the court of Veliano.

"When is Queen Leonore's child due?" I asked the girl. Her name, she had said, was Ludie.

"Cul, this very month. My mother and me, we be making an offering to the Four Gods Protector for a boy."

"King Rofdal wishes for an heir, I suppose."

The girl laughed hugely, as if I had made an irresistible joke. "And him on his third queen, to get an heir!"

"So I heard," I said, as indeed I just had. "Tell me of the first two queens."

"Cul, you be ignorant! Be all the harpers from the Silver Cities knowing so little?"

Her question was genuine; she could not imagine places not breathless for news of Veliano. I looked at her broad, honest, unattractive face and said gently, "I am ignorant, I know."

"Don't be letting them hurt you on it!" she cried, and began to pull feathers furiously, her face sullen. The feathers flew up on the warm air in a smelly cloud. "*I* don't be letting them hurt me on it, cursed girls!"

"Then I won't, either," I said soothingly. "I won't. And I am not a harper; I am a Storygiver, the Storygiver Fia." I waited for her to ask the difference between a harper and a Storygiver; she did not. She bent over her chickens, old hurts on her plain face. "You can call me Fia, Ludie, just as I call you Ludie. Won't you tell me about the first two queens, Ludie? I would like to know."

"First be good Queen Nitira. She be queen since his grace's youth, and she died but three years past."

"Had she children?"

"Four slips," Ludie said succinctly. "And died of the last."

"And then . . ."

"Queen Janore." Ludie's face changed; she began to pluck faster. "I saw the flaying."

Something grew cold in my stomach. "The queen was flayed?"

Ludie stared at me as if I had lost my senses. "Cul! The queen! No, no, her serving woman that poisoned her! And when I remember I been *that* close to her, times she come to get herbs from the kitchen garden!" She plucked furiously for a moment, then added in a low voice, "Not that the serving woman be not deserving it. We don't want no soul-beseters here."

The cold thing in my stomach crawled. Soul-beseter—no one had been put to death for that sorcery, that ancient religion, in two hundred years. In the cities a "soul-beseter" had become a vulgar figure of fun. Playwrights put a soul-beseter into a play when they wanted the audience to laugh derisively; children were told stories of soul-beseters to give them a harmless, delicious thrill; I had heard the women of wealthy merchants consider the term a flirtatious compliment, tribute to their power to capture a man's attention with their charms. Soul-besetting was a joke, an unsophisticated superstition, an exaggeration of commonplace uses of the mind into impossible ones to scare our unsophisticated ancestors. It was the stuff of stale stories.

But not to this girl.

As we worked, Ludie told me about Janore, the former queen. Cousin to this one, not that a soul be saying a word against Queen Leonore, may the Four Gods Protector protect her.

"Once I be beating a rug in the stable-yard, the old stable-yard, and Queen Janore she be there, and the dust flew over her from the rug. She had me beaten, and I be just a child-one! The king, he come to hear of it, and he be angry. Over *me*," Ludie said, her eyes wide. "He be protector to his people, my mother says, like the Four Gods Protector be to him, against soul-beseters. It be a red rug with blue cyrets woven in."

"And soul-besetting—"

"Cul, don't talk of it, Storygiver!" she cried, and her shudder was real, no stage gesture.

I sat plucking, wondering if this girl really did not know that Storygiving was the one legitimate art of the ancient superstition she called soul-besetting.

No, of course she did not. After I had forced myself to calmness, I could not see why not. Even in the Silver Cities, the street crowds do not connect Storygiving and soul-besetting. Storygiving is a harmless, vulgar illusion, a little more interesting than sword swallowing or juggling because rarer, a little less interesting than traveling plays because without words and songs. Soul-besetting is a dusty religion, dead two centuries, even its ruined altars gone.

To even the Storygivers themselves, who know of the connection, it is not important. Why should it be? Only historians care for what has passed and gone.

The historians say the old religion and Storygiving happened to enter the world at the same time: Storygiving, the talent that a few—how few!—people are born with, to make visible in figures of light the simple fancies of their minds; the old religion, one of bloody sacrifice and absolute control by dark epopts. So what happened was not complex: the epopts merely used the art to convince simple people first that the epopts could see into others' minds, then that the epopts could enter into others' minds, and finally that they could control others' minds. And the people, like people everywhere, believed their priests. "Soul-besetting" was thus a useful lie, a political use of a simple human oddity no more remarkable than the human oddity of possessing one blue eye and one brown. No more than that. Thus say the historians.

The priests of the Four Gods Protector say soul-besetting was real in the world, but Storygiving is not part of it. The ancient epopts invaded the minds of men, and in Their mercy the Four Gods Protector came to the world to preach that men's minds and bodies are Theirs and must not be invaded. Storygiving, however, uses only the mind of the Storygiver; he enters no other. Thus, there is no sin. Storygiving is an unimportant idleness. Thus say the priests.

The Storygivers say: Collect your fee before you perform.

Soul-besetting? I could have laughed, except for the solemnity of the silly child pulling pinfeathers beside me. Except for what I had seen Brant give last night: a past that lay in my mind but not in his. Except for the two flayed bodies in the courtyard.

I asked Ludie about them, as offhand as I could manage, as much the respectful and merely curious outsider.

Her round face grew troubled. "They be soul-beseters. In secret. They found an altar in the cottage and a garden of strange and wondrous plants that come from trying to grow potions to blacken minds, my mother says. Cul, all the filthy things they be finding in the cottage. All the filthy things!"

"*Who* found it all in the cottage? Who is 'they'?"

"Cul, *they*," Ludie said, and in her voice was all the vagueness of those who glimpse power from only a great distance. "The ones who be finding the cottage for the priests."

"The cottage then was not nearby the palace?"

"Nearby the *palace!*" She stared at me in amazement, a feather in her hand. "No soul-beseters dare live in cottages near King Rofdal's palace!"

"No," I said hastily, "Of course not. Only in distant cottages."

There was a little silence. "There be that serving woman," Ludie said abruptly. "To Queen Janore. But she *come* from a distant town. She be not from near the palace before. She *come from* a distant town."

She was thinking; I did not want her to think. To divert her I said the first thing I found in my head: "Does Lord Brant come from a distant town?"

"Cul, yes! Don't he be handsome? Not that I think he be handsomer than the king, of course—the king be having a better leg. Did you see the leg on the king?"

I made a vague noise, unsure whether it would be wise or unwise to have noticed the leg on the king.

"That be a *leg*." Ludie sighed, as well satisfied as if it were her own. "My lord Brant, he be from some otherwheres north, I forget the name . . . north. But he goes not there much. He be married to King Rofdal's marriage-cousin."

I was startled. "To Queen Leonore's cousin?"

"Cul, no! To a cousin of the first queen, the Four Gods Protector never forget her. But the Lady Cynda be much younger than the poor dead queen. The queen would be as old as the king. Not that the king be old, not yet. Not with that leg."

Brant had married into royalty. Distantly, and petty and provincial royalty—but royalty still. Something twisted under my heart, and I pulled chicken feathers more quickly. To prove to myself how stupid was the thickening of my throat, I said, "Has he heirs?"

But Ludie thought I meant the king. She said, very slowly, "His cousin be the heir. My lord Landril, of . . . some other where. But only till the baby prince be born."

Landril—a distant heir, perhaps younger, off the blood line. The offensiveness of my story was explained—but not why Brant had created it. Explained, too, the look of warning from Rofdal to the pregnant Leonore: his third wife, and no heir. Produce a son or you have failed me. I felt a quick sympathy for the young queen and wondered if her pregnancy were a hard one. All the little boys in the world, all the infant stablemen and coopers and ploughboys, all the little boys . . .

"Do," I asked carefully, "my lord Brant and Lady Cynda have children?"

"No. And Cul, that's strange, with the Lady Cynda as wide-hipped for breeding like she is. Not like the poor queen, the Four Gods Protector help her through her woman's time."

Ludie's last words sounded stilted, as if she were repeating something she had heard older women say. Probably she was. I looked at her and thought that she was about the same age I had been when Brant had come to Mother Arcoa's, a wild runaway lordling being searched for through all the Silver Cities by an irate family, and I an orphan sent to Mother Arcoa's because my unimportant human oddity had provided a way for my mother's brother to shed a burden he did not want. I hoped that simple Ludie would provide better for herself than had I, but I doubted it.

"Ludie, how many . . . soul-beseters have been discovered and flayed?"

"Five, now. The second queen's serving woman"—I noticed that Ludie did not use her name and guessed that she thought the name had some mystical power—"a year ago, it was, and one girl before the second queen's woman, and one man after. And then those two yesterday afternoon."

Yesterday afternoon. No wonder the court had been touchy last night. The man and woman had been flayed at the same time as Jorry and I had been riding from Veliano's major town, Velin, to its palace. I felt my gorge rise.

"They be taking the bodies away this morning," Ludie said, the trouble back on her homely face. "It be just like, a warning. So harpers would tell people not living nearby the palace." In her voice, despite its troubled tone, was a note of contempt for these rustic Velianos who did not live nearby the palace. "Harpers watched."

"Watched the *flaying*?" The servant last night had called me harper; had I come a day earlier I might have been made to watch as well. Nausea rose in me, helped by the smell of the chickens.

"Yes, harpers watched the flaying. And the stabbing, as well."

"Stabbing?"

"Yes." Ludie looked at me. "You don't think they be flayed *alive*, do you? That be what soul-beseters did! The Four Gods Protector root out sin; they don't ape it!" She brooded a minute, wide-eyed. "Cul, you thought they be flayed alive! Be that how cruel they be in the cities of the north?"

"No. No, of course not."

"But you thought it," Ludie said. "I looked it on your face. Cul, of course they be put first from their miserable lives. I be standing in the stable-yard when the men-at-arms be going out, and I heard my lord Brant give the very order."

Brant.

"He said," Ludie continued, "for the harpers to watch, order of the king's priests. Then he told the men-at-arms to make as quick and clean a death as possible."

The chickens were all plucked. I helped Ludie load them into a basket and I rose, legs trembling, to cross the stable-yard to Jorry. As he curried his pony, Slipper, the sun brightened his brown hair and lay pearly along the curve of his cheek, which was streaked with dirt from a swipe of his hand. The pony stamped, and Jorry laid a hand along her neck. He looked to me too thin, too grubby, too small—infinitely precious.

"Listen," Jorry said. "I hear a flute!"

From within the stables came a boy, playing a homemade flute as he walked. The flute looked crude, made of wood cut and shaped, but the music the boy brought from it was astonishing. Plaintive and sweet with an undertone of sadness, the tune disturbed the mind, caught at it with wordless yearnings, brought from the mind's unseen depths regrets for the absence of nameless things never even known. A squire leading a huge black horse stopped to listen, and the horse paused as well. Jorry, one hand along Slipper's neck, grew quiet, the currycomb motionless in his hand, his lips parted. I, too, felt moved by the enchantment of the music, and when it was done and the boy lowered his flute, I wished I had some coin to give him.

"You play with great skill," I told him.

"I know," he said, grinned impudently, and ran off, evidently expecting no price for his playing, his bare legs flashing brown in the sunlight.

"I wish I had a flute," Jorry said.

"Perhaps I can get you one."

"*Would* you?"

"I will try, at least."

"Then . . . Mother, while you try for a flute, will you try to get me a small sword as well?"

I felt myself grow still.

"I am old enough to learn it," Jorry said, but he looked after the boy as he said it, and I did not know which he meant: flute or sword.

3

AND SO, THAT EVENING, WE STOOD AGAIN IN THE antechamber to the Great Hall. I stared at the same arras, and this time there seemed to me no doubt that the ill-drawn, silvery figure was indeed a knight beheaded, who had died screaming in his own blood.

I had drunk the First Flask. Jorry sat quietly behind me, playing with a carved wooden dog given to him by a child he had met in the kitchen at midday meal, the young son of a dairymaid, a child with dung-caked feet and a sweet smile. Jorry had spent the afternoon among the cows and had asked me no questions. I had refused to let either child out of sight, which annoyed them both, and the afternoon had been unremarkable.

Let the evening, too, be unremarkable!

The sullen lad who last night had warned me of dinner's ending, this night did not come, presumably because I had given him no coin. I guessed for myself when the king would summon me, and drank the Second Flask.

Colors brightened, noise rose, balance grew unsteady. Then all these sensations faded and only one remained, a suspension in a single tranced moment shot through with a single elusive note. Time had ceased, but music, born of timing, took its place. The single note flowed through and around my mind while not flowing at all, and I waited to be summoned as Storygiver by people who flayed those who entered others' minds.

Or those who they thought did.

This time the table stood waiting for me. As I entered the room conversation ceased, and then began once more at a different, lower pitch. None approached my table quite as closely as before. I could feel their temper thick around me: they were cautious, but not yet afraid.

The music was still strong within me, and I allowed myself one look at Rofdal before I began. Huge in yellow silk, he lounged on his chair, the small eyes in his fleshy face watchful. Beside him sat Queen Leonore, half his bulk despite her pregnancy. Her eyes were downcast, and I received only a quick impression of smooth dark hair wrapped severely around her head, delicate young features, a dark and un-adorned dress of changeful sheen. Next to Rofdal's enormous yellow splendor, she seemed a small dark wren, preternatural-ly still.

I looked down at the table, concentrated, and spread my hands.

The pink mist formed quickly—too quickly, it seemed to me—and thickly. It swirled, coalesced, began to form figures. One, two—three. I did not recognize any of them.

The audience did not know that, of course. The court assumed this was my story, and watched the man and woman, both dressed in rough tunics but wearing rings and clasps of jeweled gold, as the tiny figures circled the table. They walked slowly, their faces intent, peering down at the road, up above them, straight ahead. Clearly both searched for some-thing. At times they moved arduously, as if climbing rough terrain; at times they drooped with exhaustion.

The Giant Killer? Could it be the folktale of the humble Giant Killer, unaccountably augmented by a sister and missing a giant?

I knew it was not the Giant Killer. These two searched for something much smaller and much more coveted than a giant. The third figure, hooded and cloaked so that neither its age nor its sex could be seen, remained motionless in the middle of the table.

The two figures continued to search. The audience, at first

intent on the novelty, grew impatient and then restless. Rofdal shifted his immense bulk on his chair. People murmured; a woman in the crowd tittered.

The figures began to search more desperately, but with no more success. Minutes dragged by. I did not understand: this was no story from my mind; or if it was, it was one I had not drawn forth before. Tentatively I tried to picture the female figure stopping her search and standing still. Even so small an alteration can be risky: begin to impose willed direction on a story's characters and most of the time they begin to fade. But I had to do something: this futile search was no story at all. Carefully I concentrated on the female, trying to picture her standing still.

She continued to search.

More recklessly, I pictured her tripping and sprawling upon her face.

She continued to search.

Frightened at my complete lack of control over her, I imagined a more drastic story: she drew a dagger and plunged it into her male companion. I pictured blood spurting forth and his mouth opening in a silent scream.

Unchanged, she continued to search.

I pictured her stripping herself naked, hurling herself on her male companion, wrapping her legs around him, rubbing her breasts in his face, her own contorted with passion. Sweat broke out on my face and neck. I pictured her rolling with him on the ground, scratching his back into long red welts with her fingernails, straddling him where he lay.

She would not do it. She continued to search.

My audience began to mock. I could not look up to see their faces, but I heard the whispered taunts, the contemptuous shifting. Someone laughed.

Then, slowly, the cloaked figure in the middle of the table raised one arm. "Cul, *finally*," a woman sneered. But abruptly the audience began to quiet. There was something both eerie and commanding about that slowly rising arm, miniature and silent though it was. And when the arm had risen completely, the brown sleeve fell back and it could be seen that the hand was folded around something.

The two figures at the edge of the table stood still.

Now the Great Hall was completely silent. No one moved except Rofdal, who leaned forward to better see the shining object in the cloaked figure's hand. But it was hard to see. It was hard to be sure it was even an object, because it seemed surrounded by a nimbus of white light which blurred not only its edges but those of the hand holding it. And yet there seemed to be more than just light within the blurred hand.

The tiny male and female figures moved to the middle of the table. For the first time their faces held expression: greed, rapaciousness, an unholy joy. The female reached out and touched the elusive object. The moment she did, the table did what no table ever does during Storygiving: exploded into a change of scene with no pink misty transition, no fading of the previous scene. Instead the white light around the cloaked figure's palm flared into a blinding blaze and then, too quickly to permit the audience to react to the explosion, vanished. In its place was a new tableau: the cloaked figure had become a sticky pool of brown cloak, the female figure stood triumphantly holding in her hand the object devoid of its light, and the male figure hung upside down on a gibbet, stripped and flayed.

Then the whole tableau vanished and Queen Leonore screamed in pain.

She screamed just once and clutched at her belly. Her women sprang to her, some of them screaming as well. A guard seized my arms and pinned them behind me. Rofdal leaped to his feet, quivering with outrage, and started toward me.

"No, no," the queen gasped. "No. She . . . *didn't*!"

At her protest, impassioned and vague, Rofdal halted. Leonore seemed to be struggling to control herself. She waved away her ladies, laid her own trembling hands on the great curve of stomach.

"It's not yet time!" Rofdal bellowed, and it was somewhere between an order and a cry of fear that he might lose his heir.

"No," Leonore said. She sat very still. I knew that look, had felt it from the inside: a woman trying to assess the life within her life. Does it move still? Is all well? Is this the time, the start of the ordeal of blood and hope?

Not yet.

"No," Leonore said to Rofdal, "Not time. Labor is not beginning. It was only the shock, my lord—the shock of seeing that . . . that abomination. The flaying. But nothing more—merely a pregnant woman's ridiculous sensitivity." And she smiled at her husband.

I have seen many types of smiles, but never, before or since, one like that. It was the smile of a dog owner before he slips loose the dog into the pit to fight for its life. He has lived with the dog, devoted countless hours to learning its ways and habits, sustained its life, slept with its breath in his face, perhaps risked his own injury in training the dog at feint and attack. And he sends the dog to kill or to be torn apart with just such a fierce and affectionate coldness as Leonore's smile at her husband the king.

"Nothing?" Rofdal said. "You cried out in pain."

"No, no. Just shock. The Storygiver has shown us strong entertainment." She smiled at me, and my neck went cold.

"Release her; she is not armed," Rofdal said impatiently. He glanced from me to Leonore, and I saw his features thicken with resentment that he had reacted so much to what was, after all, a matter for only physicians and women. When his gaze came again to me, and with it that male resentment, I stood still within the close circle of the men-at-arms. They had released me, but stood so near I could smell their leather breastplates and their sweat.

"Storygiver," the king said, "you have made a poor choice of entertainment. Flaying is a death reserved in Veliano for soul-beseters. It is not a matter to be mocked by harpers."

"Nor would I ever mock, my lord king!"

Rofdal did not answer. He moved a step closer, an immense yellow mountain, and regarded me from his small eyes.

I knew fully, in that moment, the extent of my danger. I saw myself accused of some dim connection to soul-besetting, priests of the Four Gods Protector debating the figures in the story I had not created, Jorry imprisoned. I felt the rope at my ankles, felt the sudden obscene tug to string me upside down, saw the flash of the knife before it scraped my flesh without escape or hope of escape. I heard my own first anguished scream as the knife bit, and Jorry's paralyzed face as he was made to watch, surrounded by harpers. Would Brant let me die quickly first—Brant, who had created the story between my hands and so given me over to the danger?

My terror must have shown on my face, may have contributed to Rofdal's judgment. His gaze scanned me, and again I saw what I had seen the night before: a man so accustomed to being law that he would recognize opposition only when evidence became overwhelming, and then only with baffled rage. In Veliano he was the lion beside whom mice might be an annoyance but scarcely a threat. And to that complacency, and not to any mercy, I owed my life.

"She is merely a Storygiver," he pronounced to the court. "A harper without words. The harpers have been ordered to sing of the flayings; she has but done likewise." He glanced at me. "But not in my court and not offered for my entertainment."

"No, Your Grace."

He shrugged. "I see no fault in her. Let her perform elsewhere in Veliano besides the palace, until the caravan leaves. The peasants shall not be deprived of their entertainment because of the vapors of women."

"Thank you, my lord king!"

Rofdal looked surprised that I was still there, clapped his hands, and called for music and the dance. Instantly the table in front of me vanished, musicians appeared, lutes sounded. But I could not move quite so fast. I had felt too much terror and too much bafflement. Only my eyes moved, swinging wildly around in my head, out of control. I tried to control them; I could not. They saw the small flayed figure in my story, they saw Leonore's horrible smile, they saw the men and women of the court, brilliant in silks that had never come from Veliano, forming the figures of the dance in the middle

of the Hall. The middle of the Hall. Then I *had* moved, my
legs had carried me toward the antechamber. I stood by the
arras, unable to go farther, and my eyes searched. They
continued searching. They would not stop searching.

It was the story over again—my eyes searched, and I did
not know for what.

They found Brant.

He had not moved, either. He stood frozen, his face
clenched and white, his blue eyes momentarily unguarded
and as stricken as my own. Something had jarred him as much
as my moment of terror had jarred me. Then his gaze swung
to mine, and in that locking I suddenly knew that it was not he
who had entered my mind and created that story between my
hands, not he who had thrust Jorry and me into danger of our
lives. He had been as surprised as I. I saw astonishment, fear,
and anger on his face, and something else—something that
unlocked my own immobility and let my knees move once
more.

Brant had been afraid for *my* sake.

To believe that was not reasonable. But it was true.

A hand darted from behind the arras, seized my arm, and
tugged me backward. Jorry. I saw his small terrified face
framed by curtain, and I moved backward toward him. But
my gaze jumped back to Brant.

It jumped too late. In the time I had bent to Jorry, Brant
had mastered himself. He moved toward the dancers and his
face was composed—slightly pale, but cool and bland. Had I
first seen him then, I would have gone on believing, in hatred
and pain, that it was he who had created my dangerous story
and played with my life.

Who had?

"I want to go away from here," Jorry said. "*Now.*" His
fingers opened and closed on my arm, and he looked at me
from wide eyes brilliant with tears he was too scared to shed. I
picked him up and held him. He was nearly too heavy for my
arms.

"We will go now, Jorry. This very moment. Down to a
tavern in Velin, in the town."

"*On the ponies*," he said.

"Yes, yes, baby. On the ponies. Now."

No one tried to stop us. The stable master did not even ask questions, further manifestation of the completeness with which Rofdal's orders were obeyed, but he did give us a lantern. I think he felt sorry for us, fleeing the palace without even most of our belongings, picking our way in the dark down the mountain path toward the town. But to me fleeing felt natural, as it always had: an act not of cowardice but of preservation.

The path was twisty and narrow. Rofdal could easily defend his palace, should that ever be necessary. As darkness gathered around us, Jorry began to relax. I heard his breathing change from quick frightened pants to a longer, calmer rhythm. He did not crowd his pony as close to mine or look back over his shoulder. I had been talking to him steadily in a low, confident voice, of nothing at all: the flowers by the path, the evening smells of mint and earth, a rabbit darting between rocks. At last I fell silent.

The moment I stopped talking, I began to tremble.

Who had created the story I had given? It had been someone with enormous mastery of the art, to not only alter one of my own stories, as Brant had done the night before, but to make a story that previously had not existed in my mind at all. Such power was completely beyond the art of Storygiving, as I knew it. Such power verged on the rumors of the ancient religion: soul-besetting.

But I had not been beset, not controlled; only my story had. My own mind had been free to picture whatever it would, as I had done with the tiny female figure. I had not been controlled, but only used, to present a story someone did not wish to claim himself. I had been like a harper, singing a ballad handed to him anonymously by someone in the crowd. A wordless ballad, with the sharp mystery and myriad meanings of wordless things.

But a ballad written by whom? And intended for whom to heed?

An image recalled itself to me. Just before the final tableau of the story had vanished, the female figure had held the object taken from the cloaked figure's hand. The nimbus of white light had vanished; the object was plain. But I, and the court, had been looking at the flayed man dripping blood and shreds of skin, and had not paid attention to the object. Try as I would now, I could not see what the thing was. I saw only whiteness, and a vague impression of squareness. A box? A small weapon? A book? What had been the end of that long and desperate search?

I could not see it clearly.

Full darkness, the late darkness of approaching midsummer, finally hid the trail. The night was clear and there were stars, but the moon had not yet risen. The trees swayed gently, murmuring, dark shapes beyond the trail. Below I could see the torchlights of Velin, and then we had reached the level of the town, where the tavern of the Dancing Spider stood ready to house travelers between Velin and the palace.

I went to the kitchen door, away from the evening drinkers in the ale room, and knocked loudly. A kitchen maid opened and fetched the innkeeper.

I had intended to ask only if Kalafa the trader was in the ale room; my first thought was to immediately return to the caravan and so assure myself that it, and I, were indeed leaving Veliano. But as the innkeeper approached, I hesitated. To find Kalafa once more would mean to bed Kalafa once more, and what had seemed pleasant enough to me two days ago seemed impossible to me now. I preferred to pay for Jorry's and my passage in coin, even if it depleted my small store. Kalafa would not like it.

"I wish a room for the night," I told the innkeeper.

He looked me over. "Are you a harper?"

"No," I said, too quickly. I did not want to perform again in Veliano. Who could say what else might happen? "Merely a traveler."

The tavern keeper's eyes narrowed. I saw him trying to decide who I was, why I had come to the kitchen door and not the ale room, if I could pay. I was used to this, at least; I looked at him coolly, and he gave us a small room on the ground floor at the back of the inn. The little confrontation, trivial though it was, restored some of my confidence.

"When do we leave Veliano?" Jorry asked. He seemed subdued, but his face had lost its pinched look.

"When the caravan leaves to go back through the mountains. Four days more."

"I want to go."

"So do I," I said, and smoothed the bright brown hair back from his forehead. "You should sleep now."

"Tell me a story."

Tell me a story—never, from Jorry, Give me a story. I smiled wryly. Thus do cobblers' sons prefer to run barefoot, and silversmiths' daughters choose only flowers for their hair.

"What kind of story?"

"A story about horses. There should be horses in it, and dogs, and hawks, and that's all."

"No people?"

"No people," he said firmly. Was he thinking of the three stories he had seen at the castle, my two and Brant's one, all filled with hurtful and hurting people?

I examined our pallets for vermin—there were none—made him eat some bread and cheese, and drew a blanket over him. Then I began a rambling story about two horses who befriended a dog who thought he was a hawk. Jorry's eyelids drooped. Before I had finished the story he had fallen asleep, which was fortunate because I had no idea how to end the preposterous tale.

I sat beside him in the darkness, listening to the noises from the ale room. I did not want ale, nor food, nor talk. I didn't know what I did want, only that I was tense and restless, and that the smell of the summer night drifting into the window made both tension and restlessness worse.

After a long while, the moon rose. In its white light Jorry's small face looked smooth and peaceful, and his lashes threw a faint shadow on his cheeks. I had been wrong when I had gloated that there was nothing of Brant in Jorry's appearance. The thick long lashes were Brant's.

I shook Jorry's shoulder softly; he did not awake. So I took my restlessness to the window and climbed out into the moonlight. On this side the inn backed to a side of the stable, and then to woods. I slipped into the woods, far enough not to be visible from the stable-yard but still close enough to hear if Jorry called. He would not be upset if I were gone, but he might be if he saw what I was doing. I drank of the First Flask.

The ground had been cleared for firewood, and the trees were not dense. Enough moonlight sifted through them for me to see. Around me rose small rustlings and rich, earthy smells: loam and rotting wood and the sharp sweetness of hawley flowers. I sat on a fallen log, leaned over to a mossy patch of ground, and stretched out my hands. Room enough. I drank of the Second Flask.

Brightness, color, sound. Then timelessness and the elusive, measured notes of music that entranced the mind. I tried to let the story that was not mine dwell lightly in my mind without forcing, in hopes that it would again flow through my fingers. I have never been good at willing one story rather than another to emerge during Storygiving, but this new one still had a powerful grip on my mind, and on my soul.

The pink mist formed, swirled, coalesced. On the mossy ground the male and female figures began their search. They searched, the central figure stood immobile, the arm began to rise, the female came toward it. At the moment she touched the white nimbus of light, the whole exploded in a burst of light into the flayed man, the sticky, pooled cloak, the woman triumphantly holding the object. This time I made myself gaze at it carefully and not at the gruesome, flayed body. Another blaze of light and all vanished.

That last flash, coming after the darkness of the woods, momentarily blinded me. White light danced before me. When I could see again, I looked up from the mossy ground, shaking my head to free it of both the light spots and its slight trance—and faced Brant, silhouetted between two trees black in the moonlight.

My first sensation, thrown off in a moment in favor of sense but for that moment so hot and strong that it appalled me, was desire. I desired him.

"And this time you saw it," Brant said.

I stood, feeling the warmth still flushing my cheeks, grateful for the darkness. "This time I saw it."

"And what did you see?"

I hesitated, although there was no reason except that his presence confused me and his voice even more. It held none of last night's violence, but a deadly grimness and something more I could not name.

I said slowly, "I saw pipes. Nothing more. A set of white pipes, banded in silver, carved with scrolls."

"Not scrolls, Fia. Leaves. The White Pipes carved with leaves."

"What is it?"

"Can you tell who it was created in your mind the story you gave tonight?"

I considered warily. That first mad flash of desire had passed, and I remembered that this man held great power here, and also that he had performed arts I had thought not possible.

"Fia, what you don't tell me, I can take from your mind."

"Then take it from whoever risked my life with that story!"

"You don't know," Brant said, and it was not a question. "I thought it was you."

"No. Not I." Between the black trees he remained still, and it seemed to me then the coiled stillness of danger.

"Brant, whatever arts are being practiced in Veliano—I don't want to know. Not the arts, not the intrigues. In four days more I will leave Veliano with Kalafa's caravan, and for four days more I will give no stories, nor watch any, nor hear any."

Brant closed the distance between us and put one hand on my arm. I could not see his face—he had half-turned against the moonlight—but I knew I shuddered at his touch on my flesh.

"You are not leaving with the caravan."

My head jerked upward.

"You are not leaving because I can make use of you here."

Carefully, without hasty movement, I slipped my arm away

from his hand. I had myself mastered; my voice was steady, and no fear reached my face. Men, like beasts, can sometimes be turned back by a show of fearlessness, provided they are not in packs. Brant was alone.

"I will not stay, Brant. Jorry and I leave with the caravan. You have called me a thief and a liar and a whore; I have been none of those since I left you at Mother Arcoa's ten years ago. You were enraged at me then, and perhaps you had just cause to be so. I cannot undo the past. But my life now has nothing to do with yours, and now is when I am going to fetch Jorry from the inn and find the caravan." I started from the woods toward the Dancing Spider, walking as fearlessly as I could.

Brant said, "He is no longer there. My men already have him."

I broke for the inn, throwing myself forward out of his range. But he was too fast. His body hurled against mine and we crashed together to the ground. Brant threw his weight across me and his hand covered my mouth. I fought him with both hands; he wrenched them under me and pinned them with his free hand.

"Don't scream, Fia. If you scream, I will strike you cold."

I strained beneath him, neither screaming nor answering, saving all my strength for breaking free and finding Jorry.

"Your son is safe. Hear me: I have not hurt him."

"You don't want him. You don't know him, nor need him. Give him to me, Brant, and let us go!"

"No."

My mouth found his shoulder. I bit down as hard as I could, trying to make the bite felt even through the elaborate layers of his tunic. He cursed and rolled off me, not releasing my wrists. Almost I broke free, but then he was astride me, pinning my hands to the ground with both of his, and there was no way I could move him or strike him. The moonlight was behind his head, making a nimbus of his hair and leaving his face dark; he was a weight, a harsh voice, a faceless shadow above me.

"You blundered into Veliano, Fia, and now that you are here you have already been made use of by forces you do not understand. Now I too need to make use of you."

"Take me to Jorry. Take me to him, or I will do nothing for you, Brant. Whatever it is, I will not do it, unless you take me to him."

He was silent, a dark shape above me in the woods. I could not let myself give in to panic or anger. It seemed to me that my best chance to regain Jorry lay in calmly bargaining with Brant. Did his silence mean he was considering it?

"Fia, Jorry is being taken to a place of safety. Veliano is not safe. Suspicion breeds violence; you have already seen that here, I think."

He was sending Jorry beyond Veliano, beyond the mountains! For a moment the woods dissolved to nothing, and nausea rose in me. I clutched at calmness, found it. "I will do no tasks for you, Brant, unless I have Jorry with me. You say you are sending him away for his safety; if that is so, then let both of us go for his safety. You are holding him in order to force me to do whatever this use of yours is, but I will not. Not without Jorry. Take me to him."

"No," Brant said, and in his voice I heard the will of the boy I had known, shot through with the roughness of a man I did not know at all.

"You are punishing me," I said slowly, "for leaving, all of ten years ago. Because I wounded you then, you would take my child from me now. Once you were not so heartless!"

"Once I was not many things," he said coldly. "But, no, I am not taking Jorry from any desire to punish a worthless woman, although you may believe that if you choose."

"You do not even want him!"

"No, I do not. But now that I have him, his life rests with me. Not just his whereabouts: his life, Fia. I can place him where you would never find him, tell him you are dead, turn him into a swineherd or a nobleman or a juggler, have him put to death as a thief. Do you think you could stop me? You cannot even bargain with me. You have no power, except the feeble one you have always exercised: to flee tanglement. Flee now, by even so much as refusing to obey me, and you will not only never see Jorry again, you will never so much as hear what I have done with him."

I went cold. There was no room in Brant's tone for bargaining, no possibility of appeal. For a vivid moment it seemed to me that all he said had already happened, that Jorry had been lost to me for empty agonized years, that I had looked on endless landscapes and into the faces of thousands of men and wondered in torment if each knew anything of my son, was my son, knew people who knew my son. The ground rocked under me, and when Brant's body moved off mine and he pulled me to my feet I went blindly, empty with possibility.

Brant pushed me so that I sat on the mossy log. He remained standing above, and he tipped my face upward into the moonlight to be sure I heard him. His own face was set and strained, and I thought with that odd detachment that comes to mock with irrelevance our greatest pain: I did not know that cruelty took so much out of a man.

"What have you heard of the old religion in Veliano?"

"I have heard nothing," I said numbly.

"I think you have, but it is not worth pursuing. You have seen the flayed bodies behind the palace?"

At first I took the question as a threat, a reminder of what Brant could do if he chose, but then my mind began again to move, and I saw that it was not a threat but a prologue. When I am not paralyzed with fear, my ear is good. Brant was beginning, incredibly, to tell a *story*.

"There are forces stirring in Veliano," he said. "Forces that have lain quiet for two centuries or more."

A story—he would tell me a *story*, while Jorry was even now being carried across the saddle of some armed servitor. Were Jorry's wrists bound? Did he cry?

" 'Forces'?" I said savagely, and rose to my feet. "Do you mean forces of unbodied evil, rising from the streambeds and deep lakes? I saw that play a month ago, by the south gate of Frost. An actor spoke such stuff, and the audience dumped a chamber pot over his head!"

"The forces are bodied enough—in men's minds. That has always been sufficient for evil. Don't be a child, Fia. You are no use to me as a child.

47

"Even when you and I were at Mother Arcoa's, there were rumors from those who visited the school that in some places—always unnamed, always remote—more of the old arts had been found. The plants that yielded stronger mind drugs had been discovered again, and were being distilled. Disciplines of the mind, hidden and passed down through generations, had been witnessed by someone who knew someone who had seen a child who could pull stories from other minds. But none of these travelers could tell Mother Arcoa how to make the drugs or where to find the child. Other stories, too, drifted in, stories of lost religious relics that were supposed to focus the mind trance irresistibly. You must have heard some of those stories yourself. Did you?"

"Yes!"

"But you discounted them. Have you since then become a believer in the Four Gods Protector?"

"No."

"A disbeliever?"

"No." I gave him the truth. "It does not seem to matter."

"And in the Silver Cities skepticism is so much more polished than belief. Religion—any religion—is too entangling, isn't it, Fia? Easier to flee that, too."

He removed his hand from my neck. It hurt still.

"After you fled Mother Arcoa's I heeded the stories more. I wanted something to distract me. Over the years between I learned much of the mind arts, and that brought me to Veliano. It was here I learned of the White Pipes—from a girl since flayed alive by the priests of the Four Gods Protector."

I remembered what Ludie had told me: ". . . and one girl before the second queen's serving woman." But I did not care, and the memory did not stay. I could not see it; I could see only Jorry, bound and crying across a saddle.

"The mind arts are real," Brant said. "And I am not the only one who has learned them, although the only one who learned them from the girl, Ard. She was the last of her line, an old line gone poor and hidden since the Four Gods Protector and their priests and kings came to power in the world."

It came to me suddenly that Brant could be lying. How did I know his men had taken Jorry? Brant could be merely punishing me, with the cruelest trick he could devise, for my theft and desertion. My son could still be asleep on his pallet in the tavern, his lashes throwing shadows on his moonlit cheeks.

As soon as I had this thought, I was convinced of it. Jorry was in the tavern; I had only to break from Brant to reach him. I calculated the distance to the edge of the clearing, to the edge of the woods, to the tavern window. Jorry was there.

"The mind is capable of much deception," Brant said. I started, but he was not looking at me. "Ard herself had experimented with so much, she was uncertain what lay in her own mind, what came from the drugs, what she took from the minds of others. She lived in a cottage, away from men; their minds confused her. She was perhaps a little mad."

I gathered myself for the sprint to the tavern. Jorry lay there, asleep on his pallet.

"He is not there," Brant said, and his fingers closed on my wrist.

I swung my head wildly.

"No, I did not enter your mind," he said impatiently. "Did you see any drugs, mist, anything? I merely know you, Fia. But this time you cannot flee. Or will you anyway, if I let you go?"

"Not from my son," I said, looked at him, and so made my bargain. Brant knew it. I would do whatever was necessary to regain Jorry, but I would not forget how I had been forced to it, nor forgive. And I would not hesitate to use any advantage I could gain. For the first time I set my mind to what he was saying; I could not tell what knowledge I might need.

"Ard went even, I think, into the minds of beasts," Brant went on. "She kept swine and crooned to them and slept with them sometimes when she was afraid. I would find her there in the morning, in the swine pen. She was afraid often. When she died she was only seventeen, a childlike, eerie, beautiful soul-beseter with the long blond hair of the old line."

"Why do you tell me all this, Brant?"

"Because I choose to. You mean you do not wish to know where I went after you cast me off?" His tone was mocking, but there was something wrong about it, like music slightly off-key. I listened, perplexed.

"Ard was taken while I was away from Veliano, in Erdulin. When I returned, it was too late to gain her a merciful death. I learned that she died in swirls of violent stories that raged through the cell and terrified her torturers, who dared not quit because the order had come from Rofdal's priests. She pulled from her tormentors' minds the most horrible stories she could, but she could not stay their knives. They feared Rofdal more than their own minds. Or hers."

I could see the scene; my stomach turned.

"How did they name her soul-beseter? How did they know where and what she was?"

"You do not need to know that," he said, and I was startled by the depths of pain in the harsh voice coming from out of the darkness.

Had he loved Ard? Suddenly, viciously, I hoped that he had and that he ached over her monstrous death, reliving it each time he spoke. And then I was ashamed, not on behalf of him, but of her.

"But what of me?" I said. "What has this Ard to do with me?"

"Ard was flayed alive by the priests of the Four Gods Protector not only because she knew mind arts, but because flaying alive was how the old religion was fought before. The priests hoped to release from her mind under torture any knowledge of what they really sought."

I thought of my story—not mine, but come through me—of the two desperate searchers. A chill lay icy on my spine.

I said slowly, "They sought the White Pipes."

"Yes," Brant said. "They sought the White Pipes."

"And tonight, in the Great Hall—whoever made me give that story pantomiming a search, was hoping that I—"

"Yes, was hoping that you knew something of the Pipes and it could be taken from your mind."

I shivered. My mind had been used, with no more care for

the consequences than for the bellows of a smith, to blow an
airy lie about a set of pipes. For that, my life and Jorry's had
been tossed under the knife. For that.

"But what *are* the White Pipes? And in the story—Brant, in
the story they were *found*. Have they then already been
found?"

Brant stayed silent. The silence stretched on a long time. I
thought at first he was considering his answer, but then I
began to sense in his silence an artificial quality, the deliberately prolonged silence an actor will use to heighten an
audience's interest. But Brant was not a man for actor's tricks.
I could still feel his hand squeezing my neck, and fear and
hatred of him crawled like vermin in my stomach.

I said again, "Have the White Pipes been found?"

Brant said very softly, "Yes. I have them. Ard gave them to
me."

"You have them!"

"Yes," he said. "I have them."

"But why—"

"Others do not know that. Others who would like the
Pipes."

"Who?"

"It was the queen who sent me to fetch you back to the
palace. She wishes you to entertain her again."

The queen. I saw again Leonore's delicate body swollen
with pregnancy, heard again her cry at the end of my story,
saw her smile at Rofdal as at a dangerous and tamed beast, and
her preternatural stillness. The queen.

"You have risen high," I said bitterly, "to make a rival of a
queen."

"We are not rivals. Not yet. She does not know I know
mind arts nor that I hold the White Pipes."

"Then why tell *me*?"

"Because I choose to," Brant said contemptuously. But why
contempt? And why tell anything? Would not knowledge
be a danger?

A profound powerlessness gripped me. Brant held one end
of my leash, the queen the other; and I could not fight them. I

had no mind arts to equal theirs. I could only be used—by Brant, by Leonore—as a counter in a game the more deadly for being hidden. But why hidden? There were still things I did not know, must know, if I were to have a chance to survive and to regain Jorry.

"What of the king? Is he too of the old religion?"

"No. He knows nothing; not of Leonore, not of me."

This was an unexpected boon. My face must have shown that I thought so, for Brant said softly, "If you told him of my arts, he would not believe you. If you told him of the queen, you would die for treason. You have not the credibility of Leonore's nobles who poisoned Janore and made a serving woman die for it."

"And my lack of credibility is an asset to you or Leonore," I said. "I can be made to seem trivial, if necessary."

"Yes."

"And also dangerous, if necessary, Brant? If I am sentenced to be flayed, can I depend upon you to order a quick and merciful death?"

He looked at me steadily, but I thought I heard a flicker of pain in his voice. "To whom have you talked?"

"A kitchen maid. My informant is as trivial and expendable as I am."

"You should remember that."

I forced myself to steadiness and thought I had succeeded. But the next moment I heard myself cry, "But what are the White Pipes? What could be desirable enough for such risk?"

"You know nothing of either desire or risk," Brant said harshly. "You never did. But you are a Storygiver and you know that even the simplest tale between your palms is released from the contents of your mind opened by the drugs of the First and Second Flasks. What do you hear after you drink the Second Flask?"

"Hear—"

"Yes. *Hear.*"

"Music. A faint tune."

"Sing it."

"I cannot. I can never recall it."

"You never really hear it. You only feel it, don't you, in muscle and blood."

"Yes. That is it—yes."

"The mind arts you saw when I learned that Jorry was . . . mine—" he stumbled over the word and I glanced at him in surprise, but in the silvery moonlight his face was as hard as before. "Those arts differ from your Storygiving only in the use of different drugs to unbind deeper layers of the mind. The depths must be unbound, and then they must be roused to life—and for that there are combinations of notes, certain sequences of tone and pitch, that draw from the mind movements it did not suspect it possessed."

I remembered the boy with the flute, and how I had stood entranced by his playing, and had felt then nameless and poignant sensations. Even the horses had stood still, and turned their heads to the music, and been touched somehow in their beasts' minds.

Brant said, "There are melodies to rouse and focus the bound layers of the mind and drugs to force their unbinding. Both were lost; both are being recovered."

"And the White Pipes?" I said, but I think that already I knew.

"The White Pipes play one melody only, and that the one that unbinds all the power of the mind which plays the pipes, and binds the minds which hear. But only in combination with the drug. And on the silver bands you saw binding the Pipes, are carved the leaves and blossoms of that drug. Those who hear the music, take the drug, and discipline the mind, have access to all forces of mind. Those who hear the music, take no drugs, and try to resist with nothing but the undirected impulses of their puny thoughts, are laid as open as are unarmed and naked men against an army."

"Soul-beseters and soul-beset," I said. And then, "By the Gods Protector—it was true. It was real."

"The Gods Protector have nothing to do with it. Nor the Gods anything else."

"The White Pipes. And you have them."

Brant said with great distinctness, "Ard gave them to me."

I saw again the flayed bodies strung up in the courtyard, the blackened things that had once been human. I saw Leonore's still eyes and the cruel line of Brant's mouth, and I heard the elusive music that came after I had drunk the Second Flask. Unarmed and naked men against an army—that was the image Brant had used. But I saw another: Jorry's unprotected face asleep in the moonlight, and his child's voice saying, "They must have been very bad to be hurt so much."

I pulled my wrist free of Brant's hold. He tensed as if he thought I would again try to run. I did not. But I could not bear to have him touch me. I saw his hand holding the White Pipes, lifting them to his lips, the lives of all around him subject to the will I had eluded once by simply fleeing. In a kingdom ruled by the White Pipes, a kingdom where all minds could be ransacked or controlled at will, there could be no flight.

Already an enemy had fingered my mind. Two enemies: Brant was that now, as well. When I remembered that in the Great Hall I had believed he was afraid for me and that tonight in these woods I had desired him—when I remembered those things, my flesh writhed. My mind had deceived me. I did not know the man Brant had become, this man who held the White Pipes and who wanted me, for reasons he would not voice, to know it.

"Jorry," I said, and my voice shook. "If Jorry is hurt, you will die for it. I will kill you no matter what mind forces you command, no matter if your death causes mine."

For a moment Brant said nothing. Then, shockingly, he laughed, a laugh with no amusement in it. "Not you, Fia—not you. You would turn squeamish and flee before you acted so momentously. Or so well."

Roughly he pushed me forward. In the tiny room in the tavern, I gathered my cloak and the few other possessions left to me. Jorry's cloak was gone, and the pallet and blanket beneath the window lay empty.

4

ONLY TWO HORSES AND ONE MAN AWAITED US, AND
the man was little more than a boy. He stuttered and his face
had the heavy, blurred lines of the simpleminded. I was
surprised that he, and only he, accompanied Brant. I wondered how many men Brant had sent with Jorry.

Brant led my pony himself, astride his big bay. Jorry's
pony, Slipper, was gone from the stable. We rode in silence
through the darkness. The trail was not the clear one I had
taken down the mountain but another, less well marked and
rockier. Several times one or another of the horses slipped on
loose stones. Behind me I heard the boy breathing heavily, as
if it were he and not his pony stumbling over the hard climb.
Finally the boy spoke.

"My lord Brant . . . there be an easier trail, my lord."

"This is the trail," Brant said curtly.

We stumbled on. I felt that I scarcely breathed; there had
come to me that strange, heightened calm that sometimes is
given in great danger or great pain. I was hardly aware of my
body swaying on the laboring pony. But everything beyond
my body had sprung into preternatural sharpness. Tree
branches across the moon sliced my eye; the breeze against my
cheek was a blow; the sickly-sweetness of gillyflowers suf-
focated me.

Gillyflowers: the four-leaved emblem of the Four Gods
Protector. The devout planted gillyflowers, and the priests
chanted of them at each worship of the Four Gods Protector:

Protection for the Body against Maiming,
Protection for the Senses against Corruption,
Protection for the Mind against Invasion,
Protection for the Soul against Besetting:
Gil-ly-flow-ers.

A bawdy version of the priests' chant, heard at some fashionable masque amid the snickers of lords and the titters of ladies, rose from memory:

Protection for my sins against naming,
Protection for my loins against interruption,
Protection for my lust against abrasion,
Protection for my mistress against begetting:
Gil-ly-flow-ers.

The trail turned abruptly to the right, and Brant followed it. The boy shifted and half-rose in his saddle, an aborted movement of surprise or protest, and then subsided. Through the trees I saw the dark shape of a wall.

"Bring her inside," Brant said.

The boy lifted me from my pony and led me into the hut. He smelled of sweat and manure; the hut smelled of animal dung and sour damp. The south wall had half collapsed, letting in enough moonlight to limn Brant and his servant with silver.

Brant said, "Take the horse back to the fork in the path and wait there until morning."

The boy-shape gathered itself for protest. "My lord. The queen, she be saying to bring the harper tonight. I be sorry, my lord, but that be what I hear her say." Fright scaled up his voice; he was afraid of the power of the queen.

"I say you wait by the fork in the path," Brant said, softly. The boy went. Brant turned to me.

I had heard in his words to the boy a note of strain. For a moment he held himself still in the gloom, and I caught in a shudder of his shoulders some terrible struggle with himself. Then his fist shot out and slammed into me.

The blow caught me on the upper arm and sent me crashing against the opposite wall. My head hit the logs; pain exploded along my arm. The cabin went dark. Out of the darkness Brant pulled me to my feet and said softly against my ear, "You took him, and he was mine."

He hit me again, this time in the belly. I bent double, gasping, and Brant twisted my arms until I thought the bones would break. I heard a voice screaming; it was mine.

He released my arms. I fell to the ground and lay gasping. His boot stood a hand's span from my face; I writhed to move away, and the pain in my twisted arm made me cry out again. I could not move away from his boot. My eyes closed, and when I could open them again, a long time later, Brant was gone.

I lay, my wrists bound, on the damp floor. My pain had subsided but I shuddered convulsively. I could not stop shuddering. For a long time I could not stop shuddering. Pain still divided body from mind, banishing mind, and I knew only my body and the waves of sick hurt that took it.

Eventually, mind returned.

Through my shudders rose a memory: Brant as a boy at Mother Arcoa's, beating another boy who had set fire to a cat. Brant had put out the fire, killed the agonizing cat, and beaten the boy bloody. I had been afraid of him then, watching him from a stairwell, unable to look away from Brant's pounding fists and set, relentless face. He had fought like one possessed, and in the end had not been pulled off the boy but had stopped of himself. He had left the bully bleeding and unconscious but with no bones broken, or organs permanently damaged. That was the first time I had looked at Brant with suspicion, with dread: the sons of harpers or farmers did not fight like that. They were not given the deadly, precise training called jal-un: the art of hurting exactly thus, and no more.

That night, in the tiny upstairs attic, he had taken me with great gentleness. Afterward I laid my head on his chest and wept, afraid of his physical strength and of the strength of my desire for him.

Choking back the pain, I struggled to my knees, and then to

my feet. The collapsed wall was a pile of rubble knee-high. Slowly, wincing, I climbed over it. Beyond, leaning against a tree, Brant waited.

His face was in shadow. Had I seen on it anger, or vengeance, or the lustful pleasure of causing pain, I think I could have borne it better. Hatred would have stiffened me, as bewilderment could not.

"Why now, Brant? Why now? You knew last night that Jorry—"

He seized my shoulders and dragged me back over the rubble into the hut. For a long moment he stood still, coiled with that terrible, violent tension. His shoulders shuddered. Then he drew back his arm and struck me again.

Pain burned along my chest. I was the cat on fire, I was the boy bloody and whipped. Then I was Fia, and I staggered to my feet and tried to kick him, falling into a heap that seemed to tear out my ribs.

The door of the hut flew open and the boy stood there.

"My lord! My lord! You can't! The queen—"

"Get out," Brant said. And then, "If you run off, boy, you will die for it."

He loomed over me, a massive dark blur, and yanked me up from the ground. Then his fists hit me again.

When the battering was over, I lay sobbing on the dirt. Sometime later, I dozed—or fainted. Later still I woke, gasping, and stared at the darkness without and within.

Had I been asked, before I climbed from the window of the Dancing Spider, to wager my life that Brant, relentless as he could be when angered, was neither vindictive nor vicious, I would have felt safe with the wager. I would have said that the boy I had loved might have become hard but not brutish, not a man who met disappointment with punishment. Brant's fists had proved me wrong. As I lay dizzy with pain on the floor of the ruined hut, I knew that he had beaten from me faith in my own judgment. If I had misjudged him that badly, I could not judge at all. Memory and judgment alike had become a black abyss, turning into a mockery not only the past but my ability to appraise the present. It was more than my body that Brant had battered, and I wondered if he knew it and had intended it so.

When I drew breath, I felt sharp pain. Gradually it eased. I gazed into the blackness, shivering at each noise that might be a step. Eventually I slept, and when I woke again sunlight streamed through the broken wall.

Brant sat on the floor a little way from me, his head bowed on his raised knees. I saw the thick hair falling forward from the crown of his head and his knuckles white where they clasped his legs. It was a posture of suffering and contrition, and that he should appear like that now seemed such an obscene blasphemy that I shook with outrage. He raised his head. The skin under his eyes was dark with sleeplessness; his face looked a careful blank.

"Get up. It is morning."

I rose halfway to my feet, winced, clamped my teeth over my lower lip, and struggled upright. Brant watched me with that same blank face. When he stepped closer, I shuddered, and he stopped.

"You can ride. You don't think you can, but you can." I realized that my bonds had been cut. I thought of his knife that near my skin as I slept, and clamped my teeth again over my lip.

Mounting was torture. The boy, his heavy face white and scared, helped me up, and then took my pony's reins. Brant rode ahead, retracing the trail of the night before, and then turning toward the palace. Each sway of the pony between my legs sent waves of hurt upward through spine and belly to my shoulders.

Hurt, but no longer real pain. Brant was right; I could ride. Under my clothes would be horrible-looking bruises, but none on my face; he had not hit me in the face. He had not broken any bones, he had not knocked out any teeth, he had not let his fists damage any vital organs. He had not used the most obvious male revenge, rape, though rape would not have shown, if that had been his concern. I did not know his concern. I did not know anything.

Once he turned in the saddle, and when I felt his gaze touch me, I winced and clenched my hands. I could not help it.

The sun rose higher. We rode through green summer forests dappled with sunlight, smelling of wildflowers and clean leaves. As the trees began to thin, Brant's horse stumbled.

By chance I had happened to glance up and so I saw clearly, more clearly than perhaps Brant had intended, what he had done. On a clear long stretch of trail, Brant had suddenly kicked his horse into a canter, and then a breakneck gallop. All at once his arm had shot out to the right, yanking the bridle with all his strength. The big bay had jerked to the right, forced to step far off the path and onto a soft embankment much burrowed by small animals. He neighed and went down, throwing Brant. By the time the boy and I reached them, the horse lay thrashing on the treacherous ground, and Brant stood above him with his sleeve torn open and his cheek bloody.

"He has broken his leg," Brant said, without expression. The boy stared, frightened. "Move back, then," Brant said. "I will do it. I said, *move back*."

The boy moved his pony off, leading mine. I looked over my shoulder just as the bay screamed. It flailed on the soft dirt, screamed again, and lay still, frothing blood. Brant sheathed his sword and came toward us.

Blood had spurted onto the front of his tunic, his right arm and gauntlet, his scraped right cheek. Without being told, the boy dismounted and Brant straddled his pony. The reins of my pony passed from the boy's dirty fingers to the bloody ones of Brant's glove.

I had seen it. He had made the horse stumble to break a leg. It had been deliberate.

Brant said to the boy, "Go home to your village. Do not return to the palace. Here." He drew out a coin, smearing it with blood, and gave it to the boy. On the boy's simple face I saw a peasant's fear war with a peasant's greed. He took the coin. Brant watched him retreat into the woods, and while he watched, none of us, neither ponies nor I, moved. Brant squinted at the sun, measuring its height in the sky. Then he kicked the pony's sides and rode from the forest into the broad and grassy plateau that held the palace. Around us the scent of gillyflowers, favored of the Four Gods Protector, rose on the warm air.

In front of the palace stood assembled a royal hunting party. The sun above us stood at noon.

At the head of the party rode Rofdal, mountainous astride a huge roan. Beside him on a white horse rode a woman in blue. I saw her as only a blur of velvet and veils; I ached with bruises, was light-headed from lack of sleep and food, throbbed with fears for Jorry. The Brant who had beaten me was not the Brant of ten years ago or even the man I thought I had seen across the Great Hall. What might he do to Jorry?

"Brant," the king called cheerfully, and Brant and I, bloody and ill-mounted, rode up to the king. "What of the Gods Protector has befallen *you*?"

"An accident, my lord," Brant said, and once more I had another of those reversals that come with pain and was seeing the exchange with heightened, abrasive clarity, as if each word and sign scraped the inside of my mind.

Rofdal's small eyes, bright in the fleshy bulk of his face. The blond woman, beautiful as only paintings are beautiful, glancing with blue, mocking eyes from Rofdal to Brant. Her hunting hat sported a wispy bit of blue veil; it blew over her left cheek like a shadow. And Leonore was there as well, carried in a chair litter to see her lord off to his hunting, and her gaze moved slowly from Rofdal to the woman in blue and back again.

Brant said, "My mount misstepped into a rabbit hole and broke his leg. I had to slay him."

"Your bay stallion!" Rofdal said. "A shame, Brant. A wonderful piece of horseflesh."

"I won't find his equal," Brant said.

"I had expected you to join us," Rofdal said. A shade of annoyance passed over his face, absorbed in a moment into his mood of buoyant good humor. His day was fine, his mount eager, the lady chosen to ride beside him beautiful and smiling. He clapped Brant on one bloody shoulder and bellowed, "You will miss some good hunting! I had mind to see you take again that high hedge that tumbled you last hunting!"

"It would not have tumbled me this time," Brant said, smiling. "But I was bound by the queen's order to fetch back the Storygiver."

Rofdal's eye fell on me. I suppose he had not identified me before, seeing only the shabby pony and a slight, ill-dressed form of a servant. But now he looked at me closely, and his face darkened.

"I sent that one from the palace."

Brant looked confused. He did it so well that I think only I—preternaturally alert, used to actors—suspected it was a pose. He threw a startled glance at Leonore, pointed enough to divert Rofdal's attention to her, then dropped his eyes as if in embarrassment at a petty domestic misunderstanding, and looked again at Rofdal, a frank, smiling look that invited his liege into a conspiracy of men amused by the vagaries of pregnant women.

"A whim, perhaps, of her Grace's . . . situation? I have heard it said, my lord, that females carrying boys more often seek vulgar amusements, a presage of their babies' lustier spirits. The queen specifically requested that the Storygiver perform for you before the Midsummer Masque, and so of course I carried out her request."

"You so requested?" Rofdal demanded of Leonore.

Under the shade of her curtained litter, Leonore's still face had paled. But she was able to smile, a smile cold and quiet. "It was to be a surprise, my lord. I have been told that this Storygiver, despite her unfortunate beginning here, can perform a certain story that will especially delight Your Grace. But Lord Brant, I fear, has spoiled my surprise."

Rofdal still scowled and the issue hung in doubt: his disapproval at having been flouted or his pleasure and curiosity at a surprise performance? No one spoke, and no eye met another, while the tension spun itself out. Then the blond woman leaned forward and whispered something in Rofdal's ear, and he exploded into laughter.

"Ha! That is true, you pretty cyret! How did you think of it?. Very well, then, since a masque there will be, the Storygiver shall perform before it. I thank you, madam, for the surprise, and I am only sorry Brant spoiled it. Brant, you have been decreed your punishment by the Lady Cynda, and there is no evading it. You must hunt with us without your bay, on some inferior mount, and you and I will take that hedge again!"

"Nothing could give me greater pleasure," Brant said, smiling.

A fresh mount was brought, amid much bustle and laughter. Men laid wagers on Brant's taking the hedge or coming to a fall. A squire of Brant's height stripped off his tunic and Brant changed his own, red with horse's blood, for the squire's. I saw him laugh, throwing back his head and lifting his face to the sun.

The Lady Cynda moved her horse a little to one side; I saw her lean over to speak to the squire. A moment later he passed up to her Brant's bloody glove. She did not look at it but thrust it inexplicably within the folds of her skirt, the sticky leather hidden by the blue velvet. Her face, too, was laughing and gay, beautiful in the sunlight. Brant's wife.

The hunting party rode out with a sounding of horns, Rofdal and Cynda first, Brant just behind. He did not glance back.

Left behind with the servants, Leonore turned to me. In her eyes was cold fury. She had to be aware that Brant had arranged to have me publicly committed to performing at this masque. He had brought it all into being: the performance, Rofdal's approval, the slain horse, Jorry's abduction, my secret beating at his hands, the bruises that made it torture now to sit in the saddle. He had created it all, like some intricate story between his palms, and I did not know why.

Leonore's gaze raked me. Then she lifted her hand and a burly servant took my pony's bridle and led me behind the litter, toward the palace.

He led me to circle the palace itself. I thought at first that we headed for the old castle, the Priests' Hall, but instead we went to the unfinished wing where first I had been housed. The gibbet and its grisly burden no longer stood in the dirt courtyard, which was empty save for the rubble and debris of the stonemasons and carpenters. The man took me through a rear door, and then through another, locked despite the emptiness of the half-finished passageway. I knew, then, where he must be taking me, but it was too late to run, even had my body permitted it.

Beyond the locked door were stone steps, and then a long passageway stretching into blackness. I had not lost my bearings; the tunnel stretched toward the old castle. Rofdal was prudent in his building. An airy, balconied palace might be an apt celebration of new wealth, but a fortified keep was safer. With a secret tunnel, he could have both.

The old castle would have its own dungeons. But I was not taken along the passageway to Rofdal's priests' castle. Instead I was shoved into a small room well underneath the palace itself, the only room I saw along the tunnel. The servant's push sent me sprawling onto slightly damp stone. Then the door slammed shut, cutting off the gray light from above, and I lay yet again in darkness, bruised and aching but too numb, this time, to be afraid.

I did not wait long in the darkness. With Leonore came light, lanterns that shimmered on the dark stuff of her gown where it curved over her swollen belly. With her, too, were the same servant and another man, the latter richly dressed in dark red velvet. I had only to look at him to see he must be the queen's brother. He had the same delicate body, small face, dark eyes. But not the same cold stillness.

"Bind her to a chair," he said. Even his voice, high for a man, might have passed for Leonore's.

My bonds were loose, meant to restrain rather than hurt. Leonore took a bench as well and I thought—foolishly enough, but pain and weariness had left my mind open to foolishness—that carrying such a large child as Rofdal's promised to be must make it hard for her to stand upright ɩor very long.

Jorry had been a small infant and an easy birth.

"Will you question her first?" the man asked.

"Why should I bother? I am not interested in lies," the queen said, and drew from her skirts a small flask.

I knew then that Brant had been right about her, and fear weakened my spine. Leonore practiced the mind arts—and what else? The ancient religion? The flaying that was a part of it? When she had taken from my mind all that interested her—and I did not doubt she could do it, Brant had done so easily—what would she order done with my useless body? Flaying would not be necessary. I was not a queen's serving woman, whose death must be public and justified. I was an itinerant Storygiver, and none would question my disappearance.

No. It *would* be questioned: I was to perform before Rofdal at the Midsummer Masque. I had been committed publicly to doing so; the king might remember and question my absence. I must appear, because Brant had publicly arranged it so.

Because Brant had arranged it so.

Leonore drank her flask—was it the First or Second, I wondered, or did she not need two?—and closed her eyes. Her arm rose in an odd gesture, batting away the air above her head, as if it pressed heavy upon her. Her skin flushed and tightened with what looked to me like pain. I thought with dread that her drug must be much stronger than any I knew, to affect her so. For what seemed a long time she sat as stone. Light from the lantern held high by the servant standing behind her chair shone silver on her smooth, dark hair, on the stuff of her gown, on the gray stones of walls and floor slick with underground dampness.

The queen opened her eyes, spread her hands, and the pink mist formed above the distended bulge of her belly. When the mist became figures, they stood their ground on her unborn child. Only then did she look at me, bound in my chair. Her eyes were unfocused and dim, as if they had retreated a little into her head. I knew then why, that first night in the Great Hall, she had kept her lashes cast down.

"Think about your Storygiving," she said to me. "Where did you learn to do it? Think of where you studied and with whom. Show me what happened when you learned the mind arts. I want to know how much you can do, Storygiver, beyond fables to amuse dolts. Think of the most important day of your studying, Storygiver."

The moment she finished speaking, I knew what would happen. Frantically I tried to think of something else, anything else, but of course I could not. Turning one's mind from a thought is the surest way of driving it to a deeper layer, where the rest of the mind turns slowly to converge upon it, like the ponderous shifting of great rocks toward a fault in the earth. Between Leonore's palms, the day I considered the most important among those at Mother Arcoa's formed from mist, and there stood on her belly the figures of Brant and me, naked before each other.

Leonore's brother gasped, leaned closer, gasped again. "Brant! It is Lord Brant!"

Leonore sat frozen. "It cannot be."

"It *is*. Brant—*she knows Brant*. And from years ago, it would seem." He raised his fist, an abortive half-gesture, as if he would strike but found no target. "He must then be the one that—but why did you send Brant to fetch her back last night? Why *Brant*?"

"He offered," Leonore said sharply. "No, he made himself ready to be asked . . . he guessed I would have her back, Perwold, and he wanted to go!"

"She must know much, then. She—"

"*Watch*," Leonore said.

The story between her hands, the same story Brant had wrenched from me the first night in the Great Hall, played itself again before this new audience. It was exactly as before: the tiny Fia and Brant embraced, lay down, began to caress. She removed his tunic and kissed his chest. He ran his hands over the curve of her thigh, tenderly cupped the swell of her newly budded breasts. The figures coupled. And the boy spoke to the girl, talking excitedly and without words, his hands on her shoulders. He pleaded; she shook her head dumbly. And when he slept, she took gold from within a secret drawer in a homemade carved altar, and left him, carrying a shoe and a child. She pressed the shoe to her cheek, above the curve of her belly, and cried.

I had not known that the details of that day lay so unwavering in my mind.

Leonore's brother hissed, a sharp intake of breath between set teeth. "Her whelp is Brant's."

"And Brant was with her at her training. He, too, must know . . . but how much?"

Perwold shrugged and moved toward me. He moved his leg as one piece from the hip, with the sleekness of a dancer—or a rodent. Before he reached me Leonore raised her hand, and he stopped.

"Storygiver," she said, "think of what you and Brant learned together. Show me the greatest of the mind arts *you* can perform. Now. Think of the most difficult of the old arts you yourself have ever done . . . that is it, yes . . ."

Under her hands I saw myself, standing on a marble floor, giving a story. I remembered the occasion: it had been the house of a great merchant in Pearl, the most eastward of the Silver Cities. I had been proud of myself because I had given the fable of the Princess and the Bird all the way through, all its seven scenes, two more than I had ever done before. Or since. Seven scenes of a simple story, crude enough so that even the children had known from the beginning what the ending would have to be, and had known too that the Storygiver would not create anything that might disturb or startle them.

Perwold snickered. "The height of her arts!"

"Of hers," Leonore said, "but not his. Remember what that mad girl Ard told us just before she died. Someone had been with her, had learned from her."

"It did not look like Brant."

Leonore said, "You are a fool. It did not look like anyone; you cannot create a sane story from a mad mind. It could have been Brant. What do we know of him before he married Cynda, beyond the public commonplaces of the marriage contract?" She turned her gaze toward me and leaned forward, straining over the curve of her unborn child between us.

"You do not have Brant's son with you now. Where is he, Storygiver? The boy. Think of where he is now."

Mist swirled between her spread hands. Desperately I tried to picture Jorry as an infant, to fill my mind with the memory of his big dark eyes watching my face as he nursed, his warm weightlessness—he had felt so heavy in my belly, so light in my arms—the clean baby smell of his neck. He had had little hair. He—

The nine-year-old Jorry appeared between Leonore's hands.

First he lay asleep on the pallet at the tavern. Then, beyond him, figures of Brant and I appeared, arguing. The figure of Jorry wavered, dimmed. I tried to run; Brant caught and pinned me; the figure of Jorry sat up and blinked.

Then I saw something I had never seen before, nor even imagined. Bits of mist shifted around Jorry, mist dun-colored and nearly, but not quite, transparent. Leonore squeezed shut her eyes and grunted, as if straining to bring forth. The dun-colored mist nearly, but not quite, took on translucent shapes. One moment it was horses and men, the next nothing at all. It was like watching shapes in summer clouds: now an eagle, now a flower, and none of them existing anywhere but in the fancies of the watching mind. Leonore was bringing forth not what my mind knew, but what it had imagined.

The now-men, now-horses, now-nothing mist moved off with Jorry.

Leonore gave a great gasp and slumped forward. The scene between her hands vanished. Both men knelt anxiously beside her, and Perwold put one hand—tentatively, as a man will do who has never fathered legitimate children—on his sister's belly. When Leonore raised her head her face dripped sweat and contorted with anxiety. She slipped her hand under her brother's.

"Moving still," he said.

"Moving too *much*," she whispered, and in the emphasis I caught her fright of bringing on labor before it should begin.

She had taken a risk, straining her muscles as well as her mind after my imaginings, and I wondered if her evident fear was for the child itself or for the security the child would bring to her position as queen to a king who had already had two queens before her.

"It is quieter now," the brother said.

"Not 'it'—*he*," Leonore snapped.

Perwold withdrew his hand. "Yes, of course."

"Do not sound amused. That is not a pregnant woman's fancy. The child is a son."

"You are *certain*?"

"I am certain," Leonore said, and I sat stunned, wondering how. In the lamplight Perwold's eyes sparkled. Leonore drank from a flask offered by the servant, water or wine, and leaned wearily against the back of her chair, her arms dangling loose at her sides. "Brant sent his cub away. He knew, then, Perwold—*knew* we had suspected him. He did not want to give us anything to use against him, any lever to pry from him whatever he knows of the Pipes. He must have cared for the boy."

Perwold said incredulously, "A bastard whelp off a Story-giver? I think you are fanciful, Leonore."

She straightened in her chair. "No. Why else send the child away, if not to protect him?"

"To compel *her*. A lever can goad as well as pry, Leonore."

The queen regarded me thoughtfully. "True. Or perhaps she herself is a lever, Perwold. If Brant does care for a mongrel by-blow—why not the memory of an early love?"

"Brant? He is not sentimental."

"Neither is he simple. I have looked at him sometimes—"

"Looked in what manner?" Perwold said, and I heard layers and edges in his voice. Leonore smiled.

"Not as you think."

"It would be wiser not to."

She said sharply, "Don't call me a fool, Perwold. I do not debase the power of the mind arts by thinking they can be subverted by lust. Brant would have learned too much from that mad sorceress, Ard. I will take care not to be so much as alone with him in the same room, nor anywhere he can spread his hands."

"As this whore spread her legs. Do you truly think *she* can be used to make him divulge whatever he has learned of—"

"Be quiet," Leonore said. Then, more thoughtfully, "He has no legitimate children. Cynda does not conceive. Even an unsentimental man might hesitate to cause the flaying alive of the woman who has borne his only son." She turned her head to gaze at me. Through the numbness brought by the careless mention of torture, I saw their two faces, identical in shape and coloring, different in expression. Leonore regarded me speculatively, gauging possibilities, as one might guess at the meat yield of a cow still on the hoof. But Perwold's eyes glittered, and over his face lay the shine of voluptuous anticipation. For the queen's brother, my flaying would be a sensuous enjoyment.

From her gown Leonore drew another flask, smaller, the neck set with blue Veliano gems, and drank it off. The first one had not then been inexhaustible, although she had given two stories from it—both mine—and no Storygiving drug I knew of could yield more than one. Was this dose as strong as her other? Again her small body showed the same jolting reactions, and even through my numb fear I wondered at her capacity.

"Storygiver. You were with Lord Brant the whole night, were you not—before this 'accident' to his mount. I had told him to bring you straight back to the palace, but he did not. Where did he go? Show me what transpired between you in the night, Storygiver. Were you again lovers? Show me. Last night, Storygiver."

And I showed her. Between her hands Brant brought me to the hut, drew back his fist, struck me again and yet again. I lay on the damp ground, and the face of the battered Fia-figure showed all that I had not seen in myself: fear, and pain, and the agonized doubt of having judged so badly that the faith in one's judgment sickens and festers. All that Brant had done to me, I lived again.

Perwold laughed. "Lovers! He punishes her for stealing his

spawn. There is your lever, Leonore! Probably he would be glad to have us flay her for him and save him the trouble."

But Leonore had reached me, crossing the little distance between us so swiftly that I smelled her perfume before her bulging belly was thrust into my face. She grasped my tunic and pulled it over my head. The tunic tore, snagged on my ear, tore again. When it was off, she stood staring at my naked body. Bruises, purple and blue, swelled on arms, breasts, stomach where Brant had hit me.

"Not an illusion," she said softly. Then, to Perwold, "I thought all at once: What if she can *choose* what I create? What if all I took from her mind were merely lies?"

"No mind art can do that," Perwold said.

"Evidently not," Leonore said, and poked one slim finger at a bruise just above my left breast. I cried out. Instantly Perwold was at his sister's side, his mouth a little open, his eyes flickering.

"No, Perwold. Rofdal wishes to see her perform at the masque."

"A pity," he said, and his eye lingered on my bruises as a miser would finger gold.

But loathsome as he was, I scarcely saw him. I was seeing instead Brant, and in a moment the abyss of judgment lurched again. I stumbled, like a figure caught in a quaking of the earth, clutching with weak hands at bits of memory that had suddenly changed shape and become something else, like the tree root tripped over and grabbed for in the dark that suddenly in one's hand becomes a moving snake.

Bits of memory: The shudder of Brant's shoulders, as if with some terrible struggle, just before he first struck me. The strain in his voice when he spoke to the boy, his only attendant, simpleminded and fearful, whom he had sent home to another village. The care with which Brant caused me pain and bruises but no broken bones or crushed organs. The posture in which I had surprised him when I awoke on the hut floor: head bowed on his knees, knuckles white with anguish. And, above all, the bloody farce of causing the slaying of his horse, and his actor's confusion when he revealed to Rofdal

71

that he had had an accident while fetching the Storygiver, on order of the queen.

Fabrication—all of it, fabrication. He had beaten me so that Leonore could pull from my mind the story of his beating me, and so be convinced of my real terror and pain. Real terror, real bruises—but the reason open to guessing, and Leonore and Perwold would believe punishment for an old theft, because punishment was what they understood. I had believed it myself. I had lain gasping on the sour floor of the mountain hut and thought that Brant punished me in spite and vengefulness.

Or had he been not punishing but protecting—brutalizing me so that I might show it to Leonore in a story, and so be protected from her greater brutality?

My breath rose too hard along the back of my throat.

Turn the story one way and it appeared thus, turn it another and it changed, like expensive silk angled variously to the light. Sending Jorry away—to compel me or to protect Jorry? The feebleminded boy as Brant's sole attendant—because Brant had sent his most trusted men with Jorry, or because the boy's mind would absorb only the obvious events which Brant arranged for it to absorb? My performance at the Midsummer Masque—for Brant to make use of my public story as once Leonore had, or to ensure that Leonore and her brother could not yet kill me for having seen the power of her mind arts?

Leonore was watching my face. But without a story between her hands, she misinterpreted the reality before her. "No, I will not give you to Perwold, Storygiver—he has peasants enough to play with." She slipped the torn tunic back over my head. Her brother looked at her coolly; she ignored him. "We are not yet done, Storygiver, you and I. One more."

Not taking her eyes from my face, she pulled from her gown a small packet wrapped in silk. Opened, the packet gave off a strong smell both putrid and pungent, like some concentrated herb badly decayed. But herbs prepared as concentrated powders did not decay. In the dim light I could not see clearly what was in the packet before Leonore had put its contents to her lips.

She shuddered violently and turned from me, her face averted until she spread her hands. Her voice sounded thick, as if the skin of her throat had been burned in swallowing. "The White Pipes. Lord Brant and the White Pipes. Think of what Brant told you of himself and the White Pipes."

She was going to do it again: bring to the mist between her hands events I had not experienced but only been told, this time not the easily imagined snippet of Jorry being carried off by Brant's men but a story only secondhand to me. All at once, I doubted she could do it. There was no reason for my doubt, I had seen things in this dim room that once I would have called just as impossible. Nonetheless, doubt rose before me, as pervasive as the decayed stink of what Leonore had eaten, as solid as the damp stone beneath my bound feet.

Leonore said thickly, "The White Pipes!"

The mist between her hands took shape. Perwold, now holding the lantern, bent closer, and the light slithered over Leonore's quaking belly. Her child within kicked and jerked, agitated either by his mother's agitation or by the unknown drug she had taken. And above the squirming stuff of her gown, the mist became two figures.

Blurry, nearly transparent, constantly melting, shifting in outline as commonplace story figures never do, the figures were nonetheless identifiable. One was Brant. The other was a naked girl riding a swine, the girl's blond hair long enough to fall over both her and the dirty pig. Her face constantly distorted, now melting so that the eyes ran down into the nose, now stretching from side to side in a grin as horrible as a death rictus. Brant's face wavered as well but not so wildly, not with the same keening leer. It seemed in the shifting mist that things sprouted from the girl's body: mushrooms from her breasts, a dagger from her side, long and hairy roots, thick as a man's thumb and pale as maggots, from her thighs. Still leering, not moving from the swine, she plucked the monstrous growths from her body and handed them to Brant. In his hand the mushrooms became something else, something

73

slimy and moving, that I could not see clearly. The dagger turned bloody, stuck with shreds of skin. Almost I looked away. The woman handed Brant the dagger, then snatched it back from him and gave him instead the maggoty roots, and he took them into his hands.

The pale roots became a set of white pipes.

In all that confusion of melting, transparent shapes, only the White Pipes shone clear and hard, each detail as exquisitely etched as if the whole were a marble in miniature. Perwold gasped and his hand shot forward. The moment it penetrated the mist, Leonore screamed and fell from her chair, her eyes rolling in her head and the mist-borne shapes of her story dissolving into nothing. She hit the floor hard, landing upon her side, and the load within her belly bounced and quivered.

The servant hissed, bent over her, and then leaped to me. A knife floated in his hand; for a moment I thought she was dead, and I along with her. But the servant cut my bonds and dragged me to the fallen giver. He pushed me toward her skirts, glanced up at Perwold, frozen blankly above me, and I saw that for all that he and the servant schemed to bring down a kingdom, for all that they were prepared to murder me if it would not attract attention, for all that Leonore meant to their plans—for all of that, they could not deal with her as a woman whose woman's time had come, and they turned her over to me, her captive, from whom they expected womanly aid.

I placed my hand on Leonore's belly. The child within still quivered, but it seemed to me that the muscles of Leonore herself had not tautened. A brownish spittle foamed at the corners of her mouth, but it was a scant amount. After a small and stupid hesitation, I pulled up the queen's skirts. The servant looked away; Perwold, I saw, did not. No blood showed between her legs, and I lowered her gown. Under my hand the fine stuff felt as airy as spiderweb.

She lay more still now. Her belly quieted. Her face began to return to its own delicate features, and not the thick mask it had become at the moment she had screamed.

"It is not the child," I said. "Her time is not yet. It was the drug caused this."

Assured that his sister was assailed by only poison and not birth, Perwold knelt beside her. I stood. The door to the room was not bolted; in one corner rested a staff within my reach; Perwold's head bent directly below me, the hair shiny with the sweet oils rich men can afford. But the servant watched me with hard eyes made harder since Leonore's last story, and I knew the chance was no chance at all.

"Brant has them," Leonore groaned. "He has the White Pipes. Ard had given them to *him*." She sat up, a bulging desolate heap huddled on the damp floor.

"No," Perwold said. "No. We had her mind emptied while she was flayed—no. He does not have them yet. She did not know herself where they were."

"Then she told him bits and pieces of knowledge, and he put them together and discovered for himself where the Pipes lay. Yes—she gave him roots, did you see? Roots. From that he grew the answer she could not grow herself. Roots." She shifted her gaze to me. "I did not know you had such a poetic mind, Storygiver."

Nor did I. Brant had told me nothing of any roots. Nor of mushrooms, daggers. Where had the story Leonore had created come from? From Brant's words—he *had* told me he had found the White Pipes—from dread in my mind, from pictures in Leonore's. Perhaps a secondhand story partook of all the minds through which it passed. Leonore knew these arts, and she seemed convinced—desolately so, when I would not have suspected her of the softness of desolation—of the truth of what she had seen.

But she did not know that Brant had killed his own horse to arrive plausibly late before Rofdal, or that he had—*if* he had—beaten me for the purpose of causing Leonore to see him beating me.

Hard doubt rose in me again. I could feel it in my chest, solid as something I had swallowed. Brant had lied to me. This story, too, he had arranged for me to believe so that I could be used to channel the story to Leonore. He had, in fact, kept me alive for the purpose of channeling this one story to the queen—and it was a lie.

Brant had not found the White Pipes.

How I knew this, I couldn't say. It may even have been more self-deception, more mistaken judgment, more of Brant's deliberately spawned confusion. But I did not think so. The conviction came to me, as some thoughts do, from beyond the mind entirely, born in some surer and less muddled ether and shot to the human mind on a beam of steady light. The rest of Brant's actions still confused me, but of this I felt sure enough to wager my life. Not story, but truth: Brant had lied. He did not have the White Pipes.

"If he had them," Perwold was saying, "He would have used them by now."

"How?" Leonore said.

"Had it been I, I would have at least used them to make you miscarry of the king's heir. A fall down a stairwell, a self-inflicted blow to the belly for which only you could be blamed . . ."

Leonore grew still; it seemed to me that even she was repelled by his words. Then she rose clumsily from the damp floor. On her feet, she put one hand on the servant's arm and the other at the small of her back, stretching slightly backward over the hand, trying to ease for a moment the lopsided weight of her pregnancy. My muscles remembered how that temporary easing felt—I had done the same when I carried Jorry. Partly from visceral memory and partly from having been cramped in my bonds, I also put my hand to the small of my back and arched my bruised body.

Leonore saw me. Something—perhaps the shared gesture and the shared burden behind it, perhaps the help I had been willing to give had she truly been in labor, perhaps no more than the strain of the day—made her say abruptly, "My son must be king." I heard in the words a woman's explanation, made reluctantly but made nonetheless: "Your child has been put in danger so that my child will be beyond danger, made secure on an otherwise threatened throne."

Leonore turned away. To Perwold she said, "Send her to the kitchens. Dispatch men—Ebral for one, but not Menioc, I want him here—to search for Brant's cub. Try first the pass to

Erdulin, and the road to Frost. Find out which men rode with Brant last night from the palace to that tavern and have them brought here to wait for me."

Perwold said, "I could question them."

I thought that there would be none to hold. Only the feeble-witted boy had not gone with Jorry, and Brant had sent him back to his village, wherever and whatever it was. Had Brant foreseen this, then, as well, and provided to protect the lives of his men? It seemed to me reasonable. He was giving Leonore as little as he could while still giving her—through me—his story of having the White Pipes.

Sulkily, Perwold said to his sister, "And what of that other matter?"

"It will keep. No, do not beset me now, Perwold, I am at the end of my strength!" Her voice scaled abruptly upward; in the dim, stinking room its shrillness seemed to climb as high as the rafters and then crack into dangerous shards that could slice us all. Perwold did not argue.

The servant, whose name I still had not heard, led me to the kitchen, and I was given a pallet in a room used by the washerwomen. I fell heavily on it, too tired to mind my bruises, to undress, to think. My body ached where Brant had battered me, and my mind ached for Jorry. Both gave way, and I slept the rest of that day and the whole of the following night, without the torment nor the comfort of dreams.

5

THEN BEGAN A STRANGE TIME. THE COURT WAS PRE-
paring for the queen's summer masque, and all around me
sounded that most wearying bustle: noisy energy lavished on a
trivial end. Ladies sewed costumes; ladies' serving women
sewed the costumes; ladies' serving women's maids sewed the
costumes; in the end even the kitchen maids set stitches on the
roughest of the cloths that were to cover the walkway by the
river. There were costumes for ghosts and for dead kings and
for mythical beasts, all made of the exquisite fabrics brought
by traders from more civilized kingdoms and cut in the service
of myths rough-hewn as Veliano's real tastes. A dun satin
woven with gold was fashioned by the tireless women into the
costume of a two legged boar with horns, which would be
slain in the reenactment of the legend of the founding of
Veliano by a heroic warrior. Rofdal himself, it was said,
would be under the hero's mask, although no one was
supposed to know for sure. Gossip and speculation flew as fast
as the women's needles: who would enact what part, who
would dance with whom, who had been made responsible for
what entertainment. Chickens were plucked, beasts slaugh-
tered, pastries concocted, gowns and cloaks bespoken,
created, hidden away from rivals.

Amid all this foolishness I moved like one with a sickening
fever among children fevered with merriment. I saw with
both a heightened perception of events and a heightened
isolation from them. I noted everything, because I did not

know what detail, what slipped word, what trivial occurrence
might prove useful in regaining Jorry. Desperately I hoped
that if I could talk casually to enough different people, help
with enough different tasks, I might learn something about
Brant and Leonore and Rofdal and Perwold to make me more
than a helpless coin passed among them. I thought, too, that I
might learn of likely places for Brant to have sent Jorry. So I
did whatever tasks presented themselves: grooming horses or
sewing ground covers or scouring pots or going with a
laughing group of kitchen maids into the woods to fetch
baskets of linberries, succulent and fragrant, with the bloom
fresh on their golden skins. All of this I did with one small
piece of my mind. The rest labored feverishly over Jorry and
soul-besetting, flaying, and the White Pipes.

The priests of the Four Gods Protector strolled around the
castle, patient and uninterested. I saw that they regarded this
summer masque as harmless amusement. It might dramatize
myths from the earliest of times, but such had nothing to do
with the Gods Protector, as the circle games even kings may
play with their children have nothing to do with affairs of
state. The priests could wait indulgently for the masque to be
over and men and women to return to the more serious rites of
summer worship. I watched the priests in their dun cloaks
embroidered with four-leaved gillyflowers, and it seemed
incredible to me I should know much, and they little, of the
deadly struggle for ancient powers going on beneath the
strenuous gaiety of the palace. They, no less than I, were
being used for ends they did not foresee. Once, when I passed
a novice priest on his way to the Consecrated Garden, his
cloak blew slightly in the wind and brushed my arm. I jumped
as if I had been burned. Would that novice—pink-cheeked,
scarcely needing yet to shave—be willing to flay a human
body in the service of his gods or his king? Had he already
done so?

Hours later I still felt that woolen touch, and my skin
prickled.

"What part shall the queen play in the masque?" I asked
Pial, the brightest-eyed of the berry-gathering kitchen maids.

She popped a linberry into her mouth, rolled it on her tongue, and eyed me scornfully.

"Cul, but you be ignorant!"

"She be a foreigner," said one of the other girls. "Like the caravan trading men. How should she know?"

"Agla be defending foreigners—especially trading men," a third girl said slyly, and all of them laughed, darting sideways glances at each other and covering their mouths with their fingers.

Agla swished her skirts, looked pleased with herself, and endeavored to keep the attention. "Cul, she *be* different. How many of *us* go from the chickens to the stables to the Great Hall to tell tales to the lords?"

"Is that how it be in the Silver Cities?" Pial sneered. "No one having her proper work, but be pushed to whatever tasks come to hand?"

"I am a Storygiver," I said, "and not fortunate enough to have a proper home in Veliano. I make myself useful to those with the right to live here."

The flattery won them. They all began to chatter at once, to tell me of the pleasures of dwelling in Veliano, of the excitement of serving at court rather than in the villages where they were born. I saw that the new export of Veliano gems had transformed their lives as much as those of the lords and merchants, at least in their own eyes, and that they considered themselves far above the last generation, who had never traveled more than one village away from their rocky farms. Standing or lounging among the cool trees, their hair braided with cheap ribbons and their mouths laughing around the golden linberries, they told me these were wondrous times, rich times, the best of times in Veliano. Rofdal had eased tithes, sponsored fairs and pageants, paid his soldiers and servants and royal miners very well. To them he was a king with enough imperiousness to merit their respect and enough generosity to merit their rough affection. That his power of life and death over them was absolute was no more than his kingly due; none questioned it. None seemed to know that in the Silver Cities it was no longer so. None mentioned the five flayings that had taken place in the last few years, and none mentioned Queen Leonore, until Agla remembered that I had asked a question.

"The queen be the star of the masque," Agla said. I looked puzzled, and Agla laughed, enjoying her superior knowledge. "The *star*." She pointed overhead. Above us were only green leaves, and the others began pelting her with linberries.

"That not be the sky!"

"Agla be thinking stars shine on the behinds of leaves!"

"No—she thinks it's night now, so she can see her trading man!"

The girls collapsed in laughter. Anything would set them off again. They lolled on the mossy ground, in the cool shade and laughed until tears ran from their eyes, and then they looked at each other and laughed again, hanging on each other's necks, healthy young animals with midsummer in their blood.

I picked linberries steadily and tried to force my lips to smile. My lips were dry. I licked them, they dried, I picked linberries, I licked them again. My lips would not smile.

"The star *T'nig*," Agla said, when she could speak again. "From the story of the founding of Veliano."

I said, "I thought T'Nig was a magic boar. The costume—"

"*Before*," Pial said impatiently and told me the story.

T'nig was a mythical and powerful spirit that had been born again and again in the mountains, first as a winged wolf and then an uncuttable tree, a bottomless lake, and several other incredible things, until it was born as a monstrous boar and was slain by the Nameless Warrior. Then the Nameless Warrior founded the kingdom of Veliano, and the remains of T'Nig were put into the sky as a seven-pointed star, unaccountably reckoned to be female, and shining overhead each Midsummer Night.

"Of course, it all be nonsense," Pial finished. "The Four Gods Protector be the ones making life again and again." She shrugged her pretty shoulders in comfortable superiority. "But T'Nig be a pretty masque."

A pretty masque— and the dim room beneath the palace. A

king generous and admired—and the flayed bodies strung upside down, bumping blackened faces in the wind. Teasing and amorous laughter—and Perwold's eyes upon my bruised breasts: "He has peasants enough to play with." Satin masque costumes—and the deadly, hidden mind grasp of the White Pipes. Veliano seemed to be too many stories too densely told. The desire to flee it all, if necessary alone and on foot through the summer mountains, rose in me so strongly that for a moment the green woods faded and I could see before me the south gate of Frost, nearest of the Silver Cities. Bustling traffic of merchants and farmers, a troupe of jugglers, whores and lords, beggars and the knowing, impudent grins of street children—crowds enough to become lost in, unmarked . . .

Only Jorry kept me planted before the bush of linberries, my feet still, as Brant had intended.

"No matter how close-tongued she be," Pial said, "In two more days we hear her tale. What be your story for the masque, Harper?"

"*I don't know*," I said, and they stared at my intensity, before finding it a good joke and falling to laughing again on the fragrant mossy ground.

Midsummer Day dawned hot and close. By noon black clouds piled motionless in the east and heat shimmered over the river. For long moments the air within and without the palace would seem unnaturally still, suspended in such heavy silence that a worker alone would become uneasy and glance upward, namelessly oppressed. The moment would break and a sudden breeze blow in fitful gusts, slapping the hot upturned face with more heat, gritty with dust. Then returned that oppressive calm, the thunderheads even darker above the weight of the sky.

The heat, which must have been rare enough in the mountains this far south, had moved over them in the night, bringing with it restless sleep and fevered dreams. I had dreamed or thought—half-awake, half-asleep, I did not remember which—of something buried in mind for years: a dying cat.

The cat had come to Mother Arcoa's the same year I had been abandoned there, three years before Brant had arrived. I had been ten; the cat had been ancient. "Four-lived is a cat, four-leaved by the grace of the Four Gods Protector," ran an old street ballad, and this cat looked as if he had used already three lives. One-eared and three-legged, tail hair singed to leave a naked white rope, orange fur mottled with some skin disease or worm. One of the youngest girls smuggled him inside, against Mother Arcoa's firmest rule. When the cat was discovered, Mother Arcoa banished it. We children begged and the youngest girl cried, but Mother Arcoa put the cat in the doorway and kicked its singed tail. The cat took one look outside and darted back in. Perhaps it had been abused on the street and its fear outweighed Mother Arcoa's kick. For whatever reason, it refused to go through the door and could not be forced. Beaten with a broom, it endured the blows rather than run. Carried near the door, it scratched and bit like something demented. Caught in a sack and heaved into the street, it leaked back in through windows, through chinks, through the walls themselves. Deliberately starved, it prepared to die rather than leave. Finally Mother Arcoa killed it with a butcher knife, a single clean blow.

"The creature should have gone," she said, standing over the bloody carcass, the knife still red in her hand. "Even a cat must sometimes act or be acted upon." She spoke to the wailing youngest girl, but I felt she meant her words for me.

I remembered cat and words as I rose from my pallet on the longest day of summer. I did not know if the story that formed between my hands that evening would be mine, or Brant's, or Leonore's, or if I would live beyond it. But should I live, I would wait no longer for broom or sack or knife. Even that crippled and singed cat could have chewed and bitten to strike out at its tormentors. Why had it not? Not from fear; it had lived past fear, passing beyond into some place where its capacity for fear and struggle were numbed and all it could do was wait mutely for whatever abuse would come next. The same could happen to me, and I did not dare allow it. I could not give myself to that undemanding, terrible, restful place: I had Jorry. I would need to act.

I rose from my pallet, and looked at that place, and resolved that I would.

"You, boy!" the stable master called to me as I crossed to the kitchens. I turned around and he looked confused, but only for a moment. There was no time on a festival day for confusion, and a small woman had hands the same as a boy. "What be you doing? You be the foreign harper?"

"I am the Storygiver. And I am doing nothing. What do you need help with?"

He scowled; willingness is even more confusing than foreignness. But apparently the need was pressing, for he crossed over to me and pointed, smelling strongly of manure, a squat and strong man going bald.

"See that part of the stable—no, there. The boy be absent—on *Midsummer* he be absent—and the lords be coming later for their horses. I did the stalls myself, but the floor be wanting scrubbing, and I be without time. Get a bucket and brush and scrub the flagstones."

"Yes," I said, pleasantly enough. He scowled again.

"Do not touch the horses, you hear?"

"Of course not."

"The grooms be in and out." A warning; horses were valuable.

"Where is the bucket?"

He showed me, still suspicious but even more harried. Pages and kitchen maids toiled past with endless buckets of water, water which would have lost its well-deep coolness by the time it reached the chambers of the lords and ladies for whom it was intended. Sweat darkened the pages' armpits and trickled into the cleavage of the kitchen maids' breasts.

It was cooler in the stone stables, which smelled of fresh straw. The great horses stamped, switching their tails at flies, and pigeons mourned softly in the rafters. This stable was larger, cooler, cleaner than the one where my sway-backed pony was housed.

Where Jorry's was not.

I scrubbed the stone floor in circles until my shoulders, still bruised beneath my tunic, ached. I scrubbed with determination, with anger, with a foolish giving of myself to this one task, so simple and so distracting. My rag slapped the floor, a snap like those banners in the wind that ride gaily before any army and are brought back later bloody and torn, wrapped around the mutilated bodies of lords. Despite the comparative coolness of the stable, sweat rolled from my forehead into my eyes. I was not used to this work. My knees felt scraped raw, although they were not. I had nearly reached the far end of the stable floor when I swiped my hand across my sweat-blinded eyes and saw before me a pair of polished boots. I looked up: Brant.

Neither of us spoke. I remained still for a long moment, crouching on my knees, sodden with sweat and dirty water. For ten days I had seen the members of the court only in the distance, heard them only in servant's gossip. For ten days I had not seen Brant.

Now that he stood before me, I wanted to cry out questions and accusations—but I did not. I remained kneeling dumbly on the stable floor. A servant's rank brings with it its own involuntary deference. For ten days I had been a servant in Veliano, not a Storygiver momentarily amusing a court, but a laborer, kitchen maid and stable-hand. I could not be as free with Brant as I had been my first night at the palace. Nor did I think he would answer me. And in my mind lay the knowledge of what I planned to do that night.

Brant looked down at me as if he had never seen me before, his eyes too impersonal even for coldness. He held a folded paper, sealed with green wax.

"Where is the stable-boy?"

"He did not come, the stable master said."

"And my page?"

"I have seen no page, my lord." How easily—despite everything—the title slipped out. This, then, was how it would have been ten years ago, had I gone with him to Erdulin. I had been, bitterly, right.

"Then you will have to take this message to Lady Cynda.

She is with the king in the summer garden." Impatiently, boot toe tapping, he held out the paper.

I came slowly to my feet.

"You do not need to bring an answer."

I took the paper. Brant did not wait to see me go; he was a lord, accustomed to being obeyed, and I a scrubwoman, beneath watching. He moved out of sight beyond the stable. I heard him call to one of the grooms, and then the sound of running feet. I left my bucket and rag and crossed the stable-yard. Halfway I had to stop suddenly, but only for a moment. I put Jorry's face before me, and neither humiliation nor fear could shake it.

The summer garden had been built behind the castle and beside the river so that it lay secluded till mid-morning in the shadow of one of Veliano's mountains, but that did not help. The heat was here, too, shimmering sullenly over the river like steam. The scent of flowers choked the air. Under a great tree, out of earshot of both their attendants, King Rofdal and Lady Cynda sat on a carved bench, she lazily twirling a flower that shed white petals over the glossy blue of her trailing skirts.

I saw at once that the king's mood was petulant. He glanced up at me, his small eyes distinctly annoyed in the fleshy folds of his sweating face, and I thought with a failing heart that if I had interrupted a conversation of importance, it might affect Rofdal's response to my performance at tonight's masque. He looked as if he had been interrupted. Servant's gossip said that the Lady Cynda was the king's mistress.

Despite myself, I looked closely at Cynda. She was the most beautiful woman I had ever seen; she did not even look real. Cool, faintly smiling, playing with her flower as idly as a child but with an unchildlike veiledness, as if there were between her blond beauty and the world an unseen curtain through which she peered with voluptuous glances from under downcast lashes. This, then, was Brant's wife. The boy I had known would not have tolerated sharing a woman with even a king; Lady Cynda was one more bitter reminder that no longer did I know him, nor anything else, with certainty.

I bowed to Rofdal. "Pardon, Your Grace. A message for Lady Cynda from Lord Brant."

"The Storygiver," Rofdal said irritably. "Why in the Gods Protector does he not send a page?"

"I was at hand, Your Grace." From nervousness I bowed yet again, unnecessarily, while handing the sealed note to Cynda. Thus it happened that I was bending close over her hand when it touched Brent's message, and I saw the tremor in the white fingers and the grasping way the gilded nails closed like claws upon the paper. Startled, I raised my eyes. An expression on that lovely face so unexpected I was not even certain I had seen it startled me further. Then it was gone.

"And what does Lord Brant, your husband, say to you?" Rofdal said. From another man it might have sounded jocular; jealousy from a king is never that.

"Only that he will be gone until the masque begins in the evening," Cynda said, again smiling. She had even white teeth, and a tiny star gilded on the skin by her mouth drew attention to them. The star had seven points. T'Nig?

"He neglects you."

"Ah, but you do not," Cynda said, twirling her flower, and I could detect no undertone in her voice. I had been wrong, then; I could not have seen the expression on her face that I thought I had.

Rofdal glanced irritably at the lady, and then even more irritably at me. "You are dismissed!"

"Yes, Your Grace. Thank you, Your Grace." Retreating through the summer garden, I was careful not to look back.

My bucket and rag remained where I had left them, but fresh footsteps muddied the stable floor. In the sodden heat, the water could not dry. A stall door stood open and fresh droppings were upon the floor beside it. Brant's horse, then. That had been the stall for one of his mounts, and it had fouled the stone.

I cleaned it all.

When I had finished, I crossed the stable-yard. Servants

stood in a group at the far end, among them one of Rofdal's cooks, who surely had much else to do. I heard a flute.

It was the gifted boy Jorry and I had heard play once before. Now, as then, the song he played was sad and haunting, surely not suited to a festival day, but no one stopped him. The servants stood quietly, the cook with his huge forearms hugging his chest, a page with a puzzled look wrinkling his sunburned features. He was hearing music too old for him. The flute's plaintive tune seemed somehow ancient, full of human loss thinned out into notes made sadder for the thinning out, as flowers sentimentally preserved from some passionate night thin into sad and passionless scent. While the boy played, no one looked away. I saw Brant saying that music seized and unlayered the mind, and I saw too Jorry, listening to this flute, his small face as unguarded as the page's. I walked on, into the palace, where the hysteria of preparation for the Midsummer Masque drowned all music.

Throughout Midsummer Day, the heat worsened. By evening it was a palpable entity, as smothering as wool. Even the long evening shadows lay heavily on the parched grass.

Below the summer garden, on a low and flat section of lawn near the river, canopies and benches and platforms had been built for the masque. Here the court—stuffed with feasting, woozy with wine, sweating through satin shirts and jeweled gowns, smelling of stale scent and disappointment—sat beneath a leaden sky, waiting to be amused.

The vulgar acts, jugglers and dancers and Storygiver, preceded the masque itself, which would give the ancient myth of the Nameless Warrior and T'Nig. While acrobats cavorted in the stifling heat, I stood concealed on one side and watched the movements of the members of the court before whom I would have to perform. High on a dais Leonore sat alone, fantastically garbed as T'Nig after it had been placed in the sky as a star. She wore a silver satin gown with attached headdress that broke into seven points around her face. The gown frothed over the bulge of her pregnancy, the skirt falling in shades of midnight blue—presumably the sky—for twice a man's height from the edge of her dais and clear to the ground.

A silver seven-pointed star had been painted over her face as well. Whatever expression she wore was lost in silver and distance.

Below, Rofdal sat on a smaller dais, surrounded by such lords and ladies as were not taking part in the masque, among these Perwold. The king looked as he had in the summer garden: petulant, hot, and irritable. I did not see Brant nor his wife. She, I knew, was to be in the masque and must be among those costumed and hidden, but he was not.

The acrobats ended when one of them collapsed, gasping for air, on the platform. He was carried off by his fellows, someone went running for cold water to revive him, the court sneered and grumbled, and I took from my tunic the Second Flask. I could not imagine a more unpromising audience—nor one upon which, for me, so much depended. I drank the Second Flask.

Brightness. Flush of heat. Timelessness and music made of time. Then I stood upon the stage and spread my hands.

Throughout the afternoon I had concentrated, with as much intensity as I could, upon the stories that I had given the most often and most effortlessly. I hoped for a simple tale that would neither interest nor offend anyone, and then for safe anonymity again among the kitchen maids and stable-boys. But from the beginning the mist between my hands swirled into forms over which I had no control, and that at first I did not even recognize.

But the court recognized the forms. Lords and ladies stirred in the heat, and their collective breath drew inward sharply, like wind through a cleft in stubborn rock.

The mist had become a winged wolf, white as cool snow that would have been so welcome in this heat, perfect in miniature as the forms of Storygiving seldom are. His minute fangs dripped blood, his white wings were faintly traced with blue. When he suddenly spread them and soared upward the space of my hands, those nearest the stage jerked back, then glanced at each other and laughed nervously. I was not surprised at their unease, as it was nothing to my own. Almost I believed that the winged wolf was solid, that I could touch the separate coarse hairs on that white pelt or feel the blood rush through those blue veins on his spread wings.

The wolf soared, prowled, hunted. He hamstrung a deer and brought it down. Before the court could become bored with him, he had gone back into mist but not completely vanished. The mist was both formless and still the winged wolf, but whether in outline or color or something else, I had no time to decide before the wolf-mist became a tree, hacked at by men whose axes dented it by not so much as a chip. Then the tree became a lake, so still and cool between my hands, so deep a blue, that it was not hard to believe that it was, indeed, bottomless. I was giving the story of the rebirths of T'Nig.

No—*I* was not giving it. Someone was giving the story through me, for some purpose I couldn't know, and was giving it in just the way this audience at this time would most favorably receive it: swifter than with masquing costumes, more novel than with live actors, woven with images cold and sharp in the dull heat. The court leaned forward, commenting to each other like children, the sweat on their faces forgotten. Some of those too far away to see clearly had left their benches and canopies and crowded close around the platform. Even Rofdal, on his raised dais, had lost his petulant look and was leaning forward to watch the stage. I could observe him; I could observe anything, without risk of becoming distracted from my story. It was not my story. I had no control of anything between my hands.

Far above, Queen Leonore sat motionless on her dais.

The legend of T'Nig rolled on. To me it seemed a pleasant myth, notable only for the sharpness of its images, but I was not of Veliano. The court oohed, and laughed, and looked intent, and I knew that in their minds, which had lived with the legend all of their lives, the wordless story evoked emotion and response I could not share.

Then, at one end of the table, the mist finally formed the Nameless Warrior who would slay T'Nig, and when I heard the court gasp, I heard myself gasp with them. The Nameless

Warrior splendid in his youth and glory with preternatural fire, was Rofdal.

This time, then, no guards seized my arms, no flayed figures muddied the meaning of the story. The Rofdal-warrior strode toward T'Nig, which was now a huge boar with girth and ferocity to match his own. The battle between these two stretched on and on, and during all of it the court's interest never flagged. They were not sitting on makeshift benches on a stifling evening, they were fighting T'Nig with Rofdal, and when the warrior-hero at last killed the man-boar and threw its great body upward, when it became a silver star above Veliano, the court as one man looked at the sky above, and there in a gap between the restless clouds shone T'Nig, the Midsummer star.

Then came applause.

I stood drenched in sweat and dread, with barely enough presence of mind to stumble into a bow. Lords and ladies, jugglers and squires, exclaimed about the star overhead—were they so fevered with story that they actually thought I had caused *that?*—pointed, and laughed, and called to each other. Then the king himself rose, and I was being brought off the platform and toward him, and all of it so different from the last time I had performed, save for my not having caused any of it. That had not changed.

"So you choose this way to compliment me and redeem yourself," Rofdal boomed, and his smile was both pleased and wry. "Very pretty. This is how you give us the tale of T'Nig?"

"That is how it comes between my hands, Your Grace," I said, and thought that no words could hold more truth.

"Then your hands are inventive ones," Rofdal said. "A pretty compliment and an entertaining performance. Too often the entertainment offered here is stale and worn."

I wondered if his words carried to Leonore, who had arranged the entertainment. I dared not look.

"You are wasted in the kitchens and stables, Storygiver," Rofdal said, and I started, wondering how he knew where I spent my time. I must not underestimate him. "From here on,

I will have you dine with the court in the Great Hall, and your stories will amuse us all."

He was smiling at me as if he had conferred a great honor, as in his eyes he had. I was appalled. To be constantly before Brant and Leonore and Perwold . . . the kingly smile wavered just slightly, and I sank to my knees. Rofdal gave openheartedly as a generous child; like a child, he expected lavish gratitude.

"Thank you, Your Grace, thank you . . . I have never had my art honored before by such a patron!"

"Patron, yes," Rofdal said, and I saw the term pleased him. In the Silver Cities, courts often patronized the arts; here it would be rarer. I suddenly saw the dual image Rofdal must see of himself: to Veliano, a monarch unquestioned, even by himself; to the merchants who brought Veliano its wealth, an unpolished provincial ruler. How clearly did he see their condescension, and how much did he mind? Rofdal, too, had his tethers. I would remember that.

"I am only sorry," Rofdal said, "that you have sent your lad back to the Cities with Kalafa's trading caravan." And to that I could only wonder why he thought so and from whom the covering rumor had come.

"The masque?" a voice murmured beside me, and it was a vexed question: Does the masque still go on?

"Of course, the masque!" Rofdal shouted. "Let us see how it fares next to the Storygiver's tale!" He laughed hugely. "And Storygiver, you shall be your patron's guest."

Panic swelled through me. I had planned otherwise. It was too hard for me to bring myself to action ever; I suddenly could not think quickly enough to adapt my intentions to this unforeseen invitation. Like a rider who is too fearful to turn his horse from a ditch, I must hurtle straight ahead and try to hang on.

"But, Your Grace—I promised to entertain in the stable-yard after I spread my hands here!"

Those around us fell silent; Rofdal looked displeased. People did not dispute him. Then I found the right note: "But your subjects will wait on your pleasure, Your Grace," emphasizing 'subjects' only slightly, including myself and all those rankless others among whom Rofdal was so popular.

"No," the king said, his face clearing. "No—you have the right of it, Storygiver. Entertain my subjects; let them as well see your T'Nig and your Nameless Warrior!"

Again I was appalled. Here was a fresh maggot: I could not be sure I would be able to repeat the story by myself. What would happen if I did not, both now in the stable-yard and all the nights to come in the Great Hall? It was not, after all, I who had made it.

"Probably the Storygiver is tired," another voice said—Lady Cynda, Brant's wife. She smiled at me, and the expression on her beautiful doll-like face was all careless kindness. Behind her stood Brant. His color was high, perhaps with heat, perhaps with strain and exertion. I could not be sure, but I did not need to be sure. He had made the story; there were only he or Leonore to do it, and I knew which not from the story's contents but from its effects. Had I failed again tonight, Leonore could have had me killed; Rofdal would not notice. But the legend of T'Nig had turned me into the king's pet, and I was safe. Brant had protected me yet again in the only way possible: by putting me not under his own eye but under the king's. And by now Leonore must realize it.

Rofdal dismissed me cheerfully, and I set off to betray my protector.

6

IT WAS TRUE THAT THE SERVANTS OF THE COURT WERE being entertained in the stable yard. A huge feast had been laid on for them in the yard beside the kitchen, a feast served later than the court's, after the work should be done, but nearly the twin of the court's in size, dishes, and wine. After it was consumed, the servants would stagger, as the court had staggered, outdoors to see jugglers, acrobats, harpers. In my peculiar status between servant and guest, I would be expected to join them. But not yet.

Thunder rumbled overhead just once as I made my way from the river to the castle. The Midsummer star had already become occluded. But still the rain held off, and behind me I heard the masque begin and the court, its mood transformed by the transformation in Rofdal's, calling jeeringly to those costumed and on the platform. The noble and makeshift actors would not have an easy time of it, unless they chose to play the masque as grotesque. Any beginning actor in the Silver Cities could have told them that a story told twice must ring in a new tone—as I was about to do to Brant's.

I slipped into the palace through the deserted summer garden. Most of the halls and passages were empty save for the occasional man-at-arms, left to prevent thievery and a little sullen over missing the merrymaking. In my twelve days in Veliano I had been all over the palace, performing servant's work of all kinds, and most of these men-at-arms knew me by sight. In the public quarters I passed unchallenged, but the private chambers would be more difficult.

The upper gallery held two men-at-arms, who stood together near the far end where an opened window looked toward the river. Evidently some of the town and palace merrymaking had spilled from the stable-yard to this side of the palace lawn, for I could hear shouts and laughter drifting through the window, intermittently augmented by music from a lute, badly played. An arras hung along one wall at my end of the passage, and I stood half-concealed behind it, watching the guards. Waiting.

"Give me another, Athio."

"It be gone."

"Your fud it be gone! Give it here!"

Athio passed over a flagon. The other leaned against a wall to drink, his head tipped back and his throat bobbing with each swallow. A sudden gust of air along the passage from the open window blew me their scent: leather, ale, masculine sweat. I thought how poorly suited I was for this sort of dangerous intrigue and how much I hated it. My hands sweated while my face had gone cool and dry, and I hoped desperately that I would not faint.

"You took all!"

"There be left only a few drops."

Athio cursed volubly. The two glared at each other. Athio's hand moved toward his dagger but then trailed off midway, whether from heat or boredom or unsteadiness of hand, and he turned instead to gaze sullenly out the window.

I waited for what seemed a long time. Thunder rumbled; if the rain came too soon, I would lose all chance. Finally a shout from outside, followed by a hubbub of cries and excited screams, above which soared a high-pitched shriek I recognized as Ludie's. Both men sprang to the window. I darted from the arras and hurried forward.

"Here! Guard! The Lady Cynda wants her other shawl immediately, open her chamber!"

Athio turned toward me; the other remained at the window. I held out my bit of lace, folded across my arm in such a way that it might have been a shawl. From beyond the window came the sounds of an enthusiastic fistfight, as of course there eventually would have had to be.

Athio scowled, one eye on the window. "I open the chamber only on my lady's orders."

"Rockhead, these *are* my lady's orders!" I shook the shawl at him. "Don't you see she's spilled wine on this shawl? Open so that I may fetch what she sent me for!"

The shouts beyond the window became more heated. Athio's companion said, "Aaah!" and half-pummeled the air with his fist. Athio craned toward the window, glanced at me in annoyance, and moved unsteadily along the passage to Cynda's door. As soon as he had opened it he was gone, back to the window. I brushed the door with my rump as I went through it, and it closed more than halfway.

Drawn draperies dimmed Cynda's chamber. I seized the first bit of cloth I saw, and then sprinted for the door in the side wall, a door glowing with the fresh honey-colored carvings of the new palace.

Panic grows strange fruits. As I laid my hand on the door that connected Cynda's chamber to Brant's, I did not even think: What if the door is locked? I did not think: I may not be able to find them. I did not think: How much time before Athio leaves the window to check my lady's chamber? Any or all of that would have been reasonable. But what I thought, as clearly as if I had all tranquil leisure for the thinking, was: Brant goes thus, through this carved door, to bed his wife.

His chamber was of a size with hers, but more austere. Table, bench, two chests, wide bed now without its winter hangings. And in the corner a small altar, carved all over with the gillyflowers of the Four Gods Protector. Such unexpected devoutness as the altar stopped me for a moment, until ten years dissolved and I knelt again in Mother Arcoa's loft under the damp eaves.

An apprentice Storygiver learns many things, as do all who survive in the Silver Cities by wit and daring. Having so little of both, I had been a dull pupil for the older girls' contests of thievery and lock picking. But now I needed neither. In clear memory Brant knelt naked beside me, pulled my wrists toward the altar he had built—smaller than this one and cruder—and placed my hands now here, now there, until the correct carvings had been pushed in the correct order, and the secret drawer slid open.

Back in the present, I knelt before the altar, my fingers trembling. Ten years is a long time for an inventive mind to keep a design unaltered. I placed my hands now here, now there, singly and in combination, and the small drawer, its outlines invisible among the riot of carving, slid open.

Even before I looked inside, I knew by the smell. His Flasks were there and purses of powdered herbs, and from the back of the drawer, wrapped tightly in a silk packet, came the smell of whatever Leonore had eaten in that dim room beneath the palace.

Some of the other drugs I knew, some not. Of each I took a little, pouring each into a tiny bottle, stoppering the top, shoving it into the hidden pockets of my tunic. How much before Brant would notice? There was no way to be sure, but I knew from my own powders how deceptive they could be, shrinking in quantity as they dried, appearing to be more when bottle or purse was shaken and air fluffed the contents. Haste made me clumsy, but I broke no bottles, and what I spilled I blotted from the floor with my lace, first spitting to wet it so the grains would stick. The spills unnerved me further. Although some purses remained unopened, I replaced everything as it had been, thrust the stained lace down the front of my tunic, and slammed the drawer closed. It disappeared into the carvings as completely as if I had only imagined it. Brant's door, too, I slammed, and I had barely reached the great chest at the foot of Cynda's bed when Athio stood in the doorway, blinking into the greater shadow of the chamber, his fingers curling loosely over the dagger at his belt.

"What be that noise?"

"My lady's chest slammed shut. I . . . . dropped the lid." He continued to blink, and I made myself move toward him. "My lady's shawl *would* be at the bottom of her chest!" I said, and raised my arm, still draped with the cloth I had snatched.

I shook it in his direction, and for the first time truly saw it myself.

It was an embroidered chamber pot cover.

All presence of mind deserted me. There were courses I could have taken: turned so that my body screened the cloth, crumpled it shapelessly against me, diverted him with a vivacious question about the fistfight. I did none of them. Silent, a knot in my stomach and the room bobbing before my eyes, I walked straight through the door, wearing a chamber pot cover draped over one arm. I cannot say why he did not stop me. Perhaps the wine had fuddled his vision, perhaps ladies' fashions confused him, perhaps he glimpsed the elaborate embroidery and thought—with sense—that what looked to him like a chamber pot cover could not possibly be a chamber pot cover because not even a lady would lavish so much needlework on such a thing. Whatever he saw or thought, he let me pass to the gallery and beyond. Behind me his key clicked in the iron lock.

The other man-at-arms still stood at the window. I left them both there and made my way to the noisy crowd in the stable yard, Brant's drugs close within my tunic. I had just reached the first of the shouting and brawling merrymakers when the rain finally began, pelting courtyard and palace and river with huge swift drops that splattered when they struck, bringing to an end the queen's Midsummer Masque in Veliano.

When the rain began, a great shout went up from the stable-yard. It was a shout of neither pleasure nor dissatisfaction, but merely of drunken welcome for any change: before it had not been raining, and now it was. Men laughed and drank off their ale; women hoisted their skirts above the mud; children whooped and began to run in circles, chasing raindrops. As I threaded my way to the unfinished palace wing, one boy ran full into me, his small body smacking mine hard enough to stagger us both. For a moment I held him, warm and pliant, against me, and then I let him go and he ran through the rain toward the river.

I did not know how much time I would have. Brant might

discover some of his drugs missing, or he might not. Rofdal might ask—tomorrow or the next day—for a repetition of the Storygiving of T'Nig, and when he did I would not be able to give it again. Before either occurred, I must learn what I had stolen from Brant and its use, and learn swiftly. And there was another reason for not delaying. If I paused now and thought too clearly about what I was doing, I would sink too deeply in fear to do it. Storygiving at the masque and escaping with the drugs had lent me a tingling and unnatural courage; it would vanish if I ceased to move, to act, to risk. To conquer my own mind, I dared not think.

Agla, the kitchen maid with whom I had picked linberries, walked by pressed to the side of a dark-bearded man, their arms intertwined in two X's, front and back. I doubted either noticed it rained. Half was lust but half was wine, and I thought that if Ludie were also this drunk, luck would be with me.

"Agla! Where is Ludie?"

Slowly her eyes focused; reluctantly she saw me. She frowned.

"The harper, Agla—I am the foreign harper, you remember me. Where is Ludie?"

"It be raining," Agla said, in great wonder. The bearded man whispered something in her ear and she exploded into laughter, sagging against him. He picked her up and carried her, still laughing, toward the stables. All at once thunder clapped loud as gunpowder, and the rain came down harder. I ran into the kitchens, chaotic with milling people, and there I saw Ludie sitting on the floor with her back to the wall and a mug of ale sloshing itself over the front of her gown. I squatted next to her and whispered into her ear.

"Ludie, I know a secret."

She looked at me with the same vagueness as Agla, and I thought that if every serving woman in the palace was this drunk, the ladies bedraggled from the rain would get precious little help in drying their hair and changing to fresh gowns.

"It's a secret about Agla. A very funny secret, Ludie. Come with me and I will tell you!"

"Agla," Ludie said.

"Yes, *Agla*."

"My gown is wet."

"No more than is the queen's. Come with me, Ludie. Give me your hand."

I risked taking her to my own room. No one would be sending for me to perform tonight, and I didn't think Brant would go, wet from the masque and with Cynda at his side, to immediately count his drugs. My room, like most servants' rooms, could not be locked, but I dragged its small, battered chest against the door, propped Ludie to sit against it upon the floor, and turned my back to her. She sat humming a ballad I had heard before, some sentiment about a handsome shepherd and his love. Most of the words she had either forgotten or mangled, but her voice was astonishingly sweet and true, and I thought for a moment how mocking it was that such a gift should come in such a package. It would do Ludie little good. Then all my thoughts turned to the drugs.

I was gambling that the mixture I used for the First Flask was close to what Brant used. That first night, when he had drawn from me the story of Jorry's birth, he had already drunk his First Flask before he even entered the chamber where Jorry and I waited, and I remembered that he smelled only of wine and horses and not of drugs. If both First and Second Flask were different from what I used, my chances of discovering the combination were lessened. Please, I prayed silently to no one, let the First Flask be the same, and felt foolish. It was a relief to feel foolish; it cooled for a moment my feverish other feelings.

I had drunk my First Flask on my way through the stable-yard to find Ludie. Now I pulled another of the bottles from my tunic, poured the same amount of its powder as I always used into my Second Flask, added water from the pitcher, and drank it off.

"What be you do?" Ludie asked. She had lurched up behind me.

"Drinking my wine," I said. The drug smelled bitter. I rolled the scent on my tongue, trying to identify its components. I could not. If I had misjudged the dosage and ended blinded, or worse, I would never know by what.

"Can I have some?" Ludie said.

"You have some already," I said, touched her mug of ale, and drank off Brant's drug. A jolt swept through me, seeming to come from where my fingers rested on Ludie's mug: sound, color, cold so sharp it seemed to burn my fingertips or to awaken them. Then the jolt passed, and I was left with only the music, too faint to identify and too enveloping to ignore, like a melody heard in a vivid dream.

"I be leaving now," Ludie said abruptly, and began to vomit ale. I held her head away from both of us, and when she had finished I found that the distraction had not, as it would have with the only Storygiving drug I knew, dissipated my light trance. The music was still there, no fainter and no louder, elusive as a breeze.

Ludie headed for my pallet. I captured her firmly and sat her against the wall, prattling madly of Agla and her secret love, until Ludie remembered that she had been interested in Agla's lover. Then I spread my hands on the floor before her.

"What did you see in the courtyard, Ludie? Who began the brawl on the Midsummer celebration? Think of the fight, Ludie, and whose fist struck first."

The mist took shape. But it was not the shape of men fighting. The mist formed two figures, both clear and unmistakable: the bearded man carrying Agla through the rain.

Ludie clapped her hands and laughed. "That no be Agla's trading man!" She laughed again, and I stared at her, desperately hoping that the vomiting had not sobered her too quickly. If she could recognize Agla and connect the Storygiving figures to Agla's two lovers, she was more in her own mind than she had been in the kitchen. I needed her to be in her mind enough to find the right drug to draw stories from her, but not enough to remember it tomorrow.

But this was not the right drug to draw stories from Ludie's mind. Ludie had not seen Agla and her bearded man—it was *I* who had been prattling of them, and my mind that had given this bit of a story. But how easily it had come, and how clearly! I had thought of Agla, and here Agla was. I thought of the bearded man setting Agla again on her feet; instantly he did so. The drug was simply a Storygiving drug, but far more effective than my own. With this one, I could easily recreate the T'Nig legend when Rofdal called for it.

No—I could not. Brant would see and know that such Storygiving lay beyond my unaided powers. This drug helped me not at all.

I clapped my hands, and Agla disappeared.

"Gone," Ludie said sadly, staring at my hands. I filled her mug with wine. I had hidden the wine beneath my pallet earlier, when I had planned this, when I had dared to think.

"Drink this, Ludie. Then I will make you another story." Again I turned my back, measured and diluted a flask of yet another drug, drank it off. This time the reaction was much worse. All sensation was altered; the floor, solid stone a moment before, turned soft and viscous, and I crashed through it onto my face. Terrible stinks choked my breath. Music pounded at me, this time not faint but deafeningly loud, too loud to distinguish any one note but only a discordant cacophony. I had not known that music could hurt—hurt not only by its loudness but by what it stirred in my mind, some deep layer where hitherto pain had slept undisturbed. Now, under the music's twisting, this layer woke and shrieked, as nerves will shriek when twisted by trained fingers. Had it lasted long I could not have borne it, but it did not. When pain and music—which were one—receded, I stumbled to my knees and crawled toward Ludie.

"The fis . . . fist . . . *fist*fight. In the stable-yard . . . Ludie? The *fight*." And I spread my hands.

The mist swirled a long time, not pink but a lurid and steady purple, like fruit gone bad. When figures formed, they were not any fighters Ludie could have seen in the courtyard. The figures were shapeless with menace, like those half-glimpsed in nightmare, and as they formed the music crashed into such significant pain that I clapped my hands together and plunged the room into blackness.

I could have been only a few moments in darkness. Ludie was leaning over me, dribbling the last of the wine from her mug onto my face. It trickled into my eyes and I sat up, wiping them. My head hurt from the inside. Terror seized me—what if I damaged or destroyed my Storygiving in piling these drugs one on the other?

Don't think of it, don't stop to think.

"That not be a good secret," Ludie said solemnly.

"But I . . . know a better one. Wait here, Ludie."

I crawled to the water bucket, not daring to stand upright, and prepared a third flask. As I raised it to my lips, there came to me one of those flashing pictures that seduce and weaken even the strongest resolution: how it would be if I left Jorry to Brant and fled from Veliano. I giving stories with the new drug in the Silver Cities, prosperous and safe; Jorry left a young nobleman in Brant's house, rich and happy; my memory conveniently faded. It would be so easy.

I drank the third drug.

For what seemed a long time there was nothing. I knelt in no place, heard or saw nothing around me but grayness. Then I sat beside Ludie, my hands spread, and the distant music had moved so much closer that I wanted to squeeze my eyes shut and decipher the elusive notes. So tantalizingly close, a melody so almost there . . .

"Aaaaaah," Ludie moaned, and I looked down. Mist swirled between my hands.

Quickly I said, "The fistfight Ludie—who fought in the stable-yard?" At my tone she glanced from the mist to me, her pale eyes bleary and filmed with drink, wine dribbling from one corner of her mouth, and at her glance I felt my mind ride on the music and touch hers.

Instantly I recoiled. It did not hurt, but it was such a shocking, squeamish sensation—like touching a living heart, the skin and bone of the chest stripped away—that I drew back. For the first time, I felt why the priests of the Four Gods Protector railed against soul-besetting, mind invasion. This touching of Ludie's helpless mind was a blasphemy, was a kind of rape.

I touched it again.

Ludie seemed to feel nothing. She watched the pink mist, which under my hand formed two men, one a carter I knew to be named Rhem and the other a red-haired stranger. Silently the two men slugged at each other on cobblestones slippery with ale. Rhem's fist caught the other's jaw and he went down, sprawled on the stones. When he rose again it was unsteadily, and Rhem slammed his fist into the stranger's belly.

That was what Brant had done to me. And this—this drug, this invasion, this blasphemy—was also what he had done to me.

Another figure, a woman, threw herself on top of the fallen stranger. It was Ludie herself. Her face shrieked without sound, cursing them. Rhem paused above them, fists at the ready, and then threw back his head and laughed, staggering off after more ale.

"Fair fight," Ludie moaned. "They say . . . it be . . . *fair*," and again she threw up. This time I was in no condition to hold her head.

I half-carried, half-dragged her from the palace to the cow shed. Other figures weaved past us, most in no less drunken condition. Outside, there was no one, and I lifted my face to the rain and let it steady me. At the first gentle drop on her own face, Ludie became a limp weight on my shoulder, heavy as the senseless or the dead. Somehow I dragged her the rest of the distance to the cow shed, which loomed ahead of me in the rain like a phantom and malodorous keep.

Within it was quiet and dim. I covered Ludie with clean straw against the chill that even summer nights will take on near dawn, and made for her head a pillow of sacking. The cows, tied to their posts, lowed softly. Almost I curled up beside her, but I could not afford that. The less she remembered of all this in the morning, the better for both of us. When she lay peacefully asleep in the clean straw, vomit still streaking one cheek, I stroked the other softly. I could not have said why, except that I suspected that somewhere in barn or stable or palace or hut, the red-haired stranger had recovered from his fight and lay now with some girl prettier and juicier than poor Ludie.

All over the palace, in the Great Hall and kitchens and cellars, the merrymaking and lovemaking roared on. I stumbled back to my room, jammed the chest against the door, and crawled on my knees to my pallet, my head jangling with pain, my stolen flasks piled in one corner and covered with my cloak. It was not a good hiding place, but I lacked the strength to go in search of another. And it wouldn't have mattered; if he discovered the drugs gone, Brant could simply take the knowledge of any hiding place from my mind.

As I now could, from his.

7

THE DAY AFTER MIDSUMMER I WAITED IN TREPIDATION
to see if Brant had discovered my theft. But no summons came
from his lordship, no man-at-arms seized my shoulder in a
private passage and brought me to him, no befuddled Ludie
sidled up to me in the kitchen with questions about last night.
And that night, when Rofdal sent for me to perform in the
Great Hall, I saw Brant and knew he had no suspicion of me.
Secret drawers are marvelous things; they leave no room for
weights and scales.

Rofdal had sent me a new suit of clothes, the first gift to
mark my new favor. The tunic was of blue satin, the stockings
of a darker blue, the cloak of brown wool hooded with blue.
Everything was a bit too big, made originally for someone
else. In the kitchen the satin was fingered and exclaimed over.
In the drawing back of some servants and the averted eyes of
others, I saw already evidence of a new wariness toward me,
born of that gap between those who sup by their own cooking
fire and those who do not. Rofdal had commanded me to dine
in the Great Hall, at the low table with his physician, his
armor maker, the chief page, the head gardener for the palace
park, and the woman who cast fortunes by the movements of
the clouds above the spire atop the palace roof. In the Silver
Cities such a table would have held court musicians and
dancers, royal painters and poets, chief bard, translators and
scribes. In Veliano there existed none of these save musicians,

who ate in the kitchen, where I wished I too could have stayed.

When the meal ended and I was summoned before Rofdal, I went in comparative calm. I had taken some of Brant's benign drug as my Second Flask, and while I dared not arouse his suspicion by again giving the legend of T'Nig, I needed only to think of any story interesting to Rofdal and known to Brant as a Storygiving commonplace. I needed only to think, and the story would appear. With the stronger drug, the dangers of the story disappearing halfway, or of one character growing beyond my control, or of magical and controversial events making the audience think too much, were all gone. As artist, the Storygiver became sure, needing to summon neither emotion nor invention.

As tool, I felt momentarily safe. I stood in high favor with the king, and Leonore would not call attention to herself by subverting my stories just now. She would wait. Brant had placed me in the royal favor; I did not think his purposes, whatever they were, would interfere this soon in my Storygiving. And Rofdal, no more eager than any patron to believe his favor ill-given, would be predisposed to enjoy whatever I performed, and thus even he became just one more unsophisticated provincial audience, pleased with more of whatever he had previously enjoyed.

I gave him the Princess and the Sea Dragon, with the face on the princess that of Lady Cynda. A gasp, a whoop from the court, and my success was assured. It was almost too easy. Whatever I thought of, became vivid images between my hands, alterable as will and flattery dictated. A change of one face to another, a high color and rapid movement, and the audience was content.

"Amazing!" Rofdal said when I had finished. "A most ingenious art, Storygiver. Another night we will have again the warrior-hero and T'Nig, but not until you have shown us all these new and complicated tales." And he smiled from the folds of his flesh, first at me and then at Brant's wife, who cast down her eyes and blushed like an actress on cue.

"The Lady Cynda is too modest to reward you for your

pretty compliment," Rofdal said. "She prefers to pretend she is not as beautiful as the princess in your tale. So the rewarding must fall to me, as king shouldering his subjects' burdens." And he pulled from his hand one of its many rings, set with Veliano's incomparable scarlet gems. From the way he made the gesture, eyes never leaving my face, I saw that he must have done it many times before, and that this impulsive generosity toward a commoner was one of the reasons he was so popular. And yet it was not entirely an actor's trick. He waited for my gratitude like a father who has given a favored child some longed-for plaything, and I did not disappoint him. Over and over I thanked him. Neither was I acting: the stone in the ring could have kept Jorry and me for half a year.

Except I did not have Jorry to keep.

In the midst of the court's double murmurs of pleasure at my story and assessment of my gift, I looked at last at Brant. I had not looked at him all during my performance. I had been too afraid that he would remember that always before I hadn't risked distraction from my trance by glancing around as I worked, and so would ask himself why I did so now. To forestall that, I had given my inane tale the same way I always did: head down, eyes on my own hands. But now I looked squarely at him, standing a little apart from the rest of the court, none of whom included him in their whispering and conjecturing but all of whom shot glances his way, glances amused or uneasy or assessing of the delicate public joke I had just made of his cuckoldry by the king.

He gazed back as if he had never seen me before. Unperturbed, stony, he looked as if he did not know that through me the queen's faction knew him to be searching for the White Pipes, as if I had not just mocked his wife's unfaithfulness, as if the court were not curiously watching him for any reaction. Suddenly chilled, I looked away. Was his gaze at me the self-command of a seasoned courtier, adept at concealing his real aims and loyalties? Or was it the detachment of a craftsman, appraising a tool, judging to what further uses he could yet put me?

I did not want to examine the impulse that had led me to put Cynda's face on the figure of the Sea Dragon's princess.

Quietly, clutching Rofdal's ring in my fist, I slipped from the Great Hall. Soon—I must make my move soon. My fingers closed more tightly on the ring. Brant did not watch me go. Soon.

But it was not soon. Brant had ridden from Veliano and no one, it seemed, knew where. Days slipped by. Nightly I performed in the gaudy Great Hall before the king. Often in the afternoons I was sent for by some lord or lady to amuse with a Storygiving in the summer garden, in the solarium, on a barge on the river. But never by Brant. He had ridden from Veliano, said the king's armorer at dinner, on business connected with his father's lands. Did I not know, said the king's armorer contemptuously, that my Lord Brant came from a great family to the north, in the Silver Cities?

I said that I knew.

I came to despise myself for the daily hoop-jumping of asking about Brant without being noticed asking about Brant. Keeping my question casual and inconsequential had become the severest ordeal of the dry, severe days. I seemed to myself pathetic, a moth without a flame. But if I despised myself, I despised Brant more. He had saved my life and in turn had taken Jorry. The bitterness of the trade was what sent me circling, night and day, to the flame that was not there.

I thought that Leonore, too, felt Brant's absence. The child within her was ten days past its time, although not dead. Her women reported it still active and kicking. Leonore's face, on the few occasions I saw it among my audience or dining in the Great Hall, remained still and calm as ever, but I thought I caught from her a strain that was more than a childless woman's fear of childbirth. She, too, must wonder about the purpose of Brant's long absence, and about his possession of the White Pipes.

Only Cynda did not seem to need her husband's presence. She danced with Rofdal, and rowed on the river, and gambled at dice, her doll's face flushed with gaiety and triumph. When I saw her at the parties of pleasure that demanded a Storygiving, her eyes seemed too bright and her laugh too delighted, but apparently only to me. Leonore retired into pregnant seclusion, and Cynda reigned at court. In the kitchens it was whispered that Brant's absence made it easier for my Lady Cynda to slip into the king's chamber.

For the most part, it was whispered maliciously. I saw that Brant, however loyal his own men brought from Erdulin might be, had few well-wishers at court. An outsider still, he was respected but not accepted. He had married nobility, but came himself from a great merchant family; that was held against him. He came from the Silver Cities, and thus might think himself above Veliano nobility; that was held against him. He was scornfully impatient of folly and incompetence; that was held against him. And his wife was openly the king's mistress. It was considered foreign laxness that he did not protest, although it would have been considered stupidity if he had.

One warm windy morning I performed before a royal party by the river, entertaining them with the insipid tale of the Three Green Woodcutters. Afterward I stood apart from guests and servants alike and watched. The wind blew across the swift water, rippled the grass and flowers, drew waving tendrils from the ladies' hair. Cynda, sitting with her skirts spread around her beside Rofdal, teased from him the gold-colored sash he wore around his vast waist and tied it around her blowing hair: a coquette's trick. As she raised her arms high to knot the sash, her eyes slid sideways to meet his, a pose and a glance at once provocative and triumphant, the laughing pertness of a woman with no thought of rivals. But later, when the party strolled again toward the palace, I saw the gold sash crumpled in Cynda's hand. She had folded it as small as possible and held it against her palm with the fingers held nearly straight, as if to conceal that she had it still. No one not studying her minutely would have noticed. Her lovely face smiled as if she thought of nothing but the sweet air and warm sun, as if she had never heard of care, nor loss.

That afternoon, Queen Leonore was brought to childbed.

Word raced through the castle, and probably beyond, like fire.

"Her grace the queen has taken to childbed!"

"Queen Leonore has begun to labor!"

"The queen begins—"

"The queen—"

I stood in the long shadows—the sun had just begun to set—of the gallery, not hidden but not noticed. By the flung-open windows a knot of ladies huddled, their gowns as brilliant as wildflowers, the oldest a grandmother and the youngest but a few years older than Jorry. Their voices were hushed, portentous; they might have been planning a conspiracy.

"My firstborn came with a caul, great good fortune."

"As did the king's father—or so my mother says. Do you remember it, Grand Aunt?"

"No. But I remember the king's mother with childbed fever. Four days she lingered, with a face as hollow as death itself."

"And her sister, when she bore the deformed girl—she looked like that. And the child, if child you can call it, looked . . . I can not say."

"I saw it as well," said another. "And her second birth, the child she tried to bring feet before head and could not."

"My lord's sister's first childbed—"

And so they went on, as if no woman ever brought forth without disaster. Perhaps no noble lady did. The young girl among them had paled, her jaw set. All around the palace similar excited knots of ladies whispered of fevers, of twins, of growths, of slips—all save one.

"Storygiver! Take this for me to my Lady Cynda, in the solarium. I have no time for this creature!" A serving woman of Leonore's thrust at me a silvered cage. The ladies descended on her, but she elbowed past. "I have no time, I cannot be spared, I must attend the queen!"

I thought that Leonore could probably spare her quite well—could probably spare all of them, save the physician—but I bowed and took the cage. The cyret within slept; cyrets can sleep through anything. Only lately had caravans brought them to Veliano from the Silver Cities, which imported them from across the seas, and the court ladies had taken to them because they were new, expensive, beautiful, and useless. Bred for sweetness of song, largeness of eye, and delicacy of wing, the little reptiles had become so big-eyed they were nearly blind and so frail-winged they could no longer fly. Ladies in Frost and Pearl led them on jeweled leashes. The scales on this one were pink, the dainty flushed pink of a sleeping baby, and I knew its eyes would be a deeper shade of the same color, rimmed with silver. The folded wings, beneath which the cyret had tucked its head, were nearly transparent save for the tracings of blood vessels, blue and rose. The feet had been declawed. Once, a merchant had told me, wild cyrets had hunted prey as big as themselves.

I carried the enfeebled thing toward the solarium. It was a wide-windowed room at the top of the north tower, reached by a stair steep and sharply angled, hung at the top with a tapestry. I had nearly reached the tapestry when I heard from behind it a female voice low with hissing fury.

"—forbid me! You have no right to forbid me anything." A laugh, shrill enough to make the cyret stir in his sleep. Laugh and words were Cynda's, but a Cynda I had not heard before, only seen hinted at in her too-fevered gaiety and too-bright eyes. "From where comes this sudden right to *forbid* me? Do you think that because you have pleasured yourself with my body that you can decree where I take it? You?"

Murmurs, the words indistinguishable, from a male voice.

Rofdal? Had I nearly interrupted a quarrel with the *king*? But surely he must be somewhere near Leonore, brought to childbed hours ago.

"You gave up the wish to rule my body—don't you remember? It was not so long ago. Or did you change your mind again, my lord? Did you decide to bed me again?"

More murmurs. Cynda's voice turned savage, a little hysterical. "Is that what you came to tell me, my lord? That you wish my breasts again? Here, they are yours. They have not changed."

The sound of ripping cloth. I began to back down the stairs. If Rofdal were to catch me overhearing—

"And my hips are yours, if you wish, just as before. You

112

turn away! But why, my lord? Surely my hips have not *changed*. Nor my belly, where once you did not scruple to lay your head! Nor my—"

"Stop it," the male voice said, and on the stairway I froze. Brant.

Cynda laughed again, and the laugh held in it a sound I have heard only twice in my life: once from a criminal about to be hanged in public execution, and once from a fishwoman told her soldier son was dead, and with him the reason of her life's being.

"Stop what, Brant? What is it you wish me to stop? Not merely riding alone in the mountains. Stop thrusting my body on you, you all unwilling? But you were not unwilling once. Not you, and not the king . . ."

"Cynda," Brant said tonelessly, and stopped.

"Cynda what? What would you say to me, my lord? That the king will return to me once this cursed child is born? I do not need *you* to tell me that."

"I did not think you did," Brant said coldly. If he hoped that coldness would calm her, he was mistaken.

"You did not think so! *You* did not! But what is your thought to me now? The thought of a husband who will not bed his own wife?"

"You have chosen to bed elsewhere, my lady."

"As you did, my lord. Or have you forgotten?"

Silence.

"May the Four Gods Protector curse you, Brant. You will bed your peasant bitch, yet turn from me for being chosen by the king."

Brant's voice came hard as ice. "You know why I turned from you."

"Do I? Do I truly? Or is that merely the windy excuse you give me—and yourself? Once you were not so fastidious."

"I will leave you now, Cynda, before you make greater fools of both of us. But remember what I have ordered. No more riding alone in the mountains."

"I will ride where I choose. Just as I will bed as I choose."

Brant answered nothing. Footsteps approached the tapestry

and I glanced wildly around in panic. But the steps stopped and I heard a wild impact of bodies, as if she had hurled herself against him. In her frenzied rush of words I heard again the criminal, the fishwoman who saw slipping away from them their different lives.

"I *do* choose! The king will return to me, there is no doubt of it—and so will you, my lord! You will not hold out forever. You cannot—I remember it too well, and so do you. I remember everything about you, Brant, what pleased you and what did not, what you said to me, how you looked at me—what would it take to make you look at me like that again? This . . . or this? Do not turn your back to me—don't you ever turn your back to me! The king will return, and you, too, my aloof lord. Perhaps I should bed yet elsewhere, many elsewheres—would that arouse you? Or perhaps I should merely bed with swine, as your filthy peasant Ard did—"

A quick step; she stopped. Trembling, I heard the sound of a brief scuffle, and then Brant curse, quick and low.

"Let it bleed!" Cynda cried. "I want you to bleed! I would like to see you drained of blood, hung upside down, flayed alive. I would enjoy it!"

"Then arrange it," Brant said, in a harsh voice at last empty of patience. "You have only to tell the king of Ard and me. What should stop you? You already did half of that. Why did you stop at arranging her torture, if you also want mine? Your influence with the king will return. And this time, as wife, you could watch."

Silence. Then I heard Cynda's voice, its overwrought frenzy turned to deadly malice. "*Then* you could never turn away from me."

A sharp intake of breath; Brant had not expected that. But Cynda laughed again. "Do not look so, my lord. Do you think that I am mad as Ard, that I would tell the priests you lived with her? I know you are not a soul-beseter. I only wish such a thing were possible, that I might beset yours! Did you think that because I caught you and her in that swinish cottage I must believe the castrated tales of priests? I can recognize lust. You took a peasant girl, a man's right; I destroyed her, a wife's right. But not you, beloved—not you. You belong to me. I would not destroy you, not this part of you, nor this . . ." she crooned now, seductive, a horribly erotic lullaby. I could not see through the tapestry, and was glad of it.

"Do you think me wanton, my lord? Do you? You liked that once, didn't you, why should you not like it now? But you do like it, I can feel that you do, here where you cannot lie. You cannot lie to me anyway, can you, I know every inch of you there is to know, you are *mine*—"

I began to creep down the stairs.

"—*mine*, and you know it. You cannot turn away from me, no more than can the king. I know all of you, all there is to know, all—save who was that boy you sent north just before Midsummer."

My heart froze. No sound came from above. Then Brant's voice, deadly quiet. "Which of my men do you pay?"

"Does it matter?" Lightly, triumphantly. "I have your attention *now*, don't I, my lord? Who was the child, and where were you sending him? You will not tell me. Very well, then you will not. I know your lust does not turn upon boys, and for the rest I don't care. But you will not forbid me to ride as I wish into the mountains, when you send strange boys off into them as you will."

She laughed, and now it was the laugh I had heard her give Rofdal time and again in the Great Hall or at a water party: gay, empty-headed, lightly sensual, the laugh of a woman sure she is the center of male attention. It was in this, more than all the rest of it, that I saw her story clear. A moment before she had been pleading, had been cruel, had been anything at all if it would win her his intent response. Now that she had it, her very tone of voice denied that anything else was possible, no more than it would be possible for the sun to falter in the sky. Cynda was a gracious sun, and the mortal men on earth below would warm to her, else all nature be perverted. I had seen such women before, although not so imperious as this. Nor so beautiful.

"Which of my men, Cynda?" Brant repeated, and at his voice I, crouching in the darkness of the stairs, quailed. But

Cynda laughed lightly, and there came the sound of smacking flesh, as if she had playfully struck him.

"You will let me keep nothing of yours, will you? I could surprise you on that, my lord. But very well—I will tell you. Colys. Now what will you do—have him beheaded?"

"I am not a king, to order beheadings."

"Poor Colys! And his only crime a loyalty to his mistress, which not even kings can order. Leonore gives birth tonight, I think. But then, only you at court do not much seem to care, do you? You have never favored dark women. Why do you really forbid me to ride in the mountains, Brant? It is no longer safe. Why not? Bandits? Dragons? Your mysterious hidden boy?"

The queen's men, I thought. A hidden army that practices mind arts.

"Me," Brant said, and I caught the deliberateness of the tone and the contempt beneath it. For her, or himself? "You will not be safe from me, because I forbid it."

"Ah," Cynda said, drawn out and low, and I saw that this time she took it with delight. What greater compliment from a mortal than his trying to control the sun? So had Brant intended, and his tawdry trick worked. She listened, if only to vanity.

This was the woman he had chosen to marry.

A cry came from below us, muffled by distance. Cynda said, "I go to wait on the queen, curse her. I hope the child is stillborn. Does that shock you?"

"No," Brant said, and she laughed.

Her footsteps came toward me. I tried to slip behind a corner of tapestry, but the only way to do that might make me seen within the solarium. All I could do was flatten myself into the deepest shadow, the stupid cyret cage bulking at my feet.

The tapestry lifted. Cynda swept past me. The bodice of her gown had been ripped; she held together with one hand the rent she had made herself. In the other she carried, senselessly, a rain-streaked brimmed hat, such as men wear on rough journeys. She must have taken it from Brant. Her face, briefly lit from the solarium above, looked as I had seen it at afternoon pleasure parties or dining in the Great Hall beside the king: smiling, flushed, assured except for the too-bright eyes. A woman too beautiful for squalor.

She did not even notice the cyret cage.

I watched her descend the rest of the stairs and held my breath, but Brant did not emerge from the solarium. The moments lengthened. The light at the turning of the stair, light sifting from some window below, began to pale. It must be close to sunset, or close after.

It was come, then—the desperate chance I had schemed for. Brant was alone. And everything I had just heard pushed me on. What would a Cynda who had arranged to have Ard die in agony—not for practicing mind arts Cynda did not believe in, but for bedding with Brant—what would such a Cynda do to a "strange boy" she discovered to be Brant's son?

From my tunic I pulled the First Flask and drank it. Then I drew out the pulifer of brass I had bought ten years ago, when I was carrying Jorry.

A pregnant woman of no household and no rank is an easy target, but those who live at Mother Arcoa's learn of things which others do not. From a foreign thief I had bought the rare and expensive pulifer, and then lived so carefully— passing up chances to Storygive if I scented even the smallest physical risk, choosing my companions for safety and not wit, living as long as possible with the same actors—that I had never used the pulifer. It could only be used once. I would use it now.

I slipped the brass ring over the ring finger of my right hand. The oval cylinder attached to it lay hidden along my palm, with the small knob that released the mechanism opposite my thumb. Placing the cyret cage directly in the middle of the first stair—it might distract him one vital moment, or with luck he might stumble over it—I waited for Brant to leave the solarium.

He did not.

Panic needled me. This waiting was worse than stealing the drugs with the men-at-arms in the hall, worse than Leonore's probing, worse even than the uncertainty of standing before the king, unsure whose story would spin out between my hands. This was my own story I spun now—mine and Jorry's.

Finally, I could bear waiting no longer. The stairway, dim and enclosed, would have been best for the pulifer, but nonetheless I picked up the cyret cage and drew aside the tapestry. Instantly I saw that I had been a fool.

Brant stood, back to me, at the open window. Of course all the windows would be open; the solarium was as airy as a treetop. Now all I could do was try to draw him toward the door, and I was not sure even that would help enough.

He turned as I entered. The setting sun was behind him, and his expression in shadow. But I saw on one cheek the long bloody scratches from Cynda's nails.

"I was sent to bring this cyret to the Lady Cynda."

"She is not here." Toneless—but not quite. I could not move closer to see his face, he must come to me. "Leave the cyret and go."

I held up the cage. "The cyret is hurt, my lord."

But he did not move forward. The stupid reptile cooed in its sleep, sounding contented and healthy. My panic soured to fear. Why should he cross the room for a cyret? I would not have.

"Brant," I said—and now nothing in my voice suggested "my lord"—"you were mistaken to trick the queen into letting me live."

The desired effect—he crossed the room away from the windows and was suddenly large before me, so swiftly I flinched. The smell of him brought again the mountain cabin and the power of his fists. I fought to hold myself steady, but heard the tremor in my own voice.

"I know that you arranged it all. The beating, the legend of T'Nig—all to force Leonore to keep me alive. Why?"

He said nothing, only watched me intently. Very slowly I put up my right hand, palm inward, as if to touch the bloody scratches on his left cheek. His eyes darkened, his gaze on mine, and I pressed the pulifer's buttom with my thumb in the correct pattern—two short pushes, one long—to release the catch.

At the first whiff of the vapor, he knew. He tried to throw himself toward the window, but while he had listened to me his lips had been parted, and his breath a little quickened. The pulifer acts very rapidly; if it did not, it would be both less useful and less expensive. In a few seconds Brant crashed to the floor.

The second I had pressed the pulifer, I had set my lips tightly together and began a long exhalation of breath through my nose. Now I rushed to the window, leaned out and into the breeze as far as I could, and breathed rapidly. But the breeze also blew into the wide windows of the solarium; behind me Brant already moved on the stone floor.

I gulped one huge breath, held it, and untied the sash from my tunic. I had envisioned a rope, but there was no rope. With my sash I bound Brant's hands behind him, and then wildly eyed the solarium. His eyes had already opened when I finished binding his feet with a leather cyret leash. Again I rushed to the window, exhaled, breathed once more. The smell of the vapor, lemony and deceptively clean, was nearly gone. I slipped the empty pulifer from my trembling finger. Cynda's—the leash must have been Cynda's; it was to her I had been supposed to carry the cyret.

Brant had revived, although his voice sounded still slightly thick.

"A pulifer. From *you*."

I said, unsteadily, "Veliano has not yet seen one."

"Neither has most of the Silver Cities. Where did you get that much gold, Fia?"

"I stole it from you. Where is Jorry?"

I could see his face now. In the light from the setting sun Cynda's scratches shone livid. "Jorry is somewhere safe. Untie me."

For answer, I pulled out the Second Flask and drank it down.

Again came that empty grayness, and from the emptiness the elusive music flooding my mind with sound that became wordless light and then wordless unfolding of layers I had not known there. Then time returned, and with it the solarium and Brant, staring from the Second Flask to my face. I remembered that on that first night in Veliano he had called me a thief—a thief, a liar, a whore.

I rode on the music and touched his mind.

From having been the one invaded, I knew he did not feel it. But I did, and it was as it had been with Ludie—a squeamish blasphemy, a kind of rape. I spread my hands.

"Where is Jorry, Brant? Think of where you have sent Jorry. Where is my son?"

He went on staring at me. I swung my eyes to the mist between my hands. Fear, panic, shame, rage—I pushed them all away and thought of the horses leaving the inn with my child slung across one of them. For this moment I had stolen the drugs, expended the pulifer, invaded poor Ludie's dim mind, stood again within reach of Brant's fists. I would not now lose action to my own fear.

The mist swirled faster. Then a sword slashed between Brant's mind and mine, and mist and music died.

I jerked my eyes to his.

"For every thrust there is a parry, Fia. You were never a soldier. Untie me. No, don't look so. There is nothing you can do against a mind armed with its own arts."

If he lied, I knew of no way to prove it. I stared dumbly.

"Hear me, Fia. If it were that easy, would Leonore and I circle around each other, seizing on an inept Storygiver to drag out what each knew? We would invade each other's minds directly, as I did your undefended one. You can see that; I have underestimated how much you see. Untie me. If anyone comes up the stairs and discovers us like this, you and I and Jorry will all be in even more danger."

My one plan lay in ruins around me. I did not trust him, but my trusting or not trusting made no difference. The stories and lies all of us created—he, Leonore, I, Cynda—had entangled me past where I could see to make another plan better than the one just failed. Despair filled me, as music had filled me moments before.

I pulled Brant's dagger from his belt.

As I moved the blade toward the sash that bound him, his eyes flickered in the close twilight. I stopped, both of us aware of the knife in my hand, of Brant's helplessness on the stone floor. Now his fists would do him no good, nor his rank. In the room was no sound.

"Brant," I said slowly. "Brant—why did you arrange for Leonore to let me live?"

He answered without a flicker to betray the lie. "Because I needed to make use of you before Rofdal."

"No use that would balance the danger you put yourself in when she pulled from my mind how much you knew of soul-besetting."

"Then because I could not bear to let you die."

And that, too, was a lie. "No, Brant. You needed me to let Leonore discover that you have found the White Pipes. You wanted her to believe that—and she did believe it. But I do not."

For the first time since I had pressed the pulifer, I saw on his face unguarded shock. It took him a moment to master himself.

"Cut me loose, Fia. We neither of us have anything to gain in being discovered like this."

"Where is Jorry, Brant? Tell me, and I will not tell Leonore that you do not have the Pipes."

"You will not tell her anyway. You would only die for it. Is it worth your death, to cause mine? You could do it easier now, with my own dagger. Why not? Wasn't that my own drug you tried to use on me, and my gold that bought the pulifer?"

Thief, liar, whore.

"Untie me, Fia. You have nothing to gain."

It was true—I did not. Unbidden, tears pricked behind my eyelids. Weakness, stupidity! My great plan, schemed and risked for with the schemes and risks I hated, had come to nothing. I stood no closer to Jorry than before, no more free of thwarting and manipulation by those with mind arts greater than mine, no surer of whether I was being used or protected by Brant, nor for what purpose. I had gained nothing.

My knife hovered over Brant's body. Then I slashed sharply downward, cutting his bonds. At the same moment two sounds started abruptly and swelled to fill the solarium: the cyret, awakened and suddenly pouring forth cascades of glorious music, and the ringing of bells in the east tower of the old castle, clamorously announcing that the queen had been safely delivered of a living son.

8

BRANT SAT ON THE STONE FLOOR, RUBBING HIS WRISTS where I had bound them. The bells went on and on, a joyous singing vibrancy, and now from the courtyard far below shouts arose and wild exuberant cheers whose words were blown away on the wind. Brant looked at me, and in his eyes I saw the one feeling I had not seen in all his troubling changes of mood and passion since I had come to Veliano: fear. Brant was afraid.

I said, "You did not find the Pipes on this last journey of yours."

"No."

"You did not see Jorry, either."

"No."

"And this baby, this heir . . ."

He seized my left wrist. At his touch I shrank back; my flesh remembered only that he had battered me, not why. But it also remembered other, older touches of his, and violently I pulled my hand away. He gave no sign of noticing.

"Fia. This heir . . . Rofdal has desired it above all else. If the boy be strong and whole, Leonore will gain much more influence with the king. Influence—and power."

"She has that already."

"She has had it, yes, but diluted. You must—"

I broke in on him. An ugly thought had come to me. "Leonore has had power, but diluted—diluted by the others who hold influence with the king. Such as your wife."

Brant watched me coldly, but I could not stop. "Did you know, Brant? Did you *encourage* her, to weaken Leonore's power—even if it made Cynda a tool and you a cuckold?"

He did not change expression. But his voice splintered with both anger and pain. From my own anger and pain I was glad of his: I would have increased it if I could.

"You babble, Fia, of situations you don't understand."

"And do you? Do you understand why the Lady Cynda beds the king and then begs for her husband's body? Do you arrange for that, Brant, as you arranged for me to beg for Jorry? Cynda, me—what did Ard beg for, Brant? Or didn't she beg at all, and so it didn't matter much that your wife had her killed?"

He had turned his back to me; I could not see his face. But his fists clenched by his sides, and not even that could stop me. I was as out of control as Cynda had been, and I did not care what I said as long as I might hurt him.

"Why does your wife take objects from you, Brant? Why? I've seen it: your glove at the hunt, your hat, your goblet at dinner. She takes them from you and carries them away with her. Is that passion, or does she too act in some story you have arranged, even to bedding the king? Or could it be *her* story, and all your stolen belongings part of a trap where she will tell Rofdal about Ard and you? Perhaps you should consider that, my Lord Brant. I cannot move against you, you have said so yourself, as long as you hold Jorry—but Cynda can. You hold no son of hers. A frayed link in your leashes—how can you be sure you control her if you can't dangle threats and promises about her child?"

Swiftly he turned on me. "I could promise her yours."

For a moment I thought he meant it. The tower room went black, and sick panic swept over me. Then Brant was next to me, seizing my arm, his curse low and quick with fury. "You believed it, damn you forever, Fia. You would believe even that of me, and even after what you have guessed. Don't push me too far, Fia. Get out—out of the palace and out of Veliano. You are not safe from Leonore now, not with the power she will hold over Rofdal with the birth of his heir. I can't protect you from her now. Leonore has only to tell the king she sent you to her brother's castle, as a favor to his ailing wife, or to anyone else. For a while now he will think nothing of indulging her in a matter so small, and would scarcely notice you were gone. Get out of Veliano. Go to the inn of the Green Sun, four streets from Mother Arcoa's, you remember it. It is still standing. Wait there until I can safely send someone to take you to Jorry."

"No!" I cried. "I won't leave Veliano without him! He's in Veliano somewhere, in the mountains Cynda said, and I won't go without him! Tell me where Jorry is—if you are really done with me, you have no reason not to tell me where he is!"

"Leonore could have the information out of you any time she chose. She could not get it from me. It's for Jorry's safety that I don't tell you, not for the relish of my own cruelty."

"Why should you care about Jorry's safety? I don't believe you, Brant!"

"That is your misfortune."

"I wish I had killed you when you lay bound!"

His fury was mastered, his face gone hard with mockery. He handed me his dagger, grip first. "Do you? Then do it now."

In astonishment, I took it. The grip felt hot in my hand. "Go ahead, Fia. Kill me now. That is how you meet your challenges, isn't it? By eliminating them entirely. Run away from entanglement or slay it dead—there is not much difference. You took my son and fled me at Mother Arcoa's, now you may try the other approach. You may kill me. I give you my most gracious leave. But of course then you never will find Jorry."

I turned the dagger over and over in my hands, but I could not see it. From frustration, from grief, from the withering contempt in Brant's voice, my vision had blurred. In the twilight room the dagger's grip shone gold, a melting gold that seemed insubstantial as light. I did not move.

Brant laughed, an ugly sound. He drew the dagger from my hands. "I hope our son is not such a coward as his mother. Leave Veliano, Fia. I can no longer protect you here, even if I

wanted to. It may be months, but when I find the White Pipes
I will send someone to take you to Jorry. Although not
immediately—first I want to find what you have made of him.
Your first night here I called you liar and thief, and I erred
only in underestimating how well you have become both."

"But not so well as you. Why do you warn me to leave,
Brant? I have served your purpose. Leonore believes you
possess the White Pipes. Do you really warn me away for my
safety, or because Leonore could learn from me that you do
not have the Pipes?"

"She has guessed it already."

"How?"

"If I had them, I would have used them."

"For what?"

"To force her to miscarry her child."

I caught my breath. "Would you have—"

"She would think so." His face tightened. "And so do you."

"But if she no longer thinks you have the Pipes, then she
could learn nothing from me. Why not let her examine me and
then kill me, Brant? Wouldn't that be less risky than having
protected my life?"

"Yes."

"Why did you do so? *Why?*"

He looked at me steadily, his face hard, and said nothing.
"You would believe even that of me" he had said, but I did not
know what to believe of him. Lies surrounded him like
breaths, and I did not know if he told me to leave Veliano to
protect me, to enmesh me in some use I had not yet glimpsed,
or even to bring about my capture by Leonore that he warned
me against. My fleeing Rofdal's favor with a caravan would
make such a capture plausible and easy. Was that what Brant
intended? He did not yet have the White Pipes. Was I still a
tool to somehow attain them? Was Cynda? Was even Jorry?

I did not trust Brant. He stood gazing at me, the bloody
scratches disfiguring his cheek, and I looked at the set line of
his mouth and felt the power in his hard body. I did not trust
him.

Carefully he said, "Whatever I answered, whatever reason I

gave for sending you from Veliano, you would not believe me, would you?"

I hesitated. "No."

"And you will not leave without Jorry."

"No!"

"A pity," he said scathingly, "that you had not such a resolution of character ten years ago."

"Not a pity. It kept me from becoming like your Cynda. Or like Ard."

I thought I had pushed him too far; I thought he would strike me. But he did not. He strode from the tower room, and I heard his boots on the stairs. A sudden trembling, borne of the risks I had taken and of their failure, took my legs and I fell to the floor, where I sat with my head in my hands. Then the crude bells of the small neighboring towns began to clamor, first one and then another and then another far off as the tidings of the new heir spread, until darkness fell and the night air churned with rejoicing.

For the first time since Jorry had been taken, despair took me completely. Before, there had been some hope, however small: Brant's drugs would aid me, the pulifer would aid me, some scrap of useful information would somehow come to light. Now I knew there was no help and no light. I stumbled from the solarium in sick blackness, unable to walk more than a few steps without stopping. At the bottom of the stairs, dizzy with anguish, I leaned against the stone wall and squeezed my eyes shut.

I would never see Jorry again.

There was no way to force Brant to tell me where Jorry was, no way to find him myself in all the vastness of Veliano and Erdulin and the Silver Cities. Brant had easily blunted the only thrust I had, and the thrust itself had been weak and stupid and a lie.

"Storygiver! Have you heard that her Grace the queen— Storygiver? Are you ill?"

Even after I opened my eyes I could not see who it was, could not see at all through the blackness in my mind. Then my vision cleared; a serving woman stood before me, a goblet in her hand and her round kind face flushed red.

"Are you ill?"

"No, I . . . no. No."

She laughed. "Then you began celebrating very early! I won't offer you more wine. You don't look like you need it, and I be several glasses behind you!" She laughed again and raised her goblet toward me, her whole ample body boisterous with joy. "To the prince, Veliano's heir and as fine a child as ever I set eyes upon!"

I would never see my son again.

The serving woman drank, smacking her lips loudly, and wiped her mouth across her sleeve. She clapped her hand on my shoulder.

"You best take yourself to bed, Storygiver. You've done your share of drinking the prince's health! To look like that, you must have begun well before he even crowned!" The pun pleased her; she laughed all the way down the passageway, and when she opened the door at the far end other laughter floated out to meet her.

Laughter, joy—I could not bear it. If I stood any longer against the wall, if I heard any longer the rejoicing over Leonore's son, I would vomit. I groped my way along the stone to a door, and stumbled out into the gardens.

Here, too, people shouted merrily, calling to each other for news and wine. I lurched past them in the twilight shadows and made my way through the gardens to the river, where I threw myself down on the embankment and clenched my fists in the long grass. The grass smelled fresh and cool, as if this were any sweet summer dusk, as if it were not the night Leonore had borne her son and I had lost mine forever.

I would never see Jorry again. Days would pass, and seasons, and years, and I would never hold him, never tell him stories, never scold him to wash his neck or to not dawdle or to please remember to tend the fire—all the precious petty threads out of which I had woven our life for the past nine years and which Brant had severed with a single stroke. If he had used his sword to cut off my arm he could not have maimed me more, and in anguish and fresh hatred I thought that he must know it.

And Jorry, wherever he was—what did he feel now? His mother had failed to protect him, had let him be slung over a saddle and carried off in fear and bewilderment, had not come to find him again. He was not timid, but he had a child's fears and sometimes in his sleep he had had nightmares. He would wake crying of a dark wood where black shapes moved behind the trees . . . *Jorry*—

The sky darkened and the stars came out. I had not the strength to roll over and stare at them. Tears might have helped, but my eyes felt frozen and I could not cry. I could not do anything. Feeble, stupid—all my efforts to do anything had failed, and there was nothing more to try. Misery robbed me of all strength, and I lay all night on the embankment, while below me Veliano's river slid by cold and dark as death.

The merrymaking for the new prince bore the stamp of Rofdal's personal joy. Royal coffers were opened to provide feasts and pageantry, not only in Velin but in every town, every farm hamlet, every mining camp high in the rough mountains. Debts to the crown were forgiven, criminals pardoned. Leonore's brother Perwold was advanced in rank. The child was shielded four days, one due each of the Gods Protector, from the eyes of all who had not seen him born—although that seemed half the court. The ritual shielding gave rise to the usual whisperings about only heirs: he was ailing, he was deformed. But the rumors were slight, and no one really believed them. And when the child was finally shown from a palace balcony on his Naming Day, a great shout of praise went up from the crowd below, none of whom was close enough to see him. That was one of the few times I remember seeing Leonore smile.

Later, those of the court who had stood on the balcony and so could see him, praised him even beyond what was politic. He was strong and straight-backed, a black-haired boy who already gave promise of Rofdal's enormous shoulders and his queen's dark eyes. The king had him named Rofwold, a further compliment to Leonore's family. His nursemaids said he rarely cried: a love of a baby, a perfect prince.

I had no opinion; I had not seen him close. I could not have borne it. Jorry, too, had been a dark-eyed baby, though neither black-haired nor large.

Leonore's childbed had been a hard one, but she recovered rapidly. She was carried in a litter to her son's Naming Day, and after two days more appeared again in the Great Hall at the feasting, which went on still. Rofdal was as attentive to her as to a favorite mistress, calling for her favorite tunes and sending to the cook for special dishes, and the courtiers watched as admiringly as if they actually loved her.

Cynda did not appear in the Hall. She had not appeared since Rofwold's birth.

Brant sat in his usual place with the officials of the court. He talked gravely with those nearest him, and his face showed nothing. I watched him from my low table and thought that again he had lied: day followed day, and not one of Leonore's men carried me to that dim room under the palace. Leonore clearly had gained the power Brant predicted, but she was not interested in turning it against me. I watched her face, as still as ever, but with a fullness to her cheeks, a banked glow in her dark eyes. The physician, even more self-important than before, was absent from our low table, but the king's Cloudcaster told us that the queen had dispensed with a wet nurse, preferring to nurse her son herself. "You had your son with you, I believe, the first night you were here," the Cloudcaster said kindly to me, "but not since. I have intended to ask you where he is, Storygiver."

"He returned with the caravan. To . . . to Frost. To my sister there."

"She has children to be companions to him?"

"Yes."

"How pleasant for him," she said, and I stared at the feast on my plate as if it were ashes.

The evening before the eighth day, the Protection Day on which the prince would be formally dedicated to the Gods Protector, Rofdal commanded me to perform. He would have the legend of T'Nig and the founder of Veliano, in honor of the heir of Veliano. I prepared myself woodenly. Brant had never taken from me the drugs I had stolen from his carved chest. I saw in the gesture both generosity and contempt: generosity because with the drugs I could sustain the Story-giving that brought Rofdal's patronage, contempt because Brant must think my use of the mind arts too small to threaten him. Like all he had done, this looked one way in one light, another way in another.

I had taken the First Flask and was walking up and down a passage near the Great Hall, when I was hailed by a maid called Tralys, one of Cynda's serving women. Like all the women Cynda chose to have around her, Tralys was swarthy, plain, and sweet-natured. As she hurried toward me her ill-favored face twisted with strong feeling, and she wrung her hands in the skirt of her gown.

"Storygiver! Storygiver! Be you before now in the Great Hall?"

"I sat there at dinner. Not since."

"And my Lady Cynda, sat she there at the high table?"

"No. What is wrong, Tralys?"

"Do you know where she be? She be nowhere at all in the palace!"

Riding alone in the mountains, I thought, to provoke her lord, but to Tralys merely shook my head. "What is wrong—" but Tralys was gone, skittering down the passageway.

I drank the Second Flask and closed my eyes greedily for the brightness, the timelessness, the dancing music that became light to open the furled layers of my mind. I thought of the story of the many rebirths of T'Nig, and it seemed that thinking of it after the Second Flask showed new beauties in the legend and new images with which to give it. I was almost willing to perform before Rofdal.

The moment I entered the Hall, however, I sensed that something had changed. Leonore sat with her hand on the king's arm, her head high. But Rofdal's fleshy face looked strained and weary, and his enormous vitality seemed to have deserted him. For the first time, I thought: *He is twice her age.*

He is nearly old. But it was not quite that. Rofdal's face also looked sullen, like a petted child forced to do something he abhorred. Aging and childishness—a dangerous combination.

I was announced, spread my hands, and began to give the legend of T'Nig and of the hero-warrior who looked like Rofdal. Never had I given it so well. Between my palms the bottomless lake sparkled, the uncuttable tree waved its limbs in the wind. But I could not hold them. The court, only half of which was in attendance, watched distractedly, whispering among themselves. Rofdal slumped in his chair, and one fleshy thumb moved restlessly over the chair's gem-set arm in endless circles. Only Leonore watched my story with courteous attention, and her attention I could have done without. Without the bulk of her pregnancy, she looked even smaller and more frail, and neither the straightness of her spine nor the intentness of her gaze wavered.

I had not even reached the part of the warrior-hero when Rofdal half-lifted his hand, as if to wave away my whole uninteresting performance, but he never finished the gesture. Sounds of scuffle in the passageway, a woman's shrill command, and Rofdal's hand hung in mid-air. More scuffling, the sound of feet running. The crowd parted.

Cynda ran across the Hall and threw herself on her knees before Rofdal.

"Your Grace, oh Your Grace no, tell me you have not—no—"

"Lady Cynda. Do not—"

"My lord, *no*, do not do this you are mistaken, I swear to you on all the nights we have spent together—"

"You forget yourself, my lady!"

"I forget nothing and you do not either, you could not. Your Grace, I beg you, I *beg* you, yes, you have made a mistake—oh, my lord, you *have*—if only you would reconsider, with all your discernment—"

Rofdal looked like a man trapped by his own feelings. Rising from his chair, he took one step toward the woman on her knees before him. Cynda had been weeping; her flushed, beautiful face might have melted stone, and if it did not, her pleading would. She lifted her wet face to Rofdal as if to the sun. Rofdal stretched out one hand. But at the same time he glanced around his court and saw their faces watching, and I could have named the exact second when anger and affront sprang the trap and Cynda had lost, although I still did not know what.

"Your Grace—"

"You are dismissed, my lady!"

"My lord, *no*, no in the name of the Gods Protector— reconsider, it is not even possible and Your Grace must know it is not, he is the most loyal of all your subjects. I swear to you on my heart, Brant is *innocent*—"

Slowly I brought together my hands, lifeless weights. The story between them vanished.

"He could not be what he stands accused of, you *know* it, oh, my lord—*Rofdal*—"

"Men-at-arms!"

Two guards sprang forward. They were not rough with her as once they had been with me. Respectfully they eased Cynda to her feet, and she broke their light grip as if they had been girls, and wrapped herself around the king's chest.

"No, no, *no*, he is innocent, you can't Rofdal, think what he has been to you, loyal and able and you *cannot* you cannot you cannot—"

The court stared, appalled. The men-at-arms grabbed Cynda's arms; they tightened around the king, and all the while she spoke in that intent, reasonable, passionate voice that chilled the spine. Rofdal finally was forced to break her grip himself, wrenching his body free with a great bellow of frustration and rage that set the men-at-arms to seizing her as roughly as any street thief. And even then she fought them, all the while still pleading with Rofdal, her eyes never leaving his face.

"Think on it a moment. My lord, he has never done you a disloyal act nor given an unwise advice, he could *not* be a soul-beseter, Lord Perwold is wrong, such a thing is not even possible, only think reasonably and you must see—"

The men-at-arms dragged her from the Hall.

No one spoke. The court dared not move. Rofdal swung his anger toward Leonore, who kept her eyes cast down and gave him no opening. He bellowed again, a wordless sound that seemed to shake the very stones.

"This is your doing, my lady. You may be right—you *are* right—" as she must be, or he too would be wrong and that was unthinkable "—but I do not think of it fondly!" With a last look around, he stamped from the Hall, and no one stood in the way of his passing.

I crept to the empty antechamber and collapsed against the wall.

Brant imprisoned as a soul-beseter. "With the power she will gain with the king, you are no longer safe," he had said to me—but had not forseen that Leonore's power could extend as far as himself, nor that he too was no longer safe. He had not thought she could persuade Rofdal against both his better judgment of Brant and his infatuation for Cynda—but Leonore had, with whatever narrow margin. What evidence—bribed, forged, stolen—had Perwold brought to bear? Whose mind among Brant's men had been raped for scraps of information, what witness tortured into confession about mind arts to convince Rofdal of what was in fact true?

Brant would be flayed alive.

The drug was still upon me, sharpening my visual powers: I saw it. I saw Brant scream under the knife, saw it cut first into his arms and legs, saw the priests yank with bloody hands strips of his skin until the skin would rip from him no more and again the knife would flash.

I turned toward the wall and retched violently.

The rest of the drug came up with my vomit. It was only then, as I stood wiping my mouth, weak and shaking against the arras, that I saw the thing I should have seen first: If Brant died, I would lose all possibility of discovering from him where he had sent Jorry. Without Brant, I would have to search for my son throughout Veliano, throughout Erdulin, throughout all the three Silver Cities with no help but my own, to find him perhaps years from now . . . Or not at all.

Rofdal would not relent. He had been publicly shamed—

not by Cynda's pleas, but by the moment of his own exposed doubt. A king does not doubt, and a king is not a dupe. Rofdal would erase that public moment by not wavering again, no matter what his regard for Brant, rather than to be made to feel a dupe of his wife and her brother or a puppet of his mistress. For Rofdal's kingly pride, Brant would die.

I could see no hope for him, nor for Jorry, nor for me. All I could see was the memory of two bodies strung upside down in the courtyard, obscenely flayed but for their blackened faces, twisting in the wind.

Desperation will bring to mind what reason will not.

On the infant prince's Protection Day, the eighth day since his birth and the day after Brant's imprisonment by the priests of the Four Gods Protector, I stood in the Consecrated Garden and watched Leonore's son placed under the protection of the Four Gods. I of course had not been invited. I crept in quietly, unremarked in the crowd, solely because I could not think what else to do. All night and day, the court had seethed with rumor, but although I clutched at it all, although I stayed as close as I dared to Rofdal and Leonore, although I questioned Brant's men and sat for hours outside the apartment where Cynda was kept sedated by physicians, with her own women, although I asked of lesser priests as much as I could make seem to be idle curiosity—although I did all this, I had been able to learn only what had happened at Brant's arrest, and not what had happened to him since. I could not learn if he still lived. He had been summoned by the king to the Priests' Hall, and taken there. Beneath it lay the warren of cells and prisons built when the Hall had been the old castle and used as a fortress. No one was admitted to the lower levels save the priests and their men-at-arms. The few courtiers who tried to speak for Brant—none too urgently nor too loud—had been denied audience with the king. Rofdal had not gone even once to see his former advisor and distant marriage-kin. The king moved about his court in an edgy, black humor, and no one dared cross him.

That humor softened now, as the king stood in the

Consecrated Garden with his heir in his arms, and under a bright summer sky—the best of omens—laid the baby onto the altar of the Four Gods Protector.

The altar was a flat circular rock, a full spear's length across. Living gillyflowers grew directly from the rock, but only in a deep border around the perimeter. The center was bare scrubbed stone, rubbed smooth by the sweating efforts of countless novices, and onto this the baby Rofwold was laid on his back. I had climbed into the branches of a tree just beyond the garden, and over the decorated heads of the court—women with veils of gillyflowers, men with lightweight embroidered hoods—I could see the baby clearly. It was the first time I had seen him. He blinked at the sun, as beautiful a child as rumor said, and then began to gnaw on his small fist. In a moment he lost the fist, twisted his face to cry, lost interest, and gazed at the sky from Leonore's dark, still eyes. Around him the priests chanted. They removed the prince's embroidered dress, and as they chanted they rubbed his small body with the four-leaved petals of gillyflowers, invoking for him the presence of the Four Gods.

> "Protection for the Body against Maiming,
> Protection for the Senses against Corruption,
> Protection for the Mind against Invasion,
> Protection for the Soul against Besetting:
> Gil-ly-flow-ers."

Solemnly the priests chanted and the court along with them. The baby too lay solemn, as the oily softness of the white petals glided over his new skin.

Jorry had never had a Protection Day. Unbelieving, I had scorned for him any protection but my own.

Sunlight, reflected off the gray stone wall of the Priests' Hall, hit my eyes and made them ache. I could barely see. Words came to me over the distant rush of the river, over the murmuring of the crowd below, over the infant prince's high sudden wail when he decided he had had enough of this. Priests' words: ". . . given to the Four Gods Protector, guarded in body and in mind, reborn under the vigilance of the Four-Leaved Protection which does not fail . . ."

Reborn. Between my palms the ancient legend of T'Nig, older than the Gods Protector or than soul-besetting both, had been reborn in a form never before seen in Veliano: Story-giving. I had created the tale anew, under the vigilance of Brant my protector, who had failed this time to outguess consequences far enough ahead. And the story of T'Nig itself was one of rebirth, of the same soul coming again in different forms, its knowledge of itself intact . . .

Reborn. Rebirth. Vigilance.

Reborn.

Thus do all desperate and foolish ideas begin.

9

MY WORST ENEMY WAS TIME. FOR THE LONG FIRST PART of the afternoon, the infant prince lay outdoors in the Consecrated Garden, although now he was shielded by a canopy and rested upon silken pillows instead of flowered rock, while the court and the Priests of the Four Gods Protector feasted his religious health. Part of the time Rofwold slept, part of the time he gazed around him or sought his own small fist, part he was nursed by Leonore herself, in a discreet curtained litter at one side of the garden. She was mother enough to nurse her own child rather than trust him to a wet nurse. Or was it that the sight of the heir at her breast was intended for Rofdal, an image in the story she gave for his benefit? I didn't know. I thought it was possible that both motives might be true, or neither; I did not understand the queen.

The afternoon wore on—endless, endless. At last Leonore began to look weary, and soon after, she retired from the Consecrated Garden. To her apartments, or to Brant's prison? She could hardly risk the latter. Perwold would have to act for her. Perwold, who gained sensual pleasure from the sight of pain.

Perwold had not left the feasting.

Soon after Leonore's departure, the baby was carried into the castle. Two noblewomen, two men-at-arms, and three nursemaids were required for this. They formed a laughing procession, seven people in high spirits on a bright summer day. I followed them, and in the coolness of a passageway, in the shadow of a turning stair, I drank the First Flask. Then I closed my eyes and summoned up what I remembered of the young actors at Mother Arcoa's being told how to act drunk. It must not be overdone. Any audience is more firmly convinced if it can deduce the drunkenness for itself, rather than have the drunkenness thrust upon it. There must be a slowly dawning realization. The worse course was honesty.

Especially, I thought bitterly, in Veliano.

The passageway led to the nursery. On either side of the nursery door stood a man-at-arms. As I approached, one of the nursery maids emerged from the chamber.

"What brings you here, Storygiver?" She was large and comfortable, with a scrubbed responsible face, neither young nor old. I would have chosen her for a nursery maid myself, and wondered if the choice had been Leonore's or Rofdal's.

"Cul, I was sent for."

"Sent for? By who?" She glanced over her shoulder at the two noblewomen within.

I tried to look befuddled. "I can't remember. I knew, I was told . . ."

The nursery maid squinted at me. I saw the men-at-arms exchange glances of amusement.

"Someone," I said, a shade too carefully, "*Someone* wanted a story."

"No one here," the woman said sharply. "The prince must sleep now."

Did that mean he was not asleep yet? I jutted my chin. "I must give . . . a story. Someone called for a *story.*"

The woman was sure now: I was drunk. Her honest face wrinkled with disgust. But I had occupied such an ambiguous position at court, neither servant nor guest, that she was reluctant to order me away herself. Disappearing into the chamber, she returned with one of the noblewomen, the elder of the two.

She was Lady Triwen. Of this choice I had no question: Lady Triwen would have been appointed by Rofdal. A distant cousin of the king, she was a middle-aged widow of the same honest, plain stamp as the first nursery maid. Remove the silks, the flowers absurd on the drab hair, and the accent of rank, and she and the nursery maid could have been older and younger sister. Lady Triwen would not have sent for a Storygiver.

Behind her in the doorway stood the younger noblewoman, watching me with amused eyes. Lady Kaleena, former attendant to the queen.

Something turned over in my chest. How widespread among the nobility were Leonore's allies? It did not seem reasonable that her brother Perwold was the only one. Did Lady Kaleena know the deeper mind arts? Would she recognize them if she saw them?

"You were not sent for *here*," Lady Triwen said. "Someone else must want you. Go ask in the summer garden."

"It was . . . here?" I said. I put one hand against the wall, withdrawing it with exaggerated dignity.

Lady Kaleena laughed. "Perhaps she should stay. I have never heard a harper drunk."

Lady Triwen gave her a freezing look and then swept the frost toward me. "You are dismissed." I bowed jerkily. The door closed.

I had failed again.

"Storygiver," one of the men-at-arms said, "I would have a story. Later."

They were both young; the one who had spoken threw a roguish glance at the other, and then at me. His blond hair fell in a slanting line across his forehead, and I saw his tongue moisten his upper lip. It was only another type of acting, and easily recognizable. I never hesitated.

"A . . . story, you want?"

"But later. When my duty be done." He smiled at me boldly, and his companion snickered. Veliano had few women harpers. What had been the speculations about me in the guardroom?

"Later?" I said, as if drunkenly considering. I took a step toward him. He smelled of horses but not of ale. I had hoped for ale. "Later I be sleeping."

"Cul, alone?" he said.

I smiled. "Maybe."

He laughed and seized me. His mouth was warm and thorough, and the hand on my breast gentle enough. Over his shoulder I saw his brother-at-arms keep watch for them both down the passage and at the nursery door. When I judged he had tasted enough, I pulled a little away from him and pouted. "But I want to give . . . a *story*."

"For me, sweetheart. Later. A . . . *story*," he mimicked, but the mockery was lighthearted, with no malice.

"*Watch*," the other said, and the guard released me and sprang straight against the wall as the nursery door opened. Immediately he relaxed again. A serving girl, as young as he and with the same coloring, came out with an empty bucket.

"Cul, Lessy, you be sudden," the guard said. He reached for me again, and Lessy's eyes widened. I saw that she was shocked: the king's Storygiver! The man-at-arms deliberately prolonged the kiss for her viewing, and I realized that he must be even younger than I had thought.

"No, *no*," I pouted, "a *story*. I must . . . give . . . a *story*."

"*Rog*," Lessy said, scandalized and delighted.

Rog smiled at her, at me, at the stone passageway, and swaggered a little, very much the lordly male granting whims. I thought that he must not be very observant; few true lords swaggered with women who were not ladies. They did not have to.

"Then a story it be, sweetheart," Rog said. "Go begin now."

"Not *here*!" Lessy said. "If Lady Triwen come out . . ."

"I come back later," I said, with great and drunken dignity. "I come back when the ladies be gone. When?"

"They never both be gone," the other man-at-arms said. He frowned a little, and I guessed he was having doubts about this. They were none of them irresponsible servants. They could not know how I was using them.

But Rog saw it all slipping away from him: the prestige of being sought by the king's Storygiver, of being the first to bed her. "No, no. The Lady Triwen will join the crowd in the Great Hall, there will be masquing at dusk. And the nursemaid captain goes to her dinner."

"Lady Kaleena?" the other man said, and Rog and Lessy looked at each other and muffled grins. "No," the other said, "Even she would not leave a post at the prince's chamber."

"If she be going to a better post . . ." Lessy said, and giggled.

The man-at-arms remained unconvinced. "Not for any man. If the king heard—"

"For the queen's brother?" Lessy cried, and then looked at me as if she had said too much.

The queen's brother—Kaleena left her duty to meet Perwold. From lust, or from politics? Did Leonore know?

Lessy frowned nervously, and I looked greatly stupid and leered at Rog.

He said quickly, "Then come at the start of the dinner watch, sweetheart. Your word?"

"My word."

"*Watch*," the guard said. Rog sprang against the wall, Lessy hurried away with her bucket, and I drew back around the turning to the stair and crept then to my room to wait till the long, unbearable hour till dusk should come.

This time I swallowed not the benign drug of Storygiving, but the stinking, powerful mold I had stolen from Brant and had never yet used. I knew from the smell that it was the same that Leonore had taken in the dim room under the palace to question me about the White Pipes. She had pulled from my mind a story I had not seen, but had only been told: the woman riding a swine, giving the White Pipes to Brant. He had told me Ard gave them to him, and because then I had believed it, Leonore had drawn that belief from my mind in a grotesque, blurry story. I understood now why the story had been so blurry and had been made of such nauseous images: like a nightmare, it had been bits of knowledge told me by Brant but seen through the terror and fancifulness of my own mind. I had never seen Ard, had only been told of her anguished death, and when Leonore pulled from my mind a scene I had never witnessed, she pulled not clear memory but distorted and dreamlike impression. Thus will a lake reflect clearly the trees that lean over it, but distort into blurry ripples when an object is thrown in from the outside. And should the object be retrieved from the mud at the lake's bottom, it will be found to have been altered, sometimes beyond recognition, into something else, sea-changed by the lake itself.

All this I thought as I held the stinking mold on the palm of my hand. When Leonore had eaten it, she had pulled from my mind Brant's lie of the White Pipes. But she had also put herself in great pain, fallen to the floor senseless, foamed at the mouth. Brant had said she possessed great defenses of mind, and practice with the old arts. What would the mold do to me, who possessed neither?

If I hesitated, I would be lost. Quickly I crammed a bit of the mold—how much to use? how could I know?—into my mouth. It tasted putrid, like meat gone bad, and I thought for a moment that I felt it wiggle on my tongue. *Worms?* I gagged, swallowed, gagged again. Then violence assaulted my mind.

Terror and music, and the music *was* terror. I was seized by the music, imprisoned in a wild melody that had awakened in myself and now swelled in great crashing chords to deafen my mind itself. *Mind deaf*—and mind blind as well, for the sound became light, a shower of splintered light with each splinter sharp and deadly as a blade. I clutched my head with both hands and I think I cried out, but I couldn't be sure in the exploding light-sound. I was caught inside the music, and my mind dissolved in it as living tissue imprisoned in acid will dissolve and become the acid itself. At the last moment, before my mind went from me completely, the music stopped. It did not soften, nor echo, nor trail away: it simply stopped.

I lay on the floor of my room. The light from the window was oblique and fine textured; the dinner watch had well begun.

Half-running, half-dragging myself, I made my way through the palace to the nursery chamber, not knowing if already I was too late and the guard had changed. But Rog and his companion still stood against the wall; the watch had not yet changed. I was not too late. Through the shadows I saw in Rog's face that he had given up expecting me, that he had sulked, but that he could be worked around.

"I was detained by the king!" I said, and that was all that was needed. He threw an arch glance at his companion—see, she comes to me from the *king*!—and kissed me more gaudily than necessary. He was so young.

Again I teased, again I said I must give my story, again I cajoled him and his brother-at-arms, and all the while impatience clawed at me—hurry, hurry, someone will come—and the wild music crouched beyond the edges of my mind. I could feel it, and feel also how narrowly I held it at bay.

"Lady Kaleena?"

"Gone to her love," Rog said and gave me another squeeze.

"Lady Triwen?"

"Still at her dinner. And the nursery captain with her, eh, Amian?" Amian nodded, speculatively watching me held in the curve of Rog's arm.

"Cul, then tell your story," Rog said indulgently. "Amian and me be watching."

"Lessy, too," I said, opened the nursery door, and was through it before he could stop me.

"Here, now!" Amian said.

"Is the prince asleep?" I cried loudly. I dared not approach the cradle; they would not have let me.

"Hush!" Lessy said, and the other nursery maid moved uncertainly between me and the cradle. But I had heard the soft gurgle that followed my shout; Rofwold lay awake.

"You best be back in the passageway," Amian said, and now his look held no dallying speculation. Suddenly older, harsher, he too moved between me and the cradle. I smiled at him.

"Just one story," I said, and abruptly I sat on the floor. The four of them glanced at each other, still uncertain. But one small fuddled woman collapsed on a floor at the feet of an armed soldier does not look menacing. They merely thought me drunker than they had supposed; they could not know that holding back the music that surged at the edge of my mind, took all my strength.

Lessy said hesitantly, "My Lady Kaleena *did* say she be liking to have a story, so if *she* come back . . ."

"Lady Triwen be gone till sunset," Rog said eagerly.

"Till sunset," echoed the other nursemaid.

Amian said nothing. But he did not order me from the chamber.

I spread my hands.

Immediately the music rose. It was as if all the notes in the world sounded beyond a closed door, and if I opened the door I would be overwhelmed and deafened. Sweat slid down my cheeks and between my breasts, while my lungs labored in my chest. So much will did it take to keep the door closed that for a panicky moment I thought I would have none left to touch the mind of the infant prince where he lay unseen in his canopied cradle.

Reborn. The rebirths of the legendary T'Nig. The rebirth into the protection of the Four Gods Protector. Was rebirth no more than a story created in the minds of men, or was there— as there had been in the story of the White Pipes—an underlying root of truth, barely glimpsed through the jungle of fantastic foliage grown onto it over the long centuries? And if rebirth was a hidden truth, what memories of it lay still unclouded in the mind of Leonore's son? He was only eight days old. What did he remember of other births and of what those other creations of himself knew of the mind arts?

I would try to reach those memories of Rofwold's life-before-life, if they existed, if they had not faded in eight days, if they could be made pictures through all the mind drugs Leonore had taken while she carried this infant within her body. I would try with the strongest mind drug *I* knew, the stinking mold with which she had invaded me. This was the desperate idea that had come to me in the Consecrated Garden.

Within a few moments I knew that, like most ideas born of desperation, this one failed.

The baby's mind felt different from Ludie's, or from the brief touch I had had of Brant's. It was the difference between touching adult flesh sliced to the bone in some unnatural tearing and touching childish flesh that was whole but still so pliable, so supple that it gave under probing without needing to tear. I thought of the feel of Jorry's head as an infant, when the skull was still soft. His small skull had yielded under my cautious and marveling fingers, with the same sensation that the infant prince's mind yielded now. But the yield, like the skull, was mostly formless. Between my palms the pink mist had turned black, a velvety living blackness that pulsed regularly but yielded no images, no stories, nothing but regular cushioned dark.

I was looking at Leonore's womb.

Lessy said doubtfully, "That be a story?"

"Leave to her some time!" Rog snapped.

The dark mist did not change. If it held memories, they remained hidden. Then, all at once, the mist exploded into light—a blinding white explosion of sunlight. My audience leaned forward: "Aaaaah!" Breathless, they waited for something else to happen.

Nothing did. The pulsing blackness of the womb had become the pulsing, lighted mist of Rofwold's birth, and thus it remained.

"Cul, she took strong drink," Rog said defensively. "It be not a fair chance at a story."

Again I had failed. Brant would die under the knife. I would never find Jorry.

In desperation, I opened the door of my mind, and the wild and cacophonous music flooded in.

"Catch her!" Lessy cried. "The fits be on her!"

"Don't—touch me!" I screamed, over the agony of music, and they did not. And between my palms the image formed.

But not from the baby Rofwold. This image came from my own mind, from the only other time I had been touched by this mold drug, from the mingling of Brant's lies and my terror and Leonore's hopes, and I recognized the image, for I had seen it before.

Brant, nearly transparent, constantly shifting in outline as commonplace story figures never did. Beside him was a naked girl straddling a swine, long blond hair falling over both her and the dirty pig. Her face constantly distorted, now melting so that the eyes ran down into the nose, now stretching from side to side in a grin horrible as a death rictus. Brant's face distorted as well, but not so wildly, not with the same keening leer. It seemed in the shifting mist that things sprouted from the girl's body: mushrooms from her breasts, a dagger from her side, long hairy roots thick as a man's thumb and pale as maggots along her thighs. Still grinning, not moving off the swine, she plucked the growths from her body and handed them to Brant. In his hands the mushrooms became something else, something slimy and moving, that I could not see clearly. The dagger turned bloody, stuck with shreds of skin. The woman handed Brant the dagger, then snatched it back from him and gave him instead the maggoty roots, and he took them into his hands.

The pale roots became a set of White Pipes.

"Oh, stop her!" Lessy groaned. "She be dying!" Rog grabbed for my arm; I slapped him away as if he had been a fly. In the slapping my hands flew apart, the images vanished, and the wild deadly music rushed in on my mind.

Rog's face bent over me. I felt wooden boards beneath me, slickness on my face.

"Be you alive?"

"Yes, I be alive."

"Need you anything?"

"No. No. Just rest."

"I must go back. My *post*."

"Go, then," I said, and tried to smile at him. He did not smile back. On his face I saw concern, uneasiness—and distaste. My spit-foamed face and stinking sweat had destroyed his youthful ardor, and he could not leave me fast enough.

"Go protected by the Four Gods," I whispered after him, but he was already beyond my voice. I did not believe my own blessing, but I meant it. All acts Rog had shown me had come from exuberance of blood or from kindness, including the seclusion of the storeroom where I now lay, and his having remained with me in it. Such kindness in the young is rare. Rog had showed me more kindness than Brant and I ten years ago, avowing love, had shown each other.

Gingerly I sat up. My head was clear, my mind intact, the wild music gone. Intact, too, was the image it had given me, the story that had been Brant's lie to Leonore.

A lie, yes. But a man's lie may tell more than do his truths—more, indeed, than he knows himself. Lies are more his own creations, made from those living layers of mind inaccessible even to the arts that Brant valued so highly. Truth is recognized; lies are birthed.

Perhaps it was the deadly music, perhaps the powerful stinking drug acting upon my untrained mind, perhaps no more than having seen in shifting lights everything Brant did. Whatever the cause, as I clutched the wooden trunks in the storeroom and dragged myself to my feet, my mind clutched no less tightly at the disgusting story that had come between my palms, turning it this way and that, seeing it in shifting lights. It would save me.

For I knew now where to find the White Pipes.

10

THE WING OF THE NEW PALACE THAT HOUSED BRANT'S and Cynda's apartments did not overlook the Consecrated Garden. Its windows gave onto a courtyard, and beyond that the vast stone bulk of the Priests' Hall. If Cynda, secluded in her chamber ever since Brant's arrest, sat by her opened window to despair, she would at least be spared hearing from the Consecrated Garden the merriment of Rofwold's Protection Day. No sounds of laughter and celebration would have reached her. But she would be faced with the sight of the scarred stone battlements of the old castle, beneath which her husband might lie in chains. Did she sit glassy-eyed and stare at it, I wondered, or were the draperies drawn across the windows as tightly as they had been the day I stole drugs from the carved altar?

Unlike that day, this time I needed no ruses to enter a chamber of rank. Cynda was a disgraced mistress and also a foolish wife to an imprisoned heretic. No one cared who entered or left her apartments so long as she did not leave herself to spoil anyone's celebration. The men-at-arms waved me through with only a faint surprise that my lady should have a visitor on this celebration evening. Few enough others had come at all, on any evening.

I had been afraid that Cynda would be drugged into sleep, but she was not. She sat hunched on a low stool in a shadowed corner. I smelled her before I saw her. Her beautiful hair hung lank and greasy by her face, and she wore only a shift, torn at one shoulder. Bruised shadows spread under her blue eyes, as though she had not slept. But she was not mad. Those eyes, though dull and despairing, were clear and sane. Her stinking apathy was not that of madness, but that of a weak mind that has known only one light and has seen it go out. Rofdal had cast her off, Brant was gone, the courtiers who danced attendance and fawned on her had melted away. Without men, the light of her self had no reflection, and she huddled afraid in the darkness, unable to see ahead. But she looked up at my approach.

"Storygiver."

I bowed before her. She went on waiting, without curiosity or interest, for me to say whatever I had come to say. Bowing, I gazed at her feet, the only part of her that moved: slim white bare feet, the toes knotting and unknotting on the polished floor, the nail of the largest toe painted with a rose so intricate that it must have taken someone a day's work. The feet stank. Ceaselessly the toes worked, knotting and unknotting. This was the woman I had feared, and envied.

"Leave us," I said to the maid, and she did. She looked a raw country girl, frightened, no more than fourteen. Where were Cynda's women, those plain-faced and meek attendants she had chosen to surround herself? Dancing in the Great Hall, or fawning on the mother of the heir, or simply lying low in fear and confusion.

"Lady Cynda, could you drink some wine?"

She did not answer. But when I brought her the filled goblet, she took it from me and drank, lapsing afterward into the same dull-eyed apathy. Moved by a feeling nowhere as kind as pity, I thought of bringing her soap, water, a comb. But there was no time.

She said nothing when I drank my Second Flask and crouched on the floor halfway across the room from her, my open palms hidden from her sight by the chest off which I had once snatched an embroidered chamber pot cover. Then came the only dangerous part.

"Lady Cynda, when you ride into the mountains—when you ride alone into the mountains, where do you go?"

She started violently and half-rose from her stool. Color swept her cheeks, her mouth twisted, and for a moment she looked a coarsened and grotesque travesty of her own beauty. "Guard!" she croaked, but only once. Her gaze caught itself on a gold-framed mirror hung on the wall. Moaning, she sank again on her stool, and her head lay buried in her hands.

"Think," I said, "of riding in the mountains, of when you ride to Ard's cottage."

From beneath her hands, the collapsed Cynda moaned.

Between my hands, a vibrant and lovely Cynda rode to Ard's cottage. I watched carefully, keeping my gaze on the twisting of trails and markers of cliffs and fords, keeping my mind in touch with hers, although it made me shudder. I invaded a place not mine to take, and it felt as if I invaded flesh with a sword and left it hacked and savaged. Cynda, however, never moved. When I had seen all I needed, I called the girl from the next room. She did not know that I carried no rank, that I had no right to the imperious commands of the rich.

"Get her washed. And fed."

"My lady—she will not. I have tried—"

"Try again. She must at least eat. I hold you responsible."

"Yes, my lady!" She looked terrified, and I felt shame. It came so easily. Yet I did not soften my orders.

Cynda looked up at me as I left. I thought that in the dullness of her eyes, beneath the whining helplessness, I saw a flicker of something not yet quenched, something of cunning or sharpness. Then again she buried her head in her hands. I thought that I despised her, and that I had no right to do so. A mind that can create but one story for itself did not choose to be so. Nor did she choose that one story's collapse.

But I despised her still.

I rode to Ard's cottage against the fall of night. The long summer sun was finally setting, blood red against the dark shapes of mountains, and already the twisting trails were half in shadow and hard to follow. My pony had had little enough exercise since we had first stumbled with Kalafa's caravan through the mountains to Veliano, and his sides heaved with exertion. The trail darkened. When I lost it altogether in the gloom and could no longer be sure of matching Cynda's images with the landmarks around me, I dismounted in a little clearing. I saw no choice but to wait in one place for moonrise. My palms sweated as I threw my leg over the laboring pony, and the saddle was sticky between my knees.

Trees rustled in the night breeze. Somewhere nearby gillyflowers bloomed; I could smell them in the darkness, sweet and heady. With the smell came insect noises, heard even over the panting of the pony and the thudding in my chest. The insects droned unseen, and the drone rose and fell as monotonously as a chant.

> Protection for the Body against Maiming,
> Protection for the Senses against Corruption,
> Protection for the Mind against Invasion,
> Protection for the Soul against Besetting:
> Gillyflowers.

But I had no protection against such harm, no more than had Brant, despite his mind arts. There existed no protection, not when crushing forces stirred in the world—and no matter that those forces came, as Brant had sneered to me the night he took Jorry, not from some evil, unnatural womb but only from men's minds. That made force enough. I had been right, and Brant wrong: the only recourse for the small when larger forces moved was to get out of the way. To flee entanglement.

All this I told myself to bolster my courage, waiting alone in the dark clearing, which of course did not care. Eventually the moon rose, gloriously full and low, shedding more than enough light for my ride. I mounted and rode again toward entanglement.

I had been on this path before, and not only in Cynda's story. For a long way the trail was the one between the castle and the ruined hut where Brant had beaten me. Then the path forked, and I rode on a narrow track up the side of a steep and wooded hill and in the opposite direction to the hut. Thereafter the climb became steeper, the growth wilder, the trail more tenuous. Several times I thought I had lost it. When that happened I kept climbing, knowing from Cynda that I must crest the low mountain. No travelers could have stumbled on the cottage by accident.

At the crest of the hill, the woods ended and the ground sloped into a hidden dell, once a farm. I rode past fallen fences, ruined byres, the shape of an empty swine pen, all preternaturally still, all silvered over by the moon. Here no insects sang, no breeze blew. Yet I felt the soft hairs at the back of my neck stiffen and rise.

The cottage stood whole, the door locked. I smashed at the door and its leather hinges, older by far than the lock, gave way and sent the door crashing inward. The crash made me—who had caused it—gasp in fear, so wrong did it seem in that silver silence. Heart pounding, I listened intently. Nothing stirred.

I left my pony chomping grass, lit a torch, and stepped over the fallen door into Ard's cottage.

By day, without the darkness and the moonlit silence, it might have seemed different, might have appeared only pitiful. But in the shadowed silence of night the objects in the cottage were half-glimpsed, remote. Smell became my strongest sense, as if I were a beast: the smells of molding cloth, decayed flowers, animal droppings, and musty velvet. In a corner gleamed something metallic. I raised my torch and circled the room, and the edgy light slid over the burden on tables and dirt floor, one object at a time.

A wine goblet.

The coulter piece from a suit of armor.

A short cloak of red velvet, embroidered in gold: the crown of Veliano worked in a circle of gillyflowers.

A sticky glove. I recognized it: Brant's, with the blood of his slain bay stallion dried on the leather.

A dagger, bearing on the hilt the emblem of one of the richest lords of the kingdom.

A battered and rain-streaked brimmed hat. That too I recognized.

A crumpled gold sash.

A man's purse. Empty.

A satin pillow and satin nightcap.

Flowers, all dead, wrapped with the sprung string from an archer's bow. The bow lay beside it.

Another dagger, this one with the device of the *king*. Taken how? When? A king's dagger is not easy to take.

A ring of Brant's. Old, valueless, a mere thin circlet—but I knew it. I had seen it on his hand ten years ago, at Mother Arcoa's.

There were more, all male belongings. I leaned my torch against the table edge and picked up the ring. It slipped from my fingers and I bent to the floor to search for it. More objects lay here, under the table, thrust back to the dirty wall. I pulled them into the light.

A wool gown, so eaten by damp and rodents that it tore under my fingers. It had been rough-spun and shapeless, the sort worn roped at the waist and by only the poorest and most miserable of hill peasants. Wrapped in the gown were bones. They rattled when I shook them out, for all were the same size. All were the same bones: the knuckles of swine.

I stared at the pile of white bones. When Ard had been taken, who had killed Ard's swine for Cynda? Or had she just waited until they starved in their pens, and then waited yet more until the winter snows and summer heat had done their work and the bones needed only to be gathered and washed in the well?

A naked girl, straddling a swine, long blond hair falling over her face, grotesque objects sprouting from her body, giving them to Brant.

The image had come from Brant's mind. He meant it for a lie. And so it had been, and most of all to himself. A blond woman, grotesquely giving and taking. *Two* blond women, grotesquely giving and taking, from and to him and each other, and among the bloody objects fingered was each of their lives. A mind may see farther than it can bear, and so make a story of its seeing, and believe it is just a story.

I reached farther under the table, groping for more of Ard's belongings where Cynda had thrust them. Her trophies on the tables, Ard's life underneath in the droppings and mud. How much satisfaction had it given Cynda's jealous mind to arrange it thus? And how much did Brant know without knowing, so that his lie of the woman on the swine should carry so much agonizing truth?

Never again would I be able to think of my profession as a childish and vulgar amusement.

My fingers found a rotted and stinking cloak, some farm tools Ard must have used, a cooking pot. Everything metal had gone greenish with age and damp. A hair comb, a wooden trencher. A well pulley—Cynda must have searched the entire farm, carrying to the cottage anything her rival had used or touched. The search must have been thorough, for among the pathetic leavings outlasting the dead were two wooden boxes, both encrusted with dirt and chewed by animals, as if they had lain long hidden.

I opened the first. Within lay a square of rotted wool, and within the wool two long locks of hair, tied with ribbon that broke at my touch and sent the locks mingling in a cascade over my lap. I brought the torch close, and bent close myself. All the hair was yellow, but there were two different shades: a bright gold and a paler blond the color of ripe wheat. The brighter I knew for Cynda's. For a long moment I stared at the mingled locks, and I could see no story that would lead her to cut hair from the doomed Ard and enclose it with her own. Yet Cynda had done so. She had brought here these stolen belongings from men who had loved her, and come to visit them over and over where Brant nor any other of her lovers would never know, and with them she had obsessively kept the belongings of the rival from whom she had stolen life.

On a sudden thought, I brought my torch higher and passed it over more of the objects in the room. And under another table they were there: Leonore's handkerchief, embroidered with the queen's emblem of a gray falcon with intertwined R and L. A shawl in her favorite dark silk. A goblet. The goblet had been smashed.

But a queen is herself untouchable. A mad peasant girl is not.

Bitterly, I lowered the torch. There remained among Ard's

poor belongings the second box. From its rusting, the lock had been smashed long ago, but the wood of the box had swollen with damp and would not open. I pried with all my strength and box and lid parted, splintering into shards of wood that drew blood from my fingers. Over the dead locks of hair in my lap spilled a pure shining.

The White Pipes.

They looked *alive*. Alive, as if they had been fashioned from a substance so vibrant it burned with a mysterious life of its own: forged starlight. Yet when I lifted them they felt cold, and much heavier than they looked. Their whiteness was that of exposed bone.

Seven pipes, bound with two bands to one mouthpiece, and that of the same cold and white substance as the rest. Each band was exquisitely carved with leaves and flowers and roots, carving so precise that the foliage seemed no less alive than the Pipes themselves, and just as whitely cold. Two roots, leaves prepared just so, stems and flowers. These carvings which Brant had said showed the steps for brewing the drug that, together with the music from the Pipes, could seize and control men's minds beyond hope of their own will. I stared at the carvings, and then traced them with wondering fingers.

They were of gillyflowers.

It needed the whole of the night to gather the gillyflowers, prepare the drug, decant it into flasks from the hidden pockets of my tunic. I worked at the edge of the dell, by torchlight and moonlight, unable to bear the shelter of Ard's cottage: dead belongings in dead silence.

Once, I put the White Pipes to my lips and blew. There came not one note but a sequence of notes, a melody, high and plaintive. It reminded me of the poignant song of the flute boy in the castle stable-yard, but no more than that. Without the drug and music together, to the blower of the pipes the mind was teased but not unlayered, and I wondered if this made for the unsatisfied yearning aroused by even the sweetest of songs, the most skillful of musicians.

The White Pipes felt cold against my lips. For this, then—

this warmth-stealing, ordinary music—for *this* Ard had been tortured, Brant imprisoned, Jorry taken. For this.

Loathing alone could have given me strength to shatter the White Pipes then and there. Instead I shoved them into my sash and rode at first light for the palace.

Two nights had passed since Brant had been imprisoned in the Priests' Hall. Did he still live? Fear, never absent from me since the caravan had brought me to the Great Hall, swelled as I rode, pushing me from behind, so that I urged the pony to a trot, and then to a canter, possibly fatal on the twisting trails and holed meadows. Branches snapped at my face, twigs tangled in my hair, the pony shied and tried to slow, and I dug my heels into his sides and forced him on. Stumbling, panting, scratched, we tore into the palace stable-yard where I threw myself off my mount and ran toward the palace. My legs, curved too long around the pony, buckled under me and I fell. A stable-boy watched with astonishment.

"Cul, Storygiver—you took an early ride. Be you hurt? Let me help you—Cul! There be no cause to strike!"

I left him scowling after me and lurched into the palace, past men-at-arms who glanced up sharply to see if I were pursued. I was, but they could not see how.

In a dim passageway I leaned against the wall, regained my breath, and drank the first prepared flask of the white drug. White—the drug itself had distilled as white as the Pipes. The color of my fear was white.

I felt nothing.

No music, no brightness, no pain nor exaltation. I stood ordinary against the stone, and the passageway stood ordinary before me. Had I made an error in distilling the drug? Or did the drug change nothing until the White Pipes sounded? Carefully, more slowly now—it had been madness to attract as much attention as I already had—I closed my eyes and tried to think. Then I went back to the stable-yard and led my panting pony around to the other side of the palace, in the shadow of the Priests' Hall but not too close to it. The groom was gone. Except for a few men-at-arms, I saw no one. It was very early, barely sunrise, and those servants already at work would be on the other side of the palace, near the wells and the kitchen yard. Above me the sky stretched blue and cool, without clouds, and in the east the pink had already faded.

I walked to the gate of the Priests' Hall. Two men-at-arms blinked at me sleepily.

"Open the gates. I have business inside."

They grinned at me, thinking it a jest. Priests did not send for stories.

"Open the gates," I said again, louder. One man scowled, the other grinned still. I drew the White Pipes from my sash and raised them to my lips. The moment before I blew, the thought came clearly: *if this fails, I can still pass it off as a jest. I can still throw down the Pipes to call off Leonore, and then flee.*

I blew.

The melody sounded high and sweet, and tears sprang to my eyes. This was not mind music but *the* music, all the music at the heart of the world, all that every other shabby song had reached for, only to fall miserably short. The flute boy's playing—how could I have been moved by it? *This* was the music vainly sought by the soul of man, because this was the music that matched soul, note for layer, layer for note, and fused the layers so that for the first time I stood whole. I blew on the White Pipes again and yet again, and three times I was made whole in a flood of rich splendor for which there were not, nor could be, words. I was the master of the music, and of mind, and of all creation grown from time.

The men-at-arms stared at me with blank faces and uninhabited eyes. I saw that they, drugless, had been made not whole but more fragmented, and it seemed to me that I understood, without words or reason, why that should be.

"Open the gates."

They did so, instantly. A part of my mind thought that I, who had built a makeshift life from powerlessness, should tremble as I gave orders to armed men, but I did not tremble. I held the White Pipes.

"Stay here," I said to one, and he stayed. "Lead me to Lord Brant. If we should meet other men-at-arms or priests, tell them I have been sent by the queen. Have you keys to open Lord Brant's cell?"

"No," he said, and the ordinariness of his voice was the first shock.

"Who does?"

"I don't know."

"Lead me to Lord Brant."

He did so, and no one questioned us along the steep stairs and long passages until we reached Brant's cell. It stood alone at the end of a passage sharply angled and very deep in the earth; no one would have heard Brant scream. No one would hear me now, save the two guards before the door. The senior drew his sword, and I my Pipes. His weapon was the faster but mine the more unexpected. I blew my melody, and his hard-eyed face went stiff and still.

"Open the cell!"

He had the key. He opened the cell. I took the torch from the wall, and entered.

Brant lay on his side, naked on the floor. At first I thought him already dead. Bruises and bloody welts swelled on his chest, legs, groin, belly, but not as badly as on his face. What Leonore could not obtain from his head by her arts, she had tried to beat from it. The flesh of his face was so swollen and bloody that had he been anyone else, I would not have known him. But this man I knew. I dropped to the floor beside him, kneeling in his blood, and touched the still body. He did not move.

"Brant."

I listened to his torn chest; one arm had been broken, and lay twisted beneath him. But his heart still beat. I found water and splashed it on his face. He groaned, and when his eyes opened I saw that despite his pain, he knew me.

"Brant!"

He fainted again. I had not foreseen this, had not planned beyond finding Brant flayed or not flayed and, if not flayed, forcing him with the Pipes to tell me where Jorry was hidden. Toward that aim I had driven myself, clutching at it as a drowning man clutches a floating bit of debris without questioning whether it will hold. But the moment had not held. What Brant knew, he could not tell me, and what I thought I had known—that I could walk in and take from him Jorry's whereabouts and walk out again from his prison, leaving him to Leonore—had been only a story my mind had clutched at to quiet fear. I could not leave him. Had he been still whole and powerful, and I as weaponless before him as ever, I could not have left him. Not to Leonore.

I ran my hands over his body. He lay without moving, and in panic I searched again for a heartbeat and again found it, stronger than I expected. The broken arm—the right, his sword arm—had been shattered above the elbow, to the pale bone. I wrenched it straight, knowing that I was not doing it properly, that it could probably not be done properly by anyone. I bound it with my sash to the stiff handle of a whip, all I could find. The whip thong was sticky with blood. If Brant lived, he would never wield a sword again.

When I called the guards they moved so naturally, without any stiffness of body or limb to match their stiffness of face, that violence rose in me like burning and I wanted to smash each of them over and over, beat them not senseless but into the sensing of crushing pain, as one of them—all of them? —had beaten Brant.

"Carry him. You, and you. And carry him as gently as you can. If you increase his pain, I will kill you. Do you understand me?"

"Yes."

"Yes."

"Yes."

"Yes."

Four answers. In each one I heard fear. It was monstrous. Despite their calm and pale faces, some part of their minds witnessed their own loss of will and they were terrified of it, and I was bitterly glad.

In the highest of the passageways, just before we emerged above ground, we met a priest. I blew on the White Pipes, and he and the two men-at-arms beyond him went white faced and still. I ordered them to hide themselves below, and they went.

But at the gate I stopped, blinking at the sunshine. Where to now?

The sun was well up. Servants worked busily. I could get Brant onto a horse and away from the palace only by using the White Pipes on at least a dozen more people. But Leonore would learn from seven men already that I had the Pipes and Brant; adding another dozen would not matter. However, I did not know how long the white drug would stay active in my mind, nor where I could take Brant if I did flee. Anywhere we went, we would be easy to track. I didn't know any methods to avoid being tracked. And with Brant I could not travel very fast. This was not what I had intended, this was not what I had foreseen! Time pressed in on me, choking the sunlit air.

"Get five horses—you. Saddled. Bring priests' horses that you can take without question, as if for a hunting party, strong horses, and bring them swiftly. Or you die."

The last was unnecessary. The man went swiftly, compelled by the Pipes. For how long? I waited with the others, all of us drawn back inside the shadow of the gate. In the guards' arms, Brant groaned. I looked at his naked, savaged body, and then away.

When the man returned with horses, I had him wrap Brant in his own cloak, Brant's head loosely covered, and then hoist Brant before his saddle. I took the other three men with me as well. We clattered away from keep and palace, a procession seen by servants, peasants in the fields, men-at-arms, anyone else watching from open windows. I did not have to make use of the Pipes. As I rode they remained clutched in my hand, a white shining, cold as death.

I took him to the ruined hut where he had beaten me. Where else should I go? In all Veliano, I knew only two locations away from people, and Ard's cottage was much the farther. Riding to the hut took all morning. We had almost reached it when the oldest man's arm began to twitch toward his sword, moving jerkily and uncertainly, first toward and then away, while his mouth grimaced just as wildly. I blew once into the Pipes, returning him to powerlessness and myself to another burst of healing joy that left me afterward trembling with anger. Joy should have no place in this vicious business. But I had now the answer to at least the question of how long my control over the strongest-minded of the men would last: half a morning. No more.

So we rode on through the summer morning, and around us leaves glistened in the fresh and clean-scented air.

At the ruined hut I set the four men-at-arms to watch, three fanned among the trees and one, the slightest in strength, just beyond the collapsed south wall, at the top of the cliff that I hoped would protect our back. Brant I had carried inside and laid on the dank floor, where I knelt beside him.

He lived still, and his heartbeat had not weakened. Perhaps only his right arm bore any severe damage, and for the rest he had been caused pain but not maiming. Even his face, swollen and purple, looked battered rather than broken: the results of jal-un. But I had seen mangled limbs develop gangrenous infections that eventually killed, and I had neither medicines to treat Brant's wound nor even enough water to clean it. And he kept fainting from weakness. Had he not, the pain might have been much worse, and I wondered if all during the ride to the hut he had revived, fainted when the jolting of the horse became too much, revived, fainted again. Shivering, I brushed the dark hair back from his forehead. The hair was sticky with blood. His eyes opened, and he watched me.

"Fia . . ."

I bent closer to hear. A spasm of pain distorted his face, but when it had passed his voice was stronger. "Jorry. In . . . Erdulin. Go to . . . my sister Malda. *Not* my father. Demand see Jantro. *Jantro.* Tell . . . him this: 'The sprig blooms—in the mountains.' He'll take you to Jorry."

Another spasm of pain, and his eyes closed. I made him drink a little water.

"Turn me . . . left."

I did so, very gently, and he seemed then to lie more easily. I saw in his eyes the moment when first he realized where he was, and what walls leaned precariously around him.

"Brant. What you said of Jorry—is that the truth?"

His gaze met mine. For answer he whispered, "The day I was taken, I gave—" a spasm of pain, while he fought for breath "—orders to have you carried from Veliano. By force. You would not go of . . . yourself."

He closed his eyes. I sat back on my heels and again brushed the hair from his forehead. I did not believe him.

But even so—even as he lied—Brant broken and in pain moved me as he had not done when he stood whole and threatening between Jorry and me, and I thought how stupid it was of women like me to feel tenderness now, because a man lay helpless. Cynda went soft toward him when he turned his whole attention on her; I did so when he could turn it nowhere. And yet he had. He had told me where to find Jorry, had said he would have further exposed himself to Leonore to remove me from danger. But were those utterances—either, or both—the truth, or had Brant said them because he thought they were what I wanted to hear—what he needed me to hear to keep himself alive? Was Jorry's location yet another story, and again the listener meant to be convinced for as long as the illusion could be sustained?

He groaned softly, and before I knew I would do so, I put my fingers to his lips. The upper was split and bloody, both were swollen. I had loved him, feared him, fled from him, hated him—except for Jorry, Brant had been the person who had most shaped my life, even during the ten years I had spent escaping him. And yet I could not tell if he lied.

"Brant." I leaned over him, and my hair brushed his bloody cheek. "Brant, open your eyes."

He did, and I pulled from out of my tunic the White Pipes.

His eyes widened, and I saw in them both what I had expected and more than I expected: shock, greed, wonder, calculation. He tried to lift his left arm toward that white shining, but he was too weak and the arm fell back.

"Cynda had them," I said, and then, ashamed of my cruelty, put the Pipes to my mouth.

He had been in a faint when I had blown them before; he was not now. His eyes became as fixed as the men-at-arms', his face as blank. But I had not known the men-at-arms' minds, and I knew Brant's. This, then, was what the Priests of the Four Gods Protector had named blasphemy, and in the names of the gods I did not believe in, *they had been right*. Brant had been reduced to an object, a tool, more than I had ever been. He was without will or life, yet not dead. I could have done anything I chose with his broken body. And that body had made me suffer. I remembered, now, the feel of his fists on my flesh, the terror and humiliation. And I could do as I chose with him.

My sudden cruel fancies sickened me. And if I could not keep free of seeing such lurid fancies dance in my mind, what would such as Perwold do with the White Pipes?

That, too, I could see.

Quickly I drank the Storygiving flasks, one after the other, not pausing between to see if either warred with the white gillyflower drug. The risk to my body, if there was one, might once have chilled me but now seemed lost in so many greater risks. I had to know if Brant lied, and no longer only to regain Jorry.

"Brant. If you hear me, close your left fist."

The fist closed. With that fist he had battered me.

"Brant. Think of where you have sent Jorry. You hear me, your mind arts cannot match the power of the White Pipes—think of what I would have to do to reach Jorry. Now, Brant."

Pink mist swirled between my palms. It became two figures—a tiny Fia, and a tiny richly dressed woman who looked so much like Brant I was startled. Malda, his sister. I had never even known he had a sister. She led the Fia-figure to a third character, born suddenly of a wisp of mist, who wore the leather armor of a man-at-arms in a great city house. His face was guarded and honest, with the eyes of a loyal dog. He and the Fia figure mounted ponies and began to circle between my hands. The circling went on endlessly. The ponies labored, as if climbing hard. When finally they halted and the two figures dismounted, he was there, running toward me.

Jorry. Whole, healthy, tanned, dressed in the satins of a young nobleman, and his face alight with joy.

I did not close my hands. I watched as the tiny Fia and the

tiny Jorry embraced, for long after they had ceased to move and merely stood there in place. After a long while, the figures began to fade, but still I watched. When finally I closed my hands, there was nothing in them any longer.

Brant had told me the truth. Unasked, before he knew I had the White Pipes, before he had any reason to think that a lie would not have worked as well in keeping me bound to his needs. He had told me the truth.

Outside the hut, shouts arose. I ran to the door. The closest of my men-at-arms clashed swords with a stranger, and beyond them an archer drew his bow. So soon! How could Leonore's men have come from the palace so soon!

The archer let fly, and the man I had stolen dropped forward, an arrow in his back. I saw his face as he fell, and frantically I blew on the Pipes again and again, mindlessly, more than necessary, seeing only the eyes of the man released from my spell only at the moment of his death.

The archer and swordsman both froze.

"Come here!" I screamed. "All of you come here, all of you within sound of my voice, come here, come here now!"

They came, moving toward me with natural gaits and empty, unnatural faces. There were at least two score men, and I recognized not one. None came from the palace. I noted their weather-bruised faces, their leather jerkins stained with old grass and streaked with old rains. One man carried a sword much superior to the others', the basket hilt encrusted with silver floral scrolls.

"You. Who sent you here?"

"Leonore the queen." His voice, too, was so natural I would have feared him broken free from the Pipes' spell, except for his eyes.

"And the other?"

"The same."

"What were your orders?"

"To kill the Storygiver and Lord Brant and bring back the White Pipes."

"Do you know what the White Pipes are?"

"I do," he said, and such iron fervor grated in his voice that spasmodically my fingers clutched the Pipes.

"Can you practice mind arts?"

"No."

"Can any of these others?"

"Some can."

"How many? Exactly."

He thought. "Eight."

"Where do you come from?"

"A hidden place in the woods."

"Does Leonore have more men in these woods?"

"She does. Also deep in the mountains. And at court."

"How many nearby enough to receive a message from court and arrive here by nightfall?"

Again he thought. "As many again as I command."

"And how many at court?"

"A handful of men-at-arms. Plus the queen, Lord Perwold, Lord Evtor, Lady Kaleena—" my heart clutched at itself, remembering the nursery "—Lord Sarpir, Lady Caidela—"

"Enough. No priests?"

"No!" he said violently, and cursed. I looked away from the passionate curses coming from the passionless face. The priesthood, then, was Leonore's tool, manipulated to flay her enemies, but not her ally. They did not know what deeper game she played. I tried to think what else I needed to know.

"And the king? Has he been told that the White Pipes have been found, or did Leonore command you in secret unknown to him?"

"In secret."

"Has she commanded more men than these to come here?"

"They be commanded if I fail to send back my messenger."

I could not put his messenger under the spell of the Pipes and send him myself to deceive Leonore; the spell would wear off his mind at just about the time he reached court. By fleeing so mindlessly with Brant, I had lost the only plan I could now think of to save us.

"Command your men to surround the hut and fight off all who approach. At the outermost ring of men post a messenger to run to tell me as soon as any fighting begins. Let the men protect the three wooded sides of the hut." I added slowly, "But not the cliff face. Put no one to observe the cliff face."

"Yes," the man said.

"What is your name?" I asked. It was stupid; it could not matter. Men bear names, and he was no longer a man. I had taken manhood from him.

"Eallow."

I went back into the hut. Through the hole in the ruined rear wall I could see the cliff, descending in stony ledges, with the small river at the bottom. The cliff face would leave no footprints to follow. Neither would the river, if I took care where I left it. I had perhaps three hours before the spell wore off Leonore's men and they followed. Longer if they did not realize at first how I had gone because none had seen me. They might even ascribe it to some superstitious vanishing; most were peasants after all, and only eight knew any mind arts. And if I were tracked and found—I would still have the White Pipes. The Pipes, and the knowledge of Jorry's whereabouts, and none other would know how to follow me there.

None other save one.

Brant lay quietly, eyes open and fixed on the sagging ceiling, the spell still upon him. I knelt by his side.

"Brant. Leonore knows that Jorry is your son. When she . . . questioned you last night, did you tell her you had sent Jorry away to keep him safe?"

"Yes."

The strongest man will break under torture; it is sentimental to think otherwise. Leonore knew that, and so had taken the risk of calling attention to herself by openly imprisoning Brant. I had known it, too, in my mind—but not in my bones, muscles, viscera.

"Did you tell her where Jorry is? Does she know?"

"No," he said, and I breathed again.

"Why did she not have me imprisoned as well?"

"No need . . . to further push Rofdal. *I* would do."

And so he had. But not completely, not yet.

Not yet. But if he were retaken and tortured again, in greater earnest? Except for Brant's arm, Perwold had thus far merely been playing. He had thought he had time. But by now Perwold—and Leonore, who did not play—knew that time had run out. And by now they knew that I possessed the White Pipes, and also that I would try to get to Jorry.

To identify a whole tree, one need see only a single leaf. Brant had told me the truth of Jorry's location. Overwhelmed by pain he could not assess, he had wanted to give me back my son before he died, and it seemed to me that from that one act I finally knew how to tilt toward the light all his other acts since I had come to Veliano. He had not killed me at the inn, although my life risked his; he had sent Jorry away for Jorry's own safety and had not told me where so that Leonore could not take the knowledge from my mind; he had twice maneuvered me into Rofdal's favor so I would have protection from Leonore; he would have had me carried by force away from her reach, had he not first been imprisoned himself.

But Brant could not flee with me now. Already he had fever; a sheen of moisture filmed his forehead and cheeks. And already he had told Perwold that Jorry lived and had been sent somewhere believed safe.

Rising from the dank floor, I walked from the hut back along the path to the closest of Eallow's men and drew from his belt his short dagger. He made no protest. The blade was very sharp. I kept it pointed away from me, until I held it at Brant's throat.

His body was too broken to flee with me. Left behind, he would be tortured into revealing Jorry's hiding place. Leonore's men could travel to Erdulin much faster than I, and reach Jorry first.

If they learned from Brant that Jorry hid in Erdulin.

My hand shook. Beyond the hut one man lay dead with an arrow in his back, but that was not like this. Not like this.

Then Brant turned his face toward me and his eyes were his own.

I gasped. The spell had not held him a few hours, it had not held him for even one.

He said, "Less time . . . for one with mind arts. The Pipes hold, but less time." He stared at me, and my knife trembled at his throat, and I did not pull it away.

"Jorry. You would tell them where he is. You *would*, Brant, with enough torture—"

I saw what it cost him to answer. "Yes. With . . . enough."

"I don't know how to do it clean!" I cried, and then I heard shouts outside the door, and the clash of steel on steel, and an arrow shot through the door and struck the dirt a handspan from my thigh.

The ones with mind arts! Less time!

I grabbed the Pipes and blew. The noise beyond the hut stopped. Leaping to my feet, I blew and blew again. Insane, rich, vicious joy flooded my mind.

"Eallow!"

He came. His sword was bloody.

"The ones with mind arts," I said, and heard my voice shake. "They tried to approach?"

"Yes," Eallow said calmly.

I closed my eyes. "Kill all eight of them. Now. Quickly!"

"Two are dead already."

"And how many of your . . . how many others?"

"Three."

"Kill the other six who know mind arts. Do it as mercifully as you can, but do it now!"

"Yes," Eallow said. "Now."

Brant lay as he had before. He had not tried to crawl away from me, or to arm himself with the nearby arrow. I didn't know if he had the strength to do so or not. I knew nothing of wounds or fighting—save that I had just killed six men.

I stood just inside the door of the hut, the dagger in my hand. Suddenly I could not see it clearly; my vision blurred. Sunlight from the doorway struck the dagger and through the blur it blazed, a bright sharp metallic fire. It was Eallow's sword slaying six men somewhere behind me, it was Brant's sword killing his bay stallion, it was Perwold's whip and the flaying knives that had tortured Ard. Shining, it was the

White Pipes. I must set the point at Brant's throat and draw it across as deeply as I could.

I opened my fingers and the dagger fell.

"No. No. I will not." And again, "No."

Brant watched me.

"I will not kill you," I said. "I will not. No. Not you. I will not."

"Jorry," he said.

I put my hands over my face to shut out the sight of him, of the bright dagger at my feet, of all else. "I will *not*!"

Time shuddered, passed. Then there was a noise in the hut. I took my hands away from my face. Brant crawled toward me on hands and knees, his face clenched with pain, his useless right arm dragging in the dirt, his eyes fixed on my face. He had nearly reached me when he fainted, and I sprang forward and caught him as he fell.

11

I SAT ON THE FLOOR OF THE RUINED HUT, BRANT'S bloody hair pressed to my breast, for too long. Of all that I might have felt, that would have been reasonable to feel, this twisted sweetness was surely the most unexpected. Twisted, tainted, lashed by fear—but sweetness nonetheless, and I gave way to it until it passed and I could think clearly.

This time, I would not flee.

The day had grown hot. I judged it to be past noon, and tried to think what would have happened at the palace since early morning. Each scene I pictured in my mind as if it had been a story growing between my palms. I tried to see the story as Brant would have, or Leonore—as someone used to foreseeing the actions and motives of others and then turning them to use. I tried to see as a person of rank.

Some priest would have discovered Brant gone and reported it to his religious superior. Eventually the news would have been taken to the king. The people who saw me ride from the palace—grooms, ploughmen, a goosegirl—would be questioned. Rofdal would learn who had taken Brant and in what direction we had gone.

There were also the priest and two men-at-arms I had put under the spell of the White Pipes and told to hide themselves in the Priests' Hall. Why—*why*—had I not taken them with me? Hours ago the spell would have slid from them, and they had witnessed the White Pipes. They must have gone straight to Leonore, for her to send a messenger so quickly to command Eallow to find and attack us. The queen's force, now mine.

But Eallow had said there were no priests among Leonore's followers. So her informer must have been one or both of the men-at-arms. And what of the priest? He would have carried the tale to other priests. Finally one would go to the king, to tell him that the Storygiver was a soul-beseter who had invaded minds, commanded their bodies and so stolen their prisoner. They would have described the Pipes. Rofdal, I thought, might not have heard of them, but at least the highest of the priests would have. If they fought soul-besetting, they would have kept alive its most dangerous lore in their own secret lore.

Then why had not Rofdal's army tracked us here? He was not a man of patience. He would have dispatched his soldiers as soon as he knew his prisoner was gone, and those soldiers would have expected to find only a woman, four traitorous men-at-arms, and a wounded lord. That force should have tracked us easily, and been here by now. Why was it not?

I could see only one answer: Leonore had prevented it. She wanted her own secret force to take the Pipes, kill Brant and me, and melt back into the forest before Rofdal's more legitimate army had seen anything of hers. Nor could she have her force attack Rofdal's soldiers; slaughter creates suspicion. Instead Leonore must have used her influence to persuade Rofdal both to hold back his soldiers and to forbid the priests to make any pursuit of their own. But how had Leonore been able to persuade the king? What arguments had she used?

Rofdal. I saw him as clearly as if he stood before me. A man born to power—no, more, born to that special fearlessness of power never challenged, never even questioned. I saw his fleshy body, overindulged in food and drink and women, and his broad face with the small eyes which grew smaller if he was crossed in even the smallest particular. Brant had been Rofdal's trusted adviser—but Rofdal had made a mistress of Brant's wife, and had been persuaded of Brant's guilt by whatever forged evidence Leonore had brought. Yet even she had needed the birth of an heir to gain that persuasiveness, and from Rofdal's dark mood afterward, I guessed that he regretted the imprisonment and perhaps blamed her. Only his huge pride prevented his modifying his own orders. Leonore had gained her way, but forfeited much of the king's favor doing it.

Powerful, petulant, stubborn, enraged if crossed, proud, already regretting his wife's influence, a firm believer in the Four Gods Protector.

No arguments from Leonore would have stopped Rofdal from sending a force after me and Brant. Rofdal would have ridden at the head of such a force himself, as he rode fearlessly at hedges that had tumbled his own younger lords from their horses. Not by reason nor guile could Leonore have prevented it. She had not that much power to persuade her husband, and none to compel him.

All at once I saw the answer, and knew why the king's men had not pursued me into the forest.

Brant moaned and stirred in my arms. I laid him on the ground and brushed his hair from his forehead. His fever had mounted. Again he moaned.

"Eallow!"

He stood at the door of the hut.

"Call the men here. All of them. No, wait—help me first with Lord Brant." Eallow carried him beyond the ruined fourth wall, along the cliff, and laid him in the shade of a thicket, making him as comfortable as possible, hiding him as well as we could. I did not think it was a hiding place that would have fooled anyone. Eallow's opinion I did not ask. I left Brant water and a dagger, the latter of no use. He could not have lifted it.

I blew again on my Pipes to be sure all my unwilling army was with me. The bodies of those already dead lay in the woods around the hut. Stepping over them, I led Leonore's troops toward the castle, they walking and I on horseback, all of us bunched together as we crashed through the trees because I dared not let any of them stray beyond the sound of the Pipes. They strode silently, with no complaining or speculation, their gaits easy and natural and their eyes fixed as stone. I rode at their head, armed with neither sword nor bow—what would I have done with either?—and felt as

unreal as the men behind me. Light-headed from hunger and
fatigue, I thought that we might all have been illusions
between the palms of some Storygiver skilled enòugh to create
so many figures. We were silent enough, and I, at least, felt
enough like an illusion, riding at the head of an army to
confront a king. I, Fia, who had desired nothing so much as to
slip through the world unharmed, Jorry at my side.

At the edge of the forest, with the palace in sight, I blew
again on the Pipes. It seemed to me that this time the sensation
was different. The music was even more sharp and poignant
to my ears, but in response my mind stirred more sluggishly,
and the pleasure I took in the music was less. There was no
burst of insane joy. Even through the pleasure I did feel, my
shoulders still ached and my eyes as well, so that I blinked
with grainy, crusted lids. I didn't understand why the
sensation should change; I had taken the gillyflower drug at
regular intervals, and there didn't seem to be any change in the
helpless enslavement that was the men's share of the miraculous Pipes. The altered response of mind was only mine, and
with it came doubt. I was so tired.

Change, doubt, weariness—none of it altered the choice.
This story, or Brant's death.

"Eallow, choose two men, good swordsmen and strong.
Which? These two, then. You two are mine. Mount. You will
guard me and let no one touch me, nor touch the White Pipes.

"I drive this stick in the ground here, Eallow, in the sun.
See where its shadow falls. When the shadow has moved thus
far—no more, no less—you will do with the queen's men as I
tell you. You will follow my instructions no matter what you
see."

He never blinked. I had not realized that before: none of
them blinked. Soul-beset, they had lost will over their eyes. I
wondered about the unshaded sun damaging their vision, and
then rememberd that these were men who would die. How
had I forgotten, for even a moment?

When I had finished giving Eallow his instructions, I took
my two guards and started at breakneck gallop for the palace.

Almost immediately we were seen. Men rode furiously
toward us on horseback, and when I blew the White Pipes the

men froze. Not, however, the horses. They kept charging forward, the reins slack in their riders' frozen hands, until some reflex not of mind made brought the horses, eyes rolling, to a stop.

Men, but not beasts. Beasts remained free of the White Pipes, remained themselves. I thought of mad Ard, curling to sleep among her swine, whom she could not control and so could love.

As we reached each of the frozen riders, I ordered them to dismount and walk with my guards, swords drawn. As I neared the palace, still blowing the Pipes, I gained more men, advancing through the knee-high grass in utter silence save for the high and plaintive melody of the White Pipes.

They were no longer so cold in my hand.

The music reached ahead of us. When we entered the main courtyard an armed force stood frozen before us: archers checking quills and bows, swordsmen in forest armor. Servants stood holding buckets of water to tethered horses. All the confusion of preparing to ride forth, and of it all only the horses moved. The rest was as still around me as a woven picture on a tapestry of war.

I stopped at a young soldier, his leather armor worked with the emblem of Rofdal's guard. "For what battle are you readying all this?"

"To destroy the soul-beseters who be raping our minds," he said, and his young voice shivered with fear.

"Why are you waiting? Why haven't you yet ridden?"

"I don't know. We await the king's word."

"Since when?"

"Early this morning. His word be not come."

An arrow, fired from above, struck the top of his shoulder. Frantically I blew on the White Pipes. The archer, who had been somewhere within the castle and so had not heard the Pipes before, heard them now. I went on blowing, while at my feet the young soldier writhed with the arrow meant for me.

"Stay here!" I screamed at them all, and ran into the palace, blowing on the White Pipes continuously, afraid to stop. Frozen servants, men-at-arms, ladies, and kitchen maids.

I found Leonore, Perwold, and two other men in the king's chamber, and ordered my guards to bind their hands and to tie the men's feet to heavy furniture. Then I sent them and the four men-at-arms from the passageway to roam the castle and immediately bind, or kill, anyone who stirred. I had not forgotten that whoever belonged to Leonore, and was trained in mind arts, would shake the spell of the White Pipes sooner than the rest. As soon as Brant had?

Then I waited, watching Leonore. She would shake the spell first. Dressed in dark silk, her black hair loose upon her shoulders and smooth as glass, her face set and still, she did not look so different from the times I had seen her in the Great Hall, at the Midsummer Masque, in the Consecrated Garden. She had always had a gift for stillness, if gift it was. Eyes cast down, so that their fixed blankness could not be seen through her lashes, she might have—save for her bonds—been as free and as dangerous as ever, and I could not keep fear from prickling my skin. This was all merely a lurid story, and I did not belong in such a story.

I realized that, for the first time, the White Pipes in my hand felt warm.

Leonore raised her eyes, and I saw in them shock and hatred as she stared first at the White Pipes and then at me. So soon!

"No, your men did not get them," I said. "But only because the men-at-arms with me were such good fighters. Otherwise yours might have crept in before I had warning."

Calculations flew in the dark eyes. Like Brant, she considered situations quickly and well. Often his eyes had looked like that, and I did not like to see the resemblance.

She said coolly, "You have not much time. Or didn't you know that near much stone—such as these walls—the spell does not hold as long?"

Didn't it? Then Eallow's men . . . "I do not believe you!"

She smiled. "The White Pipes do not obey your belief."

I could not tell if she lied. Panic struck me. How much time? I put the Pipes to my lips and blew softly.

This time there was no burst of joy at all. A pipe had

sounded, that was all. But Leonore's eyes had gone fixed and glassy. Why had I done that? What was I going to ask her?

I fumbled for the memory, and it came.

"Does the spell wear off more quickly near stone?"

"No," Leonore said.

"Where is the king? In the room under the palace where you took me?"

"No. He is in his privy chapel, beyond."

Of course. She would not have dared to move him about the palace. He had given the order for his soldiers to arm and await him in the courtyard, and then he had come to his own chamber to arm and to tell Leonore—who already knew—what had happened. I could see the scene clearly. Perwold and his own men, probably the same as those I had bound, had seized Rofdal then, slain those servants not of their own faction, and bound Rofdal in his own chapel, close by. When Eallow, or his messenger, had sped from the forest with the recovered Pipes . . .

"What were you going to order Rofdal to do, once you had played the White Pipes for him?"

"Lead his men as naturally as possibly after you, and then to fall from his horse upon his own dagger."

"You would order your husband to kill himself?"

"Yes."

"What of the drug? You must have known the White Pipes are useless without their drug. How did you hope to stave off his men's impatience while you did all the steps of distilling the necessary drug?"

"I knew of no necessary drug," Leonore said, and her voice held disbelief. So Brant had learned more of the ancient lore than she, after all—on at least this one point. Yet Brant lay maimed and feverish in the forest, while she sat whole.

"Come with me," I said harshly, but she had already come back to herself. I seized her by the hair and shoulder—one of my hands on each, although I still held the White Pipes as well—and pulled her with me. Despite her bound wrists, she resisted. Viciously I yanked her hair. We were about of a height, but she wore high spool heels and I soft boots. My yanking made her lurch sideways; a heel broke from her shoe and clattered across the floor. I dragged her by the hair to the door of Rofdal's chapel, which was locked. A man-at-arms whom I summoned held the key and opened the door, and I dragged her through.

The King of Veliano lay bound in the small chapel off his immense bedchamber. Before him lay the bloody bodies of his dresser, a serving girl, and a page. The page looked no older than Jorry, and at the sight of that small dead face, blue eyes still open, any mild pleasure left by the Pipes burned away. I shoved Leonore to her knees before Rofdal, and yanked from the king's mouth the cloths tied there to keep him silent.

The King of Veliano stared at me with fury and hatred—but no fear. In my hand lay the White Pipes, which his priests had surely told him were evil danger; my other hand had dragged the queen by the hair like any street slut; before him lay the bleeding bodies of his people—but still he showed none of the fear *I* felt, and his voice was deadly as a cornered boar that pauses only to gather his strength before charging.

"You take us both, then, my traitor wife and a king, with evil arts."

"No, Your Grace—*no*. The queen is the only traitor—"

He did not so much as glance at her. She might have already been as dead as the corpses beside her. "My palace is full of traitors!"

"But not I," I said swiftly. "And not Lord Brant."

"Guards!" Rofdal bellowed, and it seemed the walls shook. "Guards!" The stone echoed with his fury, and no note in it demanded rescue or help, only revenge. For the first time I realized that had Rofdal not been imprisoned in the chapel, or had the chapel walls been less thick so that Rofdal could have heard the Pipes when Leonore did, he would now be held by their spell and this shattering bellow would have been impossible—as would have been my efforts to convince him of my innocence. Trembling, I clapped my hands over my ears, and the king bellowed again, "Guards! *Guards!*"

"They will not come," I said.

Leonore cried, "She has them under spell with the White Pipes! Just as she had me when she made me seize you this morning!" She began to pull at her hair, and tears of innocent fear burned in her eyes. "Oh, I have been invaded! My mind has been beset! My lord—"

Now he glanced at her.

"Your Grace," I said swiftly, "she lies. When she seized your person this morning, it was just as you thought it—a bid for your throne. Her men followed me into the forest to take the Pipes from me and bring them back here to control *you*. It is true they put a spell on the mind, the priests of the Four Gods Protector would have told you that, and the queen planned to take the Pipes and force you to a public death by your own hand, while you rode after the Pipes yourself. You see what she would stand to gain: your heir crowned king, and she and her brother ruling through him until he becomes a man!"

With loathing Rofdal stared at the Pipes in my hand. "Those—with those you have beset souls in *my* kingdom!"

"In your very palace," Leonore said swiftly, "and of your queen." She shuddered, and it looked so real I stared at her myself. "And you could think of *me*, my lord, that I . . ."

I heard Brant's voice: *And even that you would believe of me, Fia.* He had been speaking truth and she lies, but the tone was the same.

"You will die," Rofdal said to me, and his voice was hatred made stone. "You will be flayed alive, and the traitor Brant with you."

From somewhere in the palace, barely audible even through all the opened doors, came the muffled sounds of fighting. Those who had known mind arts had shaken the Pipes' spell, and those still held were slaying them. Courtyard and passageway would turn sticky with blood.

"Brant dies already," I said to the king. "Perwold has tortured him, and no one nurses him now. I had no one to leave with him: no other conspirators, no knot of plotters such as those who killed your servants this morning—who killed this child, here, for no greater crime than loyalty to his king. What do I have to gain from killing children? What would I have to gain from seizing the mind of the queen and forcing her to kill children? I don't stand to gain the throne of Veliano, nor anything else. I am here now only to convince Your Grace of the truth, and of Lord Brant's innocence. To do that I had to seize the queen and her men and yours, else I could not even see you. But now that I do, I ask only that Your Grace see the truth and keep your own throne!"

Rofdal regarded me levelly. Leonore began to cry something, and I hit her in the mouth. I had not thought before I did so. She toppled sideways, still bound, a beautiful woman afraid and pathetic, and I saw my mistake.

"Your Grace, listen to me—please—" So had Cynda begged, and lost.

"She has beset souls!" Leonore cried. "Why do you think your guards do not answer your call? She has beset souls!"

"But never seized thrones!" I cried, and wondered which would weigh the most with a king. Rofdal looked from her to me. Bound, helpless, he was nonetheless still cloaked in that fearless power as in a royal mantle, and I saw that if I killed him he would die fearless, unable to acknowledge that even Death held greater rank. How could such a man be convinced? What could I do?

"Why should you care if Brant dies?" Rofdal said.

"He was once my lover. He fathered my child."

Leonore said, "A cast-off mistress and a bastard whelp! Does Your Grace believe she tells you the truth?"

"My *son*," I said, my gaze on Rofdal's. "Brant holds my *son*. What would you do for your son, Your Grace? All of that I would do to regain my own!"

"Does my son still live?" he said, too steadily, and I saw the effort it cost him. I jumped up, ran to the door, and shouted at the first person I saw, "Bring the prince here from the nursery!"

Rofdal and Leonore both watched me from still eyes. I knelt before the bound king.

"Do you think I would harm an infant? You are mistaken, Your Grace. I bring him so you can see he is safe, and because I don't know how to convince you that I do not lie. You have called me a beseter of souls, and I have done that—to regain my child. Would you not? But I want nothing of you, save that you let Lord Brant and me live, and that you know both the reasons that drove me and the reasons that drove the queen!"

He said nothing.

The prince was brought, and I took him from the man-at-arms. Time—time was slipping away, I was nearly empty of time.

Rofdal looked at his son in my arms. To the guard I said, "Remove the queen from the king's chamber."

He lifted her as if she had been a doll. She began to scream and cry, but he stayed as impassive as empty armor as he carried her out.

"That is soul-besetting," I said, as calmly as I could. "He is under my command, because of drugs I have taken and because of the White Pipes I have sounded. The whole palace lies under my command, save the queen and you. And I swear on the lives of my son and yours, that I would give them all for safe conduct from Veliano for myself and Lord Brant. Anything else you command I will do, not as trade but to prove to you that any sins I have performed have been only in opposition to forces that seek to enslave your throne. Yours is the rightful power. I will do anything, my lord, to convince you of the truth."

He said, "Unbind me."

I stood very still, his gaze on mine. Huge, strong, his fury barely held in leash—if he started toward me, could I blow the White Pipes quickly enough to stop him? And if I did, all was over. The only hope I had ever had here was that of all the souls I had beset, I had never touched Rofdal's.

He was watching me. With infinite care I laid the infant prince on a bit of carpet, as far from the corpses as I could. Then I picked a knife from a small table and cut the king's bonds.

Instantly he stood: enormous, looming over me, half-armored. I wanted to run, to sound the Pipes, to do anything that would bind him again. He stood rubbing his wrists, and we stared at each other across the chapel floor. Then wordlessly he held out his hand for the White Pipes.

"Your Grace . . ." I whispered.

He held out his hand.

I said, "I will give them to you. But one thing first, only one. A story. The last thing I will ask, since there will be nothing else left for me to do. A story, that you and I create together. Hold the Pipes as if you had just blown them, and I will cut the queen's bonds as if I had been brought under the spell—and you may see what she does. Your Grace—truth comes sometimes only through lies. This way you will *know*—"

"Give me the Pipes," Rofdal said.

And I did.

In the second his huge hand closed on them, I thought that I had brought us all to death: Brant, Jorry, myself. Flayed, naked, strung upside down, blackened and stinking—the end of all stories, all songs. I felt it all, and in that black moment the breath went out of me and I would have grabbed again at the Pipes had not Rofdal seized my shoulder.

"Cut the queen's bonds. Now!"

I still held the knife. Carrying it, I walked as naturally as I could through dressing room and bed chamber, up to Leonore, lying in the anteroom at the feet of the man-at-arms who had carried her there. I kept my face flat, my eyes blank. As I stooped over Leonore with the knife, she closed her eyes, but when she felt her bonds loosen, her dark eyes flew open, and her face sprang to life with desperate calculation. It took no mind arts to see her thought: All is not lost, all is not lost.

Had she taken the knife from me, I could not have kept my pose. But she did not.

In a low voice she said, "Kneel."

I knelt.

"Get up."

I rose.

"Tell me what you have done."

I said, "I unbound the king. He blew the Pipes, very softly."

"Rofdal?" she said, and, incredulously, I saw the corner of her mouth quirk in amusement. The king—a soul-beseter. It pleased some perverse streak in her, even now, even in grave danger, and I thought despite myself: she is braver than I.

"Remain here," she said. She hurried to the chapel, her

gown whispering over the floor. When she was beyond the dressing room, I followed her, hidden beyond the stone wall.

How much more time did I have?

"Rofwold!" Leonore cried, and I would have sworn my life that the maternal fear was genuine. "Is he harmed?"

"No," Rofdal said.

"Thanks be to the Four Gods Protector!" A violent rush of silk, and a squall from the baby. "My lord, I was so frightened!"

"Of me?"

"Of the *soul-beseter*," Leonore said shuddering. "I beg you, my lord—don't touch that filthy blasphemy! Oh, lay it down!"

· I was back outside the solarium, listening to the bodiless voices of Brant and Cynda locked in their deadly story, save that then it was she who hunted and he who was the game.

"No. I will not touch it," Rofdal said. I heard a soft click, as of an object laid on a table, and I rounded the corner of the wall.

Leonore snatched the Pipes and fled across the room, her child shifted to one arm. "Don't approach me, my lord. You will regret it. I control you now."

Rofdal watched her, his face blackening, his huge fists closing at his side.

Carefully, never moving her gaze from the king's face, Leonore set her son back on the carpet. She even took a moment to see that the infant's tiny hand was not uncomfortably pinned beneath him, and I saw her again at that moment in my cell when she had cradled the bulge of her pregnancy and said to me, "My son must be king."

Rofdal started toward her slowly, giving her plenty of time. "Stop!" she told him, raised the White Pipes to her lips, and blew.

She had not taken the gillyflower drug. Nothing happened, save to me.

The music sounded, ordinary pipe music, perhaps better than some. Through the music the man seized the woman and something clattered to the floor. But who the man was, who the woman, or what their story, I could not tell. I could not remember. I did not know who they were, or why they fought, or why I stood in this place watching senseless events of nameless people. The woman screamed. The man dragged her from this small chamber to the next, where armor lay. There he bent her backward by her long hair, seized a dagger, and cut her throat.

Blood gushed in a great spurt from her throat, spewing over the man, over the floor. He dropped the woman and thundered past me into the small room beyond. I could not remember why. He snatched an object from the floor and shook it before my eyes. A white object, nameless in my mind.

"Take it, curse you! Take it!"

I did. It felt hot. The man bellowed in rage and thrust me kneeling to the floor. From the cold hearth he pried a brick by main force. Veins stood out on his forehead, his face purpled, the cords of his arms strained, and still he bellowed. The brick tore free, and he thrust it at me.

"Smash it! Smash the filthy thing!"

A baby was wailing, high frightened cries. To the sound of its wailing I brought the brick down on the white thing. It shattered into four pieces, and that seemed to enrage the man even more. I looked at him questioningly.

"Again! Again!"

I struck at the object, and as it shattered into smaller and smaller pieces, I remembered that it was the White Pipes and he the king. The king glared at me with brutal fury; I hit over and over with all my strength; white powder flew upward and, when it hit my face, the flecks burned like sparks.

When the White Pipes had been pulverized and my arm could move no more, I sank against the wall and sobbed.

"You are safe," Rofdal said savagely, between his teeth. "You spoke only the truth. What is that noise!"

I thought he meant the baby. But then over the high infant wailing came the muffled shouts and clash of steel from the courtyards far beyond. "The queen's forces," I said wearily. "From their hiding places in the forest. They attack yours."

"The *queen's* . . ." His eyes shot fire, and his whole enormous body shook with rage. I heard him rush for his sword and helmet and then into the passageway, as the sound of the bloody fighting came closer. But it would not come much closer. Fallow's men—Leonore's men—*my* men—were much outnumbered, as I had known they would be. By evening there would be none left in palace nor forest, who knew mind arts.

Except for Brant and me.

The baby still cried. I moved toward the corner where it lay, wobbling on my knees over the powder left of the White Pipes. The Pipes would invade no more minds, beset no more souls—as it had beset Ard's, and very nearly mine. Neither of those most fervently searching for the White Pipes, not Brant nor Leonore, had foreseen whose soul they truly beset: not the used but the user, and not through playing them but through hearing them after taking the gillyflower drug. At that moment I despised Brant and Leonore both, my protector and my enemy, for the danger I had run in the service of their separate stories.

No wonder that Ard could not tell Brant where she herself had put the Pipes. Using them had slowly bled from the user all language, all memories, until the mind was as wordless and immediate as music itself. Emotion, image, movement—these remained, the gift of music. And in the end Ard lay with her swine, whose wordless minds were as empty of stories as hers had become. The swine must have been her comfort.

The powder beneath me had become cold. I reached the wailing baby and picked him up. At my touch he quieted a little, and more so as I put him to my shoulder and rubbed his back, my own back slumped against the wall. He felt damp and solid in my arms, a chunky bundle of warm life. He would have his father's broad body. I shifted his weight slightly and spread my hands on his warm back.

We sat that way, the two of us, until the shouting and screaming died away and the carnage I had caused was over.

12

THE FIRST TO RETURN TO THE CHAPEL WAS ROFDAL—
not for me, but for his heir. I heard his great stride in the
bedchamber and then there loomed over me his face still
thunderous with fury, his hair and garments sticky with
blood.

"Give him to me!"

I held out the sleeping baby, but at the same time I
shuddered, and Rofdal saw it. He dropped his arms.

"No. You are right, Storygiver. It is not fit that I hold him
against his mother's blood. Servants! Guards!" His bellow
brought them running. But when they had come, he waved
them all out again, only first letting a woman—I did not see
whom—take the child from my arms. Weak and a little light-
headed, I staggered to my feet and faced the king.

He said, "The dead lay two deep in the palace yard."

"Your Grace—if I had been able to think of any other
way—"

"You are a soul-beseter," Rofdal said. "Whether by choice
or not—you have done this thing. No, don't look so fearful,"
he said irritably—he, who expected fear—"I will not with-
draw your pardon. But you must leave Veliano and never
return."

"Lord Brant—"

"Is most likely innocent." He scowled.

"His imprisonment—"

But the king was not interested in Brant. He said, already

half turning, "Brant may go or stay in Veliano, as he chooses. *You* will go."

"Yes, Your Grace!"

He had started across the chapel, people pressing fearfully at the doorway to talk to him and wails of grief arising beyond, when once more he turned back to me. I saw the reluctance in his shoulders and in the slowness of his turn.

"You will make of this a story for the Silver Cities."

"I would not—"

"Yes. You will make of it some tale between your hands, or give it to some harper to set as a ballad."

"No. I will not. Your Grace, I give you my word."

He looked as if my word had not much value. Perhaps he was right—but not in this. And then came a last, astonishing flash of that consideration that made him so popular with his common subjects and that seemed so inexplicable a part of his autocratic pride: "You are exhausted. But you cannot stay in the palace, among my people mourning their dead. I will send men-at-arms to take you to a trading caravan."

"Yes, Your Grace. I thank you, Your—" He was gone. As he passed from the chamber others, waiting beyond, poured in: men-at-arms to remove the fallen bodies, wailing women— confusion and noise. The palace at Veliano mourned with screams and tears, and this too I had caused: I, and Leonore, and Brant.

The queen's body had been removed from the bedchamber.

Four men-at-arms met me in the passageway. Armored, hard-faced, they obviously disliked the duty of protecting and escorting the soul-beseter. Rofdal had been right—I could not stay in the palace. At any moment the overwrought survivors might seek a target for their grief. Most of those who knew what I had done were now dead—but not all.

The soldiers formed a phalanx around me, their silence sharp against the cries throughout the palace. At the end of the royal corridor I stopped. They stopped around me: none would touch me.

"I must talk to a man before I leave. About Lord Brant. I have the king's leave to do so."

No one answered me.

"The man is my lord's squire. Or—" I added suddenly, sickened by the thought that the squire might be dead, I did not know who was dead, so many were dead "—any of his grooms."

Still no answer. I pointed at the slightest of the men-at-arms, and only as I did so did I realize that it was Rog. In his young face was a cold hostility I would not have thought him capable of, but I saw too from his eyes that he remembered our meeting in the prince's nursery.

"You. Go bring me Lord Brant's squire or his chief groom. Tell him it is a matter of my lord's life."

He went. The others neither moved, touched, nor looked at me. I thought that I should have been afraid, but too much of both body and mind was too exhausted for fear.

When the squire reached me, clattering up the stairs at a run and with his tunic unbloodied and whole, I explained to him where to find Brant and what a physician would need to attend to him, if still he lived. The four men-at-arms listened coldly; there was no help for it, they would not move away from their duty. I thought that their hearing my concern for Brant would not help his position in Veliano—but neither was there help for that.

The men led me from the palace to the stables by a side gate, not through the main courtyard where the fighting had been the worst. I was grateful, although I did not think it was from kindness. Perhaps they did not want to look themselves at their slain brother soldiers. Perhaps a horror of me—soul-beseter, queen slayer, sorceress; I did not know what hysterical rumor already said of me, although I could guess what it would spit eventually—led them to keep me out of sight like a slimy creature of nightmares. Or perhaps the king had ordered it.

We rode to a trading caravan camped on the far side of the town. Light-headed, weary, sickened, I could barely sit my saddle. What the king's men said to the caravan leader, how many of Veliano's gems changed hands, I don't know. A woman led me to a rough tent, I crawled inside, and I slept.

The last thing I heard was the six men's horses, galloping away toward the palace. The last I saw before exhausted sleep took me was the face of the page dead in the king's chapel: blue eyes open, thin arms smeared with blood, face as childishly plump and smooth as Jorry's, my son's.

I woke to good-natured shouts and curses beyond the tent. A woman squatted at my shoulder, shaking it. "Arise now, Storygiver, we leave in the hour and the tent must be packed. Come now, wake up." Aching, I sat up. "Here, now, this is your breakfast. Could you eat it out in the sunshine? The tent must be packed."

I stumbled after her. All around us tents were collapsed and tied, men shouted, horses shied, cook fires sizzled as they were doused: all the sounds of a trade caravan breaking camp, all familiar to me for years, all here—in Veliano—as deformed as health among the scrofulous.

"You look as if you need this," the woman said, handing me a wooden plate of stale bread, fresh berries, some meat reheated from the night before. The woman was of my own age but taller, dressed roughly for the trail, with long fair braids and a weather-lined face. I saw that her kindness came from herself, and not from any perception that we differed in rank. There was about her, too, the quick-eyed look of the actor, or the thief.

She caught me eyeing her in the dazed and desperate way that came from my last few days, and did not resent it.

"I am Aralet, harper and traveler with Nishel. He leads this caravan." From her pride—a little amused at itself, light-hearted—and her frank friendliness, it seemed to me I could read her whole life. Itinerant harper, too much of the cities and the cities' underlife to take much very seriously, never having much wealth but seldom missing it, living lightly with this man or that. Except for a certain lack of wariness, she might have been myself when first I came to Veliano.

"I am Fia."

"You look, Fia, as if you had a prickly time in this backwater kingdom."

"Yes," I said.

"Dull audiences? Poor gettings?"

"Among other things," I said, fished out a piece of meat with my fingers and put it in my mouth. The moment it touched my tongue, I was ravenous.

Aralet had a harper's quick ear; she did not press me to say more. With a friendly nod she walked toward my tent, now collapsed beside a girl who struggled with the heavy folds, and I sat on the ground cramming food into my mouth. A few steps off, Aralet turned and snapped her fingers.

"Almost I forgot! There is a messenger to see you, waiting since sunup. A messenger from the palace."

"Where? Oh—where?"

She eyed me curiously. "Over there, sitting by that piebald gelding."

It was Brant's squire, eyes exhausted, tunic stained from the forest.

"Storygiver, I bring you word of Lord Brant. He lives." The squire looked at me levelly, and I saw in his face what last night I had been too exhausted to see: this was one of Brant's trusted men, perhaps a practicer of the mind arts himself, perhaps one of those Brant would have sent to carry me by force from Veliano had not Leonore ordered differently. I wondered if he came himself, instead of sending a messenger, for that reason, or because no more casual messenger would willingly ride to a soul-beseter and exile.

"The physician—what does the physician say?"

"My lord will recover, all but the right arm. Flesh and bone are too badly damaged."

"If infection spreads—"

"The physician thinks not."

"Where lies Lord Brant now?"

"At the palace. My Lady Cynda nurses him."

I should have foreseen it, of course, but I had not. More slowly I said, "Does he send me any message?"

"He cannot. The fever is still too high upon him."

"In his delirium . . . does he talk?" I meant: does he say anything that might condemn him or might tell his wife what she could not be trusted to know? Does he tell her of my son and where he lies?

The squire knew what I meant. "No. In his fever he mutters, yes, but mostly things from his boyhood. And one of us—" he stressed the word lightly "—his men is always nearby. His body must be restrained from movement because of the wounded arm."

"Yes," I said, and could say no more. Too many images, all wordless, pressed before my sight: Brant crawling toward me on the hut floor, Cynda restored to her mind and nursing her husband, the gurgle of blood at Leonore's throat as her husband slashed it, the blue eyes of the dead page.

The squire waited a moment longer, nodded briefly, mounted his horse. I thought foolishly, as foolish thoughts sometimes make the only escape from pain, that his boots wanted cleaning.

Aralet was considerate enough not to come up behind me until the squire had ridden off. "I hope he did not bring bad tidings."

"No," I said. "Not bad tidings."

"You do not look like cheerful ones," she said, and waited curiously. When I said nothing, she moved off, whistling.

I was cut off from her. Nothing Aralet said, neither her kindness nor her curiosity, seemed to reach me, any more than the hatred of the king's men-at-arms had reached me last night. I watched them all, and the familiar bustle of a caravan breaking camp, as if they bore no connection to me, Fia, at all. It was as if all these others were figures in a huge story, one I had told often, but now my figure had been lifted out of the Storygiving mist and set apart, on another table, in a story of its own. Only Brant and Jorry shared that story with me—and Leonore, for whom it had ended. Only Brant and Jorry did not seem to me remote figures, viewed from a great distance and across a great gulf.

But Brant and Jorry were not here. Until I found them, both, until we finished this story that shifted and impaled lives, I was cut off from the figures of other men and women in their other, separate lives. I was severed from the world around me as surely as Brant's bone had been severed from itself in his cell under the Priests' Hall. This made no sense, but nonetheless it was so. Nishel's caravan surrounded me, tents and dust and cook fires, and yet for me it might just as well not have existed. I was numb to all but the two figures not there.

There was nothing to remember of the dusty journey from the mountains of Veliano to Frost, closest of the Silver Cities—save one thing.

For days we descended, through ancient wooded passes well-marked with new trails already grown wide and hard-tamped from the gem trade. The trails were dusty with summer heat. Nishel's pack beasts alternately plodded carelessly, great heads down against the clouds of dust they raised, or carefully picked their way among the stones of steep paths that fell on one side into mountain chasms. Between the passes and chasms were small villages. Once living mostly from the grazing animals, the villages had now become prosperous under this new trade in blue and red rocks, and they sported comfortable inns in which the timbers had hardly weathered and the wine tasted under-aged to Cities-bred tongues. Sometimes at an inn Aralet sang, or the two jugglers and three masquers who had braved the mountains with Nishel's caravan would perform for the local yeomen and peasantry. I never performed.

"Give us a story," Nishel said to me one night at some such inn. The caravan had camped just outside; their songs and merrymaking drifted through the open window where I sat in firelight with Aralet, Nishel, a half dozen traders and their women of a season, and two of the masquers. The trestle tables before us were wet with spilled ale, and the firelight flickered on Aralet's pale braids and on the blue Veliano gem Nishel had knotted with a strip of leather into his long hair.

"I no longer give stories," I said.

"What? A Storygiver who has forgotten her art?" Nishel mocked.

"Or ruined it with her own foul temper," said another trader, Caphad by name.

"I thought, Caphad, that you thought all women had foul tempers."

"Especially when they will not bed him," Aralet said slyly, and there were barks of laughter. I had refused him, and not as gently as I should have.

Nishel tipped back his head to pour ale down his throat; the blue gem flashed in his hair. "Just the same," he said, swiping ale from his mouth with the back of his hand, "I should like a story. What is your price, Storygiver? For the right price, could you give us a new tale, one we haven't all seen unto death, from that backwater kingdom? Or don't they have any stories?"

I was silent. Finally I said, "They have stories."

"There, you hear?" someone said. "Veliano is not so laggard as we thought. They have stories."

Nishel said, "But none that you wish to give."

"No," I said. "None that I wish to give. I told you—I give stories no longer."

"How will you live?" Aralet asked, and her voice was both curious and kind. I had no answer for her. Her question, though astute, seemed to come from a great distance, another country.

Shortly after, I left the inn and picked my way through the gloom to the small tent given over to my use. The night was moonless, but the stars shone bright, sharper and colder in the mountains than in the Cities; the fires of the caravan's servants, travelers, gem guards, and followers dotted the field with flame. From around me drifted snatches of song, bits of argument, the talk of love-play, the rattle of dice. All of it was familiar—thus I had lived every summer for the last ten years—all of it save the figures I thought I could see just beyond the last glow of the last fire. Five score men-at-arms with bloody heads and chests, and among them a queen. I turned my head sharply, and the figures became a grove of small trees, silent against the sky.

Would I look for them all my life?

Reason told me not. Reason told me that strong happenings produced strong fancies, but that both passed with time. With time I would find the living figures I had lost, and lose the dead ones beyond the firelight. They no longer existed. I had killed them all. Only I, and Brant, remained to know their story.

One of the gem guards' fires burned not far from the open flap of my tent; it lit the inside with a faint ruddy glow. By its light I pulled from within my tunic my First and Second Flasks.

The Second held the benign and powerful Storygiving drug of Brant's. I drank the First, and waited.

Maybe the fire glow brightened a little. Maybe the drunken song drifting from a distant fire turned a little sweeter, a little more in tune and out of time. But if so, the change was slight. My fingers tightened on the Second Flask. I drank it down and spread my hands on the tent floor.

The pink mist formed, swirled, swirled some more. Nothing formed within it.

I thought of the Story of T'Nig. Painstakingly I pictured in my mind the bottomless pond, the uncuttable tree, all the rest of the nonsensical, engaging tale in which triumph took little effort, heroes suffered no doubt, and death cost no suffering. I pictured each action, each outline, each color. Nothing formed between my palms.

Next I tried another tale, a simple one standard at market days and summer fairs, one I heard and learned as long ago as Mother Arcoa's. Nothing formed from the mist.

Finally, despairingly, I thought of Leonore and Rofdal and the cries and shouts from the palace courtyard while the king held his traitorous wife by the hair and bent her body backward to expose her white neck. But the figures my mind had conjured so easily out of a silent grove of saplings would not form between my hands. The mist remained pink and formless.

I closed my palms.

I think I had suspected, even before this dismal trial. The White Pipes had destroyed something in my mind, killed with their violent joy some delicate and frivolous layer, or perhaps fused it inseparably with some other, harsher one, and I could no longer make the facile images of bold princes, comic beggarwomen, beautiful ladies, stalwart knights. Or perhaps it had been not the Pipes at all, but the nature of the story we had made, Brant and Leonore and I, in Veliano. We had turned all within the palace into characters without will, as surely as if we had spread our six hands and cast a Storygiving mist stretching from the river to the Consecrated Garden. Soul-beseters. If truth had lain behind the ancient religion I had once scorned, could it lie also behind the newer notion that some force protected the minds of men?

I still did not believe that.

But whatever the cause, I could not form anything from the pink mist. My one gift, modest when left to itself, was gone. I was a Storygiver no longer.

The drunken singing moved closer to the fire beyond my tent flap. A shout, a woman's high laughter. I closed the flap, laced it, and drew my blanket over me in the darkness. Against all reason—for how was I going to earn my bread and Jorry's, without Storygiving?—I felt a great heaviness lift from my heart. In the night the dead figures came again, the bloody soldiers and bloodier queen, and I looked at them steadily, without fleeing the sight, until wordlessly they went away.

I left Nishel's caravan, having hardly been a part of it, at the gates of Frost. The ring Rofdal had once given me, changed at a goldsmith's for enough coin to make graphic why Veliano waxed so rich, bought a horse, clothing, and a place with a retinue of a prosperous tavern owner traveling rapidly north. His well-armed guard would provide as much protection as a trading caravan, with thrice the speed. In six days we had reached Albastrina, silver-towered by the sea; in two days more we reached Erdulin; the next day I stood before Brant's sister Malda.

In the dumb show I had taken from Brant's mind to my spread palms, his older sister had looked like him: tall, dark, strong faced. But now, standing across from her in the

magnificent garden of the manor I had refused to see ten years
ago, she reminded me not of Brant but of a darker Aralet. Her
face under its silk headdress was kind and unthinking.

"A messenger came to tell me to expect you, Storygiver."
I said sharply, "A messenger?"

She frowned slightly—I should not, with our difference in
rank, have addressed her so—but the frown was slight, and
soon gone. Whatever rigidity had driven the boy Brant to the
wild rebellion of disappearing to Mother Arcoa's, it had not
come from this milk-mild sister. Nonetheless, I had asked that
I be granted a hearing in the garden, not in the manor itself.
She would most likely have received me in the gralaria, that
curious truce ground where a lady could hold personal
converse with servants. I would not appear to Brant's sister in
Brant's gralaria.

"Yes, a messenger," Malda said. "Sent by my brother. He
awaits the opportunity for speech with you—why, *there*."

At her words, a man emerged from an ornamental copse
and approached us purposefully. Again Malda's slight
frown—surely a groom, for so he looked, should not be
skulking around the formal gardens. But I knew from one look
why he did so, just as I knew him. He had been one of Brant's
grooms in Veliano, sent here to lie in wait for my arrival, and I
would never shake him until Brant ordered otherwise. He was
my shackle, mine and Jorry's, and so he looked: grim faced,
watchful, strong. I smiled at him and said, "You come from
Lord Brant."

"Yes, Storygiver. To send his health to my lady and to
conduct his business with you."

"I did not know my brother did business with Storygivers,"
Malda said, with a mild edge.

"Yes, mistress," the man said. His glance told me that
Mistress Malda did not know any of her brother's business,
with Storygivers or otherwise, and that her willingness to
receive me arose from loyalty to her brother and not from
understanding.

"With your permission, then, I will take the Storygiver to

the stables, and shortly after we will set out on my lord's business."

"You are dismissed," Malda said graciously. She smiled at me, and I thought that she was as much like Brant as a garden was like a cliff and that she probably was faithful always in her devotions to the Four Gods Protector, whose protection she would never be in enough danger to need.

Alone, the groom and I looked at each other. I said softly, "My lord Brant lives, and takes no chances. How long have you waited for me here in Erdulin?"

He did not try to lie. "I did not await you here. I traveled north with Nishel's caravan."

"And with a tavern owner's guard as well, I think."

"Yes."

"Those were Lord Brant's orders?"

"Yes."

"And what are they now?"

"To conduct you to the child."

"I was to find a man called Jantro."

"He is not here now. He went ahead."

"Another of Lord Brant's orders?"

"Yes."

"And what of Brant himself?"

"He mends slowly."

"He must," I said, "or he would not still be ordering everyone at a distance," but to this the man naturally made no answer.

He told me his name was Pritar, but would tell me little else, not about anything. In his silence I further recognized Brant's hand.

In silence we spent two days' hard riding yet farther north, through Erdulin and beyond it. The flat land began to rise gently into green hills covered with wildflowers. There was nothing here of the wildness of Veliano's mountains and chasms. Farmhouses and hamlets dotted cultivated fields backed by tamed woods of oak, birch, aspen, all green with summer growth. Wildflowers—bouncing bet, daisies, hawk-weed, buttercups—bloomed by the roadside. The sun shone hot, but each morning dew lay on the grass. My protector/ jailer and I barely rested, and late on the second day we clattered through all this placid and thus dishonest scenery into the yard of a pretty cottage a little more remote than most. The evening sun slanted long and gold over the grass, and in the blue shadows near a stone wall stood three figures, who raised their heads at the sound of hoofs. Then the smallest one, arms outstretched and face alight, was running toward me and I had thrown myself off my horse and caught him to me, although through my tears I could barely see him at all. But I could feel him; Jorry's hands tight around my neck and Jorry's hair in my mouth, and in my arms Jorry's body warm and wriggling and solid and mine.

13

JORRY WORE THE TRAPPINGS OF A NOBLEMAN'S SON. When finally we stopped clutching each other, I held him at arm's length and saw the satins and velvets, the polished boots, the miniature sword. Jorry drew it proudly.

"Look, Mother—and I have lessons now! But why did you take so long to come? Mistress Tiennen said you would come much sooner than this!"

He had grown taller, and browner. His eyes had darkened, and I could swear that in this one summer his shoulders had filled out. Or perhaps it was the velvet clothing, adding bulk along with all else it was supposed to add.

"I came as soon as I could, my Jorry. As soon as I could!"

"The young master knows you had important work to do, and that is why you sent him here," said the man who had come up behind my son, and in his courteous voice I heard a warning: This is all the boy has been told. Jantro. One look at his face and I knew that this man of Brant's, like Pritar, served his master in more than one capacity, or two.

"I missed you, Mother," Jorry said. "You never sent me away before."

Jantro said courteously, "Your manners, Jorry."

Jorry colored. "My Mother, this is Jantro, who teaches me swordplay and mathematics. And this is Mistress Tiennen, who serves us so well."

Serves us so well. Swordplay and mathematics. This from a

child who had all his life slept on floors and ranked with servants.

Mistress Tiennen made me a nervous bow. Plump, middle-aged, large-faced, she had kind eyes and the anxious smile of one eager to please.

"See!" Jorry said, waving his small sword before my nose, "I have lessons every day. See, the end is blunted for practice." Well-balanced, scaled to his height, the sword shone in the last of the sun, and above it Jorry's eyes shone too.

"It is . . . very pretty."

"Tomorrow you can see me practice! Did you finish all your important work, Mother?"

"Yes," I said. "Yes. I did. Yes."

"I have a horse, too. Not a pony, a horse. Of course I still have Slipper as well, but my horse is stronger. Come see him!"

I went. I saw the horse, and the books for studying the old languages, and his room with plain wooden walls and oak floors but silk hangings around the small bed. On the floor lay wooden soldiers and a carved flute. I picked it up and turned it over in my hands.

Jorry took it from me and began to play. The tune was such as beginners learn, simple and sweet. My son played it well. There was beauty in the melody and a delicate skill in his drawing out of it. I listened as if I were stone.

"Mother . . . I missed you," he said, and reached for me again, and my arms went around the sturdiness of his body and the richness of Brant's silks, and against my leg I felt the bumping of the small bright sword.

In the days following I never let Jorry away from my sight, and Pritar and Jantro never let us away from theirs. Both men, but Jantro especially, wore under their courteous deference an air of waiting. They waited for me to object to something: to their unobtrusive supervision, to Jorry's silks and velvets, to the instruction he received in swordplay, languages, mathematics, horsemanship, archery—all the skills taught a nobleman's son. I did not object. The one to whom I would object, the one responsible, was not yet here. And until he came, I would not know what I would need to say.

Day after day I sat on the stone wall and watched while Jorry put his horse through its paces, and the world lost its jeweled summer splendor and slowly turned another kind of splendor, lemon and gold. Jorry's face glowed. Often he would turn that rapturous face, flushed with exertion and pleasure, to make sure I was watching. Less often he would call out to me. And once, when I had lapse into black memory, he peremptorily called "Hold!" to Jantro, dismounted, strode to where I sat, and wrapped his arms, sweaty in the absurd silks, around my neck.

"I'm here, Jorry!"

"Yes," he said, and a second later was gone again, running to his horse, where Jantro threw him into the saddle.

Often at noon we ate outdoors under the great trees, just the two of us, Jorry greedily gobbling Tiennen's savory meat pies and warm breads, I tasting it all as wool in my mouth.

"Mother, are you sick?"

"No, Jorry, no. I'm fine."

He looked at me with troubled eyes, and my heart smote me that I should not be able to hide my black thoughts from him, who had caused none of it, and all of it.

"You look . . . unhappy," he said. And then in a childish rush, burying his head in my lap, "Don't be unhappy! I don't like you to be unhappy! I wish I could help you, Mother!"

"You do," I said, and hoped desperately that even in his newfound maturity he was too young to detect the lie.

He could not help me. I had discovered that even he, even Jorry, was in that other great story, where time passed with the steady rhythms of music. If I felt, daily, that I was losing the son I had struggled so hard to regain, I had yet fairness enough to see that I would have lost him, anyway, to time. But not like this, not like this!

And meanwhile I stayed trapped in that other unfinished story where time had suspended itself. The story begun in the antechamber of the palace at Veliano remained incomplete, and until it ended I too was incomplete. I watched lessons in swordplay and in languages I did not understand; I picnicked in the sunshine; I sat by Jorry's silk-hung bed as he lay asleep, and watched the shadows of his lashes on his tanned cheeks, and all the while I was incomplete, suspended in time, in a story that had shuddered to a halt before its ending and trapped me in a frozen mist. It was a fearful thing.

As a girl, I had met fear with flight. In Veliano, I had learned to meet fear with my own will. But that human stories could happen that could be met with neither flight nor will—that was more fearful yet. I had not chosen this story. But Brant and I had begun it together and together we must finish it, because until we did, I remained cut off from all else, even from my son. Only this one story compelled me, was urgent, stirred me with the breath of life.

I was beset.

In the haze of sunshine over the lemon hills, I thought I saw Leonore smile. And still Brant did not come.

"Look, Mother," Jorry said. "Watch."

I had come around the corner of the cottage from the well, carrying a bucket of water for Tiennen, who would look scandalized because I had not sent the kitchen girl. The weather had begun to turn cold. But despite the chill in the air Jorry stood stripped to his waist, and Jantro, too. Jantro's massive chest, smooth and hairless, bore a long, old scar and two or three fresh, slight bruises, as if he had recently fallen. Behind him the cold sky had turned faintly yellow with autumn light.

"Now watch," Jorry said.

He stood before Jantro, his head not quite reaching the man's shoulder, and struck upward with his fist at Jantro's neck. Jantro made no effort to block the blow; neither did he flinch. But Jorry's fist hit collarbone beneath the flesh; I heard it.

"No," Jantro said. "That is not right. That way you might break the bone, but here, two fingers over, you cause a loss of balance but no damage. You must strike exactly *here*, and you must turn your knuckles and hold your thumb as I showed you."

"Like this?"

"No, like *this*. Fold that finger more. That's good. Now strike again."

"No!"

They both turned to look at me. I dropped the water bucket, not caring how it landed, and crossed the yard. My legs trembled.

"No. You will not teach him that. Not that."

Jantro said nothing, his face impassive. But Jorry set his jaw in a way I had never seen from him.

"It is jal-un, Mother. A . . . a kind of fighting."

"I know what it is."

"I need to learn how to do it."

"You do not need to learn how to do it. And you will not."

He gazed at me steadily, small jaw set. It seemed to me that the breeze stopped blowing leaves and the yellow sky froze.

"My father knows how to do it."

"Your father."

"Lord Brant. My father. He knows jal-un."

Jantro still watched. On his face I read wariness, but also a stern compassion.

"Yes," I said. "Lord Brant knows jal-un. But you are not to learn it. Do you hear me, Jantro? Cease these lessons immediately."

"Yes, Storygiver," Jantro said respectfully. And before Jorry could protest, he said in a tone that brooked no argument, "Get your flute, Jorry. The boy is coming up the road to teach you."

His flute. Was it a subtle reminder of the White Pipes, which Brant had sought and I had destroyed? Jantro's face told me nothing. But I believed that he would discontinue the lessons in jal-un—at least until Brant arrived. I walked away from Jantro and Jorry both, and from the approaching shepherd boy hired to teach Jorry, so that I would not have to hear the plaintive music.

* * *

He came at night. From my bed, through the casement opened to the chill, sweet air, I heard the clatter of hoofs in the yard and Pritar throwing open the bolt on the kitchen door. Then voices low and quick, followed by footsteps in the tiny stairwell. I lay where I was. When the door to my dormer room opened inward, a candle flame came with it, and one figure tall in the darkness.

"Fia?"

"Here, Brant."

He moved toward me, the flame moving in his left hand. When he stopped by my bed, I saw by candlelight his right arm dangling stiff and loose at his side, the fingers bent inward into a talon that could not uncurl.

"You can still ride?" I said, and heard my voice harsher than I wished, in defense. I needed the defense. I did not know who we were, either of us.

Brant of Erdulin. Fia the Storygiver. But he had become a cripple, and I could give stories no longer. I had taken his son, and he had stolen mine; I had preserved his life and lost him his arm; he had preserved my life and lost me my stories. Men and women had died. I had destroyed the White Pipes which he had sought with every means at his command. He had used me as a channel for lies. I did not know what either of us was, save that after all this destruction we both still lived and stood less than an arm's span from each other in the tiny darkened room too much like the attic at Mother Arcoa's. We were strangers and not strangers, and not the least to ourselves. So I watched the dark shape he made in the candlelight and asked a question to which the answer was obvious: You can still ride?

"Not well. But I can ride."

"And fight?"

"No."

"So now Jorry learns to do it for you."

"And is late in doing so. He is nearly ten."

"He is a child. And *my* child."

"Then let him learn his mother's courage," Brant said quietly, and the breath went out of me. I had not expected it. Of all that he might have said, that was perhaps the most unexpected. I lay on my side, barely breathing, my eyes on the candle flame flickering in the gloom and so not on his face.

"Why?" Brant said. "You could have left Veliano with the White Pipes and been able to protect yourself."

"The queen might have reached Jorry before me."

"She did not know where he was."

"She could have learned from you," I said and, as in the hut, he did not deny it. "Brant—we both know this. All of this."

"Yes. We both know all of this. But I still do not know why you did not choose the easy way: kill me and flee in safety."

"Why," I retorted, "did you not abandon me to Leonore after I had filled my purpose of telling her you possessed the Pipes?"

"Because I loved you still and could not have borne it," he said, and I saw that his was still the greater courage: I would not have said it first. I felt the foolish prickling start behind my eyes. Brant laid his hand on my cheek.

"Fia . . . tears?"

"You are maimed."

"And you, as well." Abruptly he laughed, a short harsh sound without amusement, and took his hand from my cheek. "I stand maimed by what I have lost, you by what you have discovered."

"And what is it you think I have discovered?" I said. But I had misunderstood him; he meant something simpler than what lay in my mind.

"The White Pipes, of course. Where were they, Fia? Where did you find them?"

"You don't *know?*"

"How could I know?"

Then Cynda had not told him. What *had* she told him— what had she deduced for herself? Suddenly I felt cold.

"Brant—listen to me. Tell me what you think happened in Veliano. It is important that I know, so that I can tell you the rest. Please."

For a moment he hesitated. I saw that the recital would hurt him, and that it was necessary. When he spoke, his voice was low with leashed tension.

"My men have told me you came to the Priests' Hall at first light with the Pipes. You took me from my cell to the mountain hut, which is the first thing I remember myself. Later you returned to the palace, bringing there all who had attacked you, by means of the White Pipes. You forced your way to the king, whom the queen held prisoner, and released him. He slew the queen with his own hand and his troop conquered yours, which had been hers. This much is the common story. I would guess, for myself, that you must have needed to persuade Rofdal of Leonore's treachery. When you succeeded, he pardoned you—and me—and destroyed the Pipes."

"I destroyed them. Not the king—I, though at his command."

He drew breath sharply, and I saw that he had not guessed that, and would not easily forgive it when he knew the rest.

"Could you not have saved them?"

"I would not if I could."

"*Would* not? *Why?* In the name of—why?"

I listened to his anger and loss, and grew angry myself. "Why should you want them so, Brant? They destroyed your Ard. Yes, it was the Pipes—she became as she became because she used them too much, and all her own stories were leached from her mind until nothing remained but the wordless music of the Pipes, and she forgot all else she had once known. That was why she couldn't give you the White Pipes, Brant—she *had* them, but she had forgotten that, as her mind had forgotten all but the storyless images of beasts. The White Pipes have taken my stories, too. I can give no more stories, not even with your drugs. That is my maiming from the White Pipes you wanted enough to risk your life for!"

He stood rigid, the candle trembling in his left hand until slowly he set it on the table beside my bed. The candle's movement passed it before his ruined right arm and again I saw the fingers, faintly blue, curling inward like damaged claws.

"Why, Brant? Why did you want the Pipes fiercely enough to cause . . . all this?"

He did not answer, but I already knew. He had wanted the White Pipes because he was Brant, who could not desire something without wanting ferocious possession of it. That had been his story as a boy; it was his story as a man, and I had come to know how few people could ever change their stories. Few ever saw a need to.

"Cynda had the White Pipes," I went on, cruelly, unable to stop. "She hunted them up on Ard's farm, as she hunted up every other bit of Ard's belongings and kept them. In Ard's cottage—"

"I have seen it," he said. "I have seen what was in Ard's cottage. I rode there just before I rode here. I saw . . . but not the Pipes. I did not know that Cynda had ever had the Pipes, there or anywhere."

"She did not know what they were."

"No," he agreed quietly, in a voice so full of pain that my anger shamed me. "Cynda would not have known what they were. But, Fia, I searched Ard's cottage, before her death. I searched every inch of that farm. If the Pipes had been there, I would have found them!"

"Did you search the swine?"

"The—"

"The *swine*, Brant. Ard's swine didn't die until after she had been flayed—Cynda had their bones among her other trophies in the cottage. Did you dig in the muck in the swine pen, sift with your hands through their dung, examine even the bodies of the female swine themselves?"

He said nothing, and I felt him speculating, shifting, calculating. I felt, too, in the stiffening of his back, the fastidiousness that had kept him from realizing that Ard could have stuck something so precious into a swine—a lord's fastidiousness, as much the result of his breeding as were his bones. That lord's breeding had lost him the Pipes.

"No," he said finally. "No. I did not examine the swine. Ard might have—if such a thing is possible—"

"It is."

"She might have. She was . . . I didn't see the possibility before, but she might have. But Cynda would not have found them there, either!"

"I think she found them much later, after the swine starved. Or were killed. Time and weather cleanse even a swine pen, Brant."

"You don't know that is how it happened."

"No. I don't know. But you said you searched the farm—can you see how else you might have missed what Cynda found? But of course you knew your Ard best. You would know best how her mind worked."

"No," he said, so softly that I regretted my cruelty. "Not once."

I wanted to ask if he had loved her; if he, with his lord's breeding, had been repelled those last mornings when he pulled her from the swine pen where her mad mind had led her from his bed; if his only relation with her had been expediency. But I did not ask if he had felt any love for the peasant he had not understood. I did not want to know the answer.

Instead I spoke of Cynda. "Does she know now about the Pipes? You said that you still did not know where I had found them. But surely after I left, Cynda would have heard the story, would have realized the White Pipes were the same as her relic in the cottage, would have realized that I had come back to the palace only to save you . . ."

He said nothing. I reached up to take his good hand and pull him down to me, where I could see his face in the candlelight. Not resisting, he came to sit on the bed beside me, and his fingers tightened on mine.

"Yes," he said. "You are right. She must realize all that, and more."

"That Jorry is mine," I said slowly. "And yours."

"Yes."

"She will think . . . she will think that it was like Ard, and that you bedded me in the palace."

"Yes," he said, his voice intent, and our gazes locked. Too soon—the moment had sprung on us too soon, too much was still unsettled, unknown. But I held my breath, my body taut under my rough blanket, and waited. The smell of him came to me, wine and clean, male sweat. Yet Brant did not move, and suddenly I saw in his eyes that he would not, that he was leashing himself tightly because he wanted the choice to be mine, and freely made. Ard's death, the White Pipes, his wife and my son, the very velvets he wore, badge of rank—all lay between us still, and against them all he could do was give the choice to me. And it was part of the last ten years that I did not know, even now, if his leaving me the choice was gift, or bond, or both at once.

I touched first his wounded arm, just at the elbow, and he winced.

"Even that pains you?"

"Pains me? Yes."

"I am sorry."

"Are you, Fia?"

"Do you think I still wish you pain?"

"No. How could I still think so?"

"You called me a thief, and a liar, and a whore. That first night, do you remember?"

"Yes," he said roughly.

"You have stolen from me my ability to give stories, lied to me about the White Pipes, acted the whore yourself with Ard for the Pipes' sake."

"Yes."

"But I would not pain you more, Brant. Not now, not any more. Despite what both of us have done, or been, or lost."

My mouth came up hard to his, and his good arm went around my body. A shock tore through me; I had expected to feel still some anger, or fear, or treacherous memory of his fists battering me. But not only were there none of these, there was not even the maimed arm nor the lost deceits. Ten years fell away as if they had not been, and left a boy and girl oblivious of all but the moment. I pulled Brant's clothes from his body and it became my body, and in the shaking sweetness came timelessness, and brightness, and music.

* * *

Afterward, I lay with Brant naked beside me on the narrow bed and returned to the world. Brant's head rested on my right shoulder. His good fingers twined themselves tightly in my hair. Night air, liquid as dark water, blew in the window, and somewhere a bird cried, mournful and low. Replete, we listened in the darkness.

Brant said softly, "The night was never so quiet at Mother Arcoa's."

"Street sounds. There was a vendor of apples, every evening."

"We wondered why he chose night to sell his apples."

"You said he must be blind."

"But I never really knew. I just said it, for a story."

"Your stories were better than mine, in class."

"Did you care, Fia?"

"Of course I cared."

"You never said so."

"Do you remember," I said, "that boy, Durleth—he was better than either of us. He is Master Bard now, in the house of the Lord of Frost."

"I know," he said. "I have seen him perform."

And so we were back already, to our different and unsettled stories. I said, more harshly than I had intended, "And was the coin you tossed him a generous one?"

"Lie closer to me, Fia. Lie on top of me, as you used to."

"I will hurt your arm."

"No more than we already have," he said, and so I lay with my heart pressed to his heart and my legs between his, and they cradled over me protectively. My left hand sought his ruined arm and stroked it tentatively.

"Does it hurt?"

"Yes."

"Will the arm mend more?"

"It will pain me less. I will never have use of it."

"You rode here earlier than the physician wished," I guessed. "He wanted you to give your body yet additional rest."

"Did you know I would come to you?" he asked.

"Yes, Brant. I knew you would come. But you were not so sure I would wait here for you, were you?"

He stirred under me. "Why do you say that?"

"Pritar. Jantro. You were afraid I would take Jorry and flee again." Brant stayed silent. I went on. "Jorry, too. His horse and swordplay and nobleman's clothing. Were you hoping to bind him enough to your wealth so that even if I took him away, he might come back to you on his own?"

"Yes," he said, finally. "I hoped that. But more, that his pleasure here would persuade you to stay."

"And if it does not? If I choose to take Jorry and go?"

His hand tightened in my hair. We had come, then, to the heart of it: whether I was a figure in his richer, wider story, or he a discarded one from mine. That had been the heart ten years ago at Mother Arcoa's, two months ago in Veliano, this moment in this narrow bed.

I said, with truth although not all the truth, "I am afraid here, Brant. This cottage is not that far from Erdulin. Will your wife move against me, as she moved against Ard? There is no way you can be sure she will not."

"Cynda did not travel with me to Erdulin."

I lay quietly on top of him. "Where is she?"

"In Veliano."

"You did not bring her with you? Why?"

"She has chosen to stay there."

"In *Veliano*? That is not possible."

"It is possible," he said.

"Why? Why has she chosen to stay? You have no position there any longer, no task nor honor. Rofdal will look at you and see the White Pipes and soul-besetting. And should he need a commander—"

"I would no longer be of use to him there, either," Brant said steadily, finishing what I had broken off. "No, I have no position or task or honor in Veliano any longer. I cannot return."

"And Cynda—"

"Cynda consoles the king."

I saw again the scene in the Great Hall when Rofdal had

spurned Cynda's plea for mercy for Brant. I saw her beauty and his scorn of it in the fresh triumph of an heir and the sudden anger of being publicly crossed. But if that triumph were sullied, the heir's mother a traitor, the public crossing dwarfed against a disaster of such proportions that the smaller quarrel became unmemorable, and the lady's innocent repentance very beautiful . . .

"She makes her own stories," I said, with harshness and relief and, yes, envy. "Even without any mind arts, without the White Pipes, Cynda makes her own stories more skillfully than any of us, and all the rest of us were her figures. Did you know I pitied her, once? Why did you take her to wife?"

"She was the most desirable woman I had ever seen. She was—" but I could all too easily guess. "And you were gone."

"You could not have married me, Brant. That was wild talk, an ignorant boy to a scared girl."

"You are wrong. I could have and would have. And I will not let you go with Jorry now. Cynda will never come now to Erdulin. She prefers a bereaved king to a crippled husband, and you have no need to fear her. But you should fear me, Fia. I will imprison you, if I must, to keep you and my son."

I had felt him tauten beneath me, and I thought how helpless he was, naked and one armed, to make such threats. But he said softly, "My men are below. I want you to know this, Fia. If never again do you permit me your bed, you still cannot leave. Jorry is my son, too—the only one I have."

"And this," I said, "is what would have happened ten years ago, had I not fled then. I do not like being coerced, Brant."

"I do not like being cheated."

"Your wife has cheated you. Send men to imprison her."

"I do not want her. I want you, and Jorry. But what do you want, Fia? You have danced all around my desires and said none of your own."

"Does it matter?"

"More than anything else in the world."

He meant it. He could say both: I will keep you by force; your choice is all important—and mean both. Neither was it that he did not see the contradiction. He saw it and accepted it as one more part of striving for what he chose to possess.

"One thing more, Fia. Before you make your choice. You think you can give no more stories, and thus have lost any way to earn your bread. That is both true and not true. There is more to the lore of the mind arts than you have learned, despite your being the one to find the Pipes. Watch."

Roughly he pushed me off him; I rolled against the wall by the bed. Brant climbed from the bed and relit the candle, blown out by a night breeze. Shadows leapt and shifted on the wooden walls, playing over his naked body and ruined arm.

From his cloak on the floor where we had flung it, he pulled a small flask and held it out to me with his left hand.

"You recognize it, do you not? Your own. You left it in Rofdal's chapel, by the destroyed Pipes. This is the drug you made to use with the Pipes, isn't it, Fia? What is it made of?"

I did not remember leaving it with the White Pipes; I had not remembered it at all. I shivered, without the warmth of Brant's body next to mine, and did not answer him.

"Drink it, Fia. But only half. Drink only half."

I did. Even as I drank, I knew it was in itself a kind of choice. I was acting together with him in what he chose to do. It was curiosity, and bravado, and a desire to please, and a desire for distraction from the trouble and intensity of our talk, and a hope of some resolution to the deadlock Brant and I seemed to have reached—all of these together. Like Brant, I saw all the contradictions and meant them, and so drank down half the white gillyflower drug I had never thought to touch again.

He drank the other half. Again I shivered; in our lovemaking the blanket had slid from the bed and lay useless somewhere in the gloom of the floor.

Brant said, "In Veliano you forced my mind when you held the White Pipes. But even force is a kind of story, Fia, with its own endings, and those endings do not go away—no more than the ending of Leonore's force on my arm. Do you know why soul-beseters were flayed alive, rather than beheaded or burned? It was because flaying alive removed the layers of flesh, fatally exposing layers underneath. The first priests of the Gods Protector, bloody butchers that they were, thought it a fit punishment. I will show you why."

Brant seized my left hand and held it upright, palm facing the room. I snatched my hand away, but again he wrenched it upright, and this time I left it there. Retreating across the room, Brant held his own left palm level with mine.

"You think, Fia, that you can give no more stories, because you cannot direct the Storygiving mist. But Storygiving uses only the first layers of your mind, and only those have been flayed from you by the White Pipes. The other layers lie there still, intact and now exposed—to those minds you have forced. Watch, my love. Watch."

Across the darkened room, Brant stood too far away for me to see his face. But I saw his upraised palm, ghostly in the candlelight, and it seemed to me, too, that I felt his gaze upon me. Not within my mind—I felt nothing there, not the "obscene" touch of invading another's flesh, nor the burst of timeless music of Storygiving, nor the joy of the White Pipes. The outer layers of my mind stayed as the Pipes had left them, flayed of stories.

But in the gloomy room, lit by only the single flickering candle as a twilight sky may be lit by one star, there formed between Brant's palm and mine a white mist.

"White," Brant said, his breath catching. Whatever he had known of this art, it had not included the mist's color. Between our two hands it crawled and spun, looking now like wisps of fog, now like the ghostly lights that sometime sweep across the southern sky, now suddenly substantial so that it was neither fog nor light but seemed something one could touch and hold. I reached out my other hand; the fingers passsed through the white mist.

I whispered, "What is it, Brant?"

His voice was labored; this mind art was costing him more than me. Because he and not I was the one calling it forth? Because he and not I had been the one forced by the Pipes, so that I still held a sort of effortless ascendency? Perhaps only because of his arm and the pain from bodily injury. "Can't you guess what it is?"

But I could not, or would not. The creeping white mist filled the room between our hands. Pink Storygiving mist would have swirled; this suddenly froze, motionless as death, and I held my breath and stared.

Brant said, with difficulty, "Stories, such as you and I learned to give at Mother Arcoa's, are what has never happened. Lies. Truth, such as I pulled from your mind when I learned that Jorry is mine, is what has already happened. Desires, as when Leonore thought she saw me find the White Pipes, are what someone wishes would happen. But this—this is neither lies, nor past truth, nor desires. Do you know now what you see, Fia?"

The frozen mist broke, shattering like ice covering a spring river. In the tiny room stood three life-size figures, their size shocking after the miniature figures of Storygiving. These filled the cramped space, claiming it, talking wordlessly to each other and oblivious of Brant and me.

But they *were* Brant and me—and Jorry. Brant with an unexpected beard, his useless arm dangling at his side; I in a blue gown bulging with pregnancy; Jorry a young man between us, armored for battle, laughing from under a helmet plumed with two golden feathers as glowing as light.

I screamed, "What *will* happen!" and threw myself from the bed, through the monstrous figures, straight at Brant's palm, with all my strength. We both crashed to the floor. "No!" I screamed at him, pounding him with my fists, not caring where I struck nor what damage I did. "No, no, no! I do not want to know! Not now, not ever, not ever—"

Brant cried out in pain; it brought me again to my senses. He had fallen on his arm; I had knocked him onto his arm. Gasping, ashen, he tried to rise. I grasped his body around the waist and together we staggered to the bed. Footsteps pounded in the stairwell—Jantro or Pritar. Brant called out to them to take no heed, and the guarding footsteps went away, more slowly than they had come.

"Your arm—" I said in anguish, but he rolled on the bed to clasp my waist with the other one, his face ashen but smiling.

"Never," I said. "*Never*. Hear me well, Brant—I will never do that again. If the image was truly what will be, what has not happened yet—how can it be in the mind if it has not happened yet?"

"I don't know."

"But you are telling me the truth, as you understand it." His arm tightened around me. "Yes."

"Was that the last of the drug I made for the Pipes?"

"Yes."

I stared at the darkness, breathing hard. "I will never tell you how to prepare it, Brant. Never. Not from what substances, nor how."

He said nothing. From his silence, from the tautness of his body against mine, I thought he would press the point. Instead he said softly, his mouth against my ear, "You did not flee, Fia. Jorry, you, I—you did not flee."

I had not seen it. In my outrage and fear over seeing the monstrous extent of the mind arts, I had not considered the image I had seen. Jorry, Brant, I—I, pregnant—in some time not yet come, some time when Jorry was a young man and about to ride to battle under a feathered emblem I had never seen.

"Feathers of light," I said. "Feathers of light. There is no such thing, not from birds of flesh and droppings. It is a lie, all of it!"

"Fia. Fia, love—"

"It is not what will happen," I said. "It is *not*. The mind is not capable of seeing the future. This was only another story, one brought forth differently from the rest, perhaps one given by the White Pipes themselves. Didn't you see that there was a kind of whiteness about the image? But it was not what will happen."

Brant said nothing. He believed as he believed. But it was not so. I would not believe it. The future already known, and my small son a soldier . . .

"It is not so," I said. "I will make it not so."

The arm around me, the long hard body pressed my own, grew still. "Make it not so? How will you do that?"

I said nothing.

Brant said deliberately, "Will you try again to leave me?"

"Will you try as you have said—to stop me by imprisonment?"

A long silence. In the darkness I heard both our heartbeats, mine against my ribs and Brant's against my temple pressed to his chest.

"No," he said finally. "No. I will not imprison you."

"Because you love me, Brant? Or to be fair, or merciful, or charitable? Or because you believe the white-mist image, and so see no need?"

"Does it matter which? You do not believe the image. In your mind, then, you are equally free—no matter what my reasoning."

"In my mind," I repeated slowly, and saw again the three huge figures: Jorry in the feathered war helmet, Brant, myself with child. With child . . .

Unthinking, with the protective gesture of women, I laid my palm upon my taut, flat belly. Swiftly Brant rolled himself on top of me and his mouth came down on mine. My gesture had not been one of desire, but on the instant it became so, and I reached to put my arms around him. The powerful muscles of his chest and legs lay along mine. I felt the pulse beating in the side of his neck, covered it with my lips, and said against the taste of his skin, "I will not live in your father's manor in Erdulin."

"We can live where you wish."

"Jorry will not learn jal-un. All else, but not that."

"Then not that."

"I will live neither as your mistress nor your captive, Brant. I will not be guarded by your men, nor bound even by your love. Understand this: I stay with you by my own choice, and I will live with you as your equal, despite all the badges of rank ever embroidered in the Silver Cities."

"By your choice, and as my equal."

"And I will not tell you how to make the white drug. Not ever."

But to that he did not agree. I saw—though mercifully without images—that we would struggle over it again and yet again. His fierce desire for possession would not change, nor my distrust of rank, nor the other struggles that had been only brought to uneasy truce by one weightless white image that compelled one of us to belief, one to disbelief. On this fragile image we would balance a life. I thought that it was a frightening way to live, and then that it was frightening to live at all. Then I stopped thinking and tightened my arms around Brant's maimed body, and together we formed our story. The night whispered dark beyond the window until, toward morning, the moon rose shining and whole.